A
DARK LE[

C000104359

A DI ALICE MANN CASE

BOOK 1

The Garansay Press

Katherine Pathak

Dark Origin

The Dark Isle

Dark Enough to See

The Eye in the Dark

The Dark Raven

When All Is Dark

Standalone novels:

I Trust You

The DI Alice Mann Casebook

A Dark Legacy

This is a work of fiction. Names, characters, businesses, places, events and incidents are either the products of the author's imagination or used in a fictitious manner. Any resemblance to actual persons, living or dead, or actual events is purely coincidental.

All rights reserved. No part of this publication may be reproduced in any form or by any means - graphic, electronic, or mechanical, including photocopying, recording, taping or information storage and retrieval systems - without the prior permission in writing of the author and publishers.

The moral right of the author has been asserted.

© Katherine Pathak, 2022

#ADarkLegacy

Edited by: The Currie Revisionists, 2022

© Cover photograph Unsplash Images

Prologue

Peacehaven had always seemed too good to be true as a name. He understood it was chosen because of his great-grandfather's association with the town in East Sussex, although he'd no idea even what that association was. When Zacharia Crammond, the ancestor in question, had bought this house, despite its being over four hundred miles from its namesake, it was given the designation with immediate effect.

It was a house that was expected to bring peace and stability to the Crammond family; a haven where children would play in the manicured lawns and find overgrown paths meandering down the gentle cliffs towards the shingle beach and the clear sea. Views of the islands offshore would create an impressive vista. Tea would be drunk on cast-iron tables set out on the grass where the sing-song laughter of ladies in long dresses would be accompanied by the satisfying clunk of croquet mallet on ball.

He smiled to himself, easing out from behind the large mahogany desk and moving to the foxed bay window which looked out over those very gardens which had held such promise for Zacharia. The sun was setting in a warm glow of subtle pinks and yellows over the sea. The garden sloped down towards a bank of bracken and gorse, in need of cutting back now that the summer had pitched abruptly into autumn, leaving those still enjoying the memories of mild, light evenings and sunny days spent by the sheltered cove reeling from the sudden change.

The scene as viewed from his study window looked peaceful enough. Many would see this house and its land as a haven. But impressions could be deceptive. He, of all people, knew that. A deep sigh filled the room, misting the glass for a second before evaporating into the chilly air, revealing the view exactly as it had been before. It took a moment to realise the sound had come from himself. The time was right, there was no point in questioning that fact. He'd been over it enough times in his head through a month of interminable sleepless nights where the sounds of muffled sobbing had made it hard for him to even formulate a solid plan. But when it came, he knew it was the correct one.

He reached into the old Bible box he kept on the windowsill, the dark swirls in the ancient wood still visible under a layer of dust. He lifted out the reassuringly heavy service revolver. He'd filled it with bullets the previous day, not wanting to be fumbling over the process when the actual moment arrived.

Did he want to be looking at this view when the time came? He wasn't sure now why he'd chosen this spot to place the gun. His line of vision took in the now darkening skies, casting shadows beneath the oaks which lined the southern boundary of the property. His eyes darkened in sympathy with the descent into night. Now, he remembered why he'd decided to do it here, facing his beautiful garden at dusk. He forced himself to look at the final oak tree in the line, with its gnarled lower branches, ideal for young adventurers to climb. It seemed to cast the longest shadow of them all.

His chest tightened with anguish and his face crumpled. He wondered yet again how pain which was not physical in origin could be so unbearable. This was the incentive he needed, because he hadn't really trusted himself to go through with it otherwise. Tears stung his eyes like a corrosive and his hand trembled as he raised the cold barrel to the side of his head. When the moment finally came, it wasn't difficult at all. It felt like the squeezing of the trigger was the easiest thing he'd ever done in his life.

Chapter 1

Alice woke abruptly from a light sleep. She lay still for a moment, waiting for the inevitable call from her little boy Charlie, which must surely have been the cause of her disturbance. It didn't come.

She sighed heavily, knowing that now she was awake it would be impossible not to go and check on her sleeping offspring. Fergus remained crashed out beside her, his breathing a deep rumble. The air was chilly outside of the duvet and she found herself shivering as she padded across the hallway to their small second bedroom.

The nursery door was open enough for her to peek around. The blackout curtains were tightly shut. A nightlight plugged into the wall created a subdued glow. Charlie lay in his toddler bed, his cheeks rosy and plump; long, dark eyelashes resting upon them. If her child had woken up, he was back to the land of nod now.

Alice noticed the dawn was breaking. A murky, zaffre blue light was filtering under the bathroom door, suggesting it was maybe around quarter to six. She decided to go downstairs and turn on the heating. Fergus had an early start and she and Charlie's day wouldn't begin much later.

Her dressing gown hung behind the door of the master bedroom and she retrieved it before tip-toeing down the stairs. She knocked up the thermostat, hoping the groaning and clanking of the pipes wouldn't disturb her sleeping boys.

The kettle was already full so she flicked on the switch, leaning against the counter and surveying their kitchen, with its knotted oak table and four chairs; the Welsh dresser that lined the opposite wall, filled with a set of Spode dishes Fergus's mother had given them. Alice smiled, they'd only moved into their end of terrace Victorian home a month before and she already loved it. There was no way they could've stayed in their old flat. Too many bad memories. The detective inspector knew the woman who had snatched Charlie, if only for a few, nightmarish hours several months before, was being treated in a psychiatric hospital and no longer lived near their previous property. It didn't matter. She could not have remained there a moment longer. Fortunately, Fergus agreed.

Despite spending the decade after she graduated from university trying to forge a life away from her parents, Alice had found herself searching for properties within a few miles of her childhood home in Largs, on the North Ayrshire coast. She had been an only child and had always felt stifled and overprotected growing up. It didn't take a psychologist to tell her that since Charlie's abduction, this type of protective environment was exactly what she craved for her child.

The kettle reached a boil and Alice lifted down a mug and tossed a teabag into it. She poured the steaming water on top, thinking how one traumatic event had turned her priorities on their head. Andy had suggested she place Charlie at Carol Calder's pre-school nursery, where her colleague's wife would keep a special eye on him. She appreciated the gesture, but when it came to the question of leaving her son again, it turned out that only her own parents would be acceptable for the job. Nobody was more surprised at this outcome than her.

Alice sipped the hot tea. She smiled, cradling the cup in her hands. So they'd viewed houses along the strip of west coast where genteel towns were positioned towards the undulating views of the Clyde islands. It meant a forty minute commute for her to the Pitt Street headquarters of Police Scotland and even longer for Fergus to reach his legal chambers in Edinburgh. But it had been worth it for the peace of mind.

They fell in love with a Victorian terraced house in Fairlie, a couple of miles south of her parents' bungalow. There were decent schools nearby and the house had been extended at the rear to create a light, airy kitchen, with French doors opening onto a long, lawned garden. The beach was a short walk away and Charlie loved to toddle along the shore in his welly boots and red duffle coat, leaning down every so often to collect stones which he shoved in his pockets.

The way her parents had adapted to the role of childminders for Charlie had been a revelation. They had cleared the table out of their modest dining room in order to create a space for their grandson to play, draw and be creative. When Alice returned to pick him up after a long and often arduous shift in the city, she would invariably find her son had been on a trip to a nearby castle or to watch the ferry boats from a viewpoint on the pier.

The DI marvelled at how harshly she'd judged her own childhood, clearly full of stimulation and love, when she'd been prepared to delegate the care of her own son to strangers. She knew this was probably an unfair judgement on the nursery staff where Charlie had once been a pupil, who could be deeply caring and attentive to their charges. But bitter experience had shown Alice that even the tightest of safety procedures could be breached, if someone was determined and clever enough, and the safety at these nurseries wasn't really all that tight, not if you looked closely. Most importantly, the staff didn't really know you, especially if you were a busy working mum who had to drop off and pick up their offspring on the run. It meant they didn't recognise your voice on the phone, not enough to realise it was an imposter who was ringing to give permission for somebody new to pick up your child...

She shuddered, tipping the dregs of her drink down the sink. The underlying tang of the milk turning sour on her tongue. The floorboards creaked above her head. Fergus would be about to get in the shower. Alice had maybe ten minutes to get Charlie's breakfast ready before her little boy woke up with the boundless energy he always had for the day ahead.

Chapter 2

A bank of cloud hung stubbornly over the coastal road which ran between Fairlie and Largs. The persistent drizzle meant more cars were on the roads. By the time Alice had reached her parents' house to drop off Charlie, she was late. But no longer did this make her frantic with stress. Alice still took the time to chat to her mum about the day ahead they had planned and waited for her son to remove his coat and shoes and bound away to find his grandad.

As Alice made her way along the A78, before she took the turning onto Haylie Brae and headed towards the city, the slow traffic came to a complete standstill. The DI took deep breaths and gripped the steering wheel to calm her rising nerves. The new commute was bad enough without hold-ups like this one.

She was about to radio the Pitt Street headquarters to inform them she'd be late, when Alice spotted a spiral of smoke, rising like Jack's beanstalk towards the heavens some way ahead of her car. The iron-grey clouds had finally dispersed and this artificial interloper was what remained to blight the now brightening sky.

From what she could tell, the plume of smoke was originating from somewhere beyond Castle Bay. She switched on her police radio, hoping to pick up some local chatter which might explain what was going on. It seemed that squad cars from West Kilbride had been sent out to investigate. Acrid smoke was billowing across the A78 just past the marina. Patrol bikes had closed the road. Fire crews from Fairlie were currently at the scene of a massive house blaze.

Alice picked up the receiver and reported her location to the local police station. She was told to use the hard shoulder to exit the dual carriageway and given a postcode to head for once she was clear of the stationary traffic.

Despite having grown up in the area, Alice found herself turning onto an unmarked track, heading west, that she'd never come across before. The track veered up a steep incline where the dense smoke cloud was towering menacingly above the DI's car. She was definitely heading in the right direction, even though her natural instincts screamed at her to turn back.

At the top of the slope, the track became a sweeping shingled driveway which curved back on itself and ended in front of a large brick and timber house at the crest of a lawned garden. It faced an impressive view of Great Cumbrae Island and the Arran hills beyond. The scene would have been quite idyllic if it wasn't for the fact that half of the property was engulfed in flames and the windows to the north end of the building were blackened by soot.

Alice got out of the car. She was immediately grateful for a stiff sea breeze which was directing the smoke away from the front of the property. Nonetheless, she took a handkerchief from her pocket and held it up to her face as she crunched across the stony drive in the direction of one of the fire engines, where a group of people had gathered. There were two water cannons, manned by firefighters in full gear, directing their arc of spray towards the roof of the house.

She held up her warrant card. "DI Alice Mann. Who is in charge here?"

A man in a dark blue suit stepped away from the group. His hair was a sandy blond, cropped close to his head. He looked about mid-thirties. He kept his hands firmly buried in his pockets. "DS Pete Falmer, Ma'am. I got here about forty minutes ago with a couple of PCs. We're from the West Kilbride station. The fire engines were already here when we arrived. It seems the rain dampened down the worst of the blaze, which set off the alarms at roughly 7am."

Alice pictured herself making milky porridge for Charlie at that exact same time. "Is everyone safely out of the building?"

Falmer nodded. "It was the first thing we checked." He dipped his head in the direction of a series of outhouses, not connected to the main house. For the first time, Alice noticed an ambulance was parked there. "The residents are over in the stables getting checked out by the paramedics. Apparently, the house sometimes gets rented out for the summer, so the smoke alarm systems were modern. It got the family out before the fire took hold."

"Just one family live here?" Alice furrowed her brow as she took in the size of the double-fronted façade. At a glance, she saw at least six upstairs windows.

"Aye, although, the husband is away on business until this afternoon. Mrs Golding and her three children were just getting up when the alarms went off. There is a live-in au pair who has a couple of rooms to herself in the north wing of the property, where the fire seemed to be at its worst. But she made it out too."

Alice nodded, grateful for the comprehensive update. "And there's definitely nobody else who may still be inside? The husband didn't return early for some reason, no other staff live on site?"

Falmer raised his eyebrows. "I'm sure the others would have mentioned it, Ma'am."

Alice began striding towards the stable block.

"You'd be surprised." She called over her shoulder, "the couple could have separate rooms. It's a big old place. If he returned in the early hours, the wife may not even be aware of it."

Falmer knitted his brow in concern. "We'd better double-check. I'll have a word with the firefighters." He set off for one of the bright red engines at a brisk pace.

Chapter 3

Alice approached the stables. A black and white spaniel appeared from the shadows of one of the barns and ran towards her, tail wagging, as though this was all a marvellous game. The pup followed her dutifully as she reached the forlorn congregation who she assumed where the Goldings.

A woman of around forty was huddled in a blanket, seated on a sturdy milking stool clutching a young child in each arm. An older boy stood in front of one of the paramedics, who was listening to his chest with a stethoscope through an old fashioned pair of buttoned-up pyjamas.

"Mrs Golding?" Alice ventured.

The woman nodded. Her face was drained of colour and her eyes bloodshot. She was clearly in a state of shock.

"I'm DI Alice Mann, a police officer from Glasgow. I believe the fire is now under control. I just need to check there isn't anybody else inside the property."

She shook her head violently. "Cassie and Joe are here with me, Jacob is just having his check-up over there. Maria, she's our au pair, is in one of the stable boxes with Jacob's pony. She said she wanted to check on her, but I think it's the comfort she wanted. It's been a terrible shock."

"Yes, I know. The ambulance will take you all to the hospital in Irvine soon, for a proper examination. I just need to ask you a couple of questions first."

"Okay, but I don't know what I can tell you. This has all been a terrible blur. We'd barely woken up when the alarms went off."

"The fire service will be able to tell us more about the cause of the blaze when the building is secure enough to enter. What time did you go to bed last night?"

Mrs Golding clutched her children closer to her, the little girl was weeping noiselessly into her mother's shoulder. "The kids went to bed around quarter to nine. Maria went to her rooms soon after. I stayed up watching TV in the lounge until about half ten, then I went up to bed too. I spoke to Roger on the mobile at about nine o'clock." Her voice cracked. "Oh, God. What are we going to tell him?"

"I expect he'll be very relieved you are all safe. We will need contact details for him."

"Of course, he's in Aberdeen at a conference, but he's got his mobile phone with him."

"What about this morning? Can you talk me through what happened?" Alice knew it was important to get this woman's testimony as early as possible. If the fire turned out to be a criminal act, they would need her recollections to be fresh and free from the prejudices that crept in after further information had emerged.

Mrs Golding screwed up her eyes for a moment. "The smoke alarms went off at ten past seven. I looked at the clock as soon as I'd woken up. I thought it was my phone alarm for a split second. But it was far too loud, of course." She shuddered. "I jumped out of bed and ran down the corridor to the kids' rooms. They were just starting to move about, frightened by the terrible noise. We didn't waste any time. I could smell the smoke already. This is an old, Georgian house. I know what a problem fire can be in these types of properties. Hill House has had them before, you see, when it was heated by open fireplaces. So we didn't hang about to get dressed, not even to put on shoes. We ran down the main stairs and into the kitchen where Billy sleeps."

Alice was momentarily confused. "Ah, the dog?"

"Yes, he was barking and going mad, so I unbolted the back door and we ran straight to the stables, which isn't connected to the main house at all. We also had a kitchen of sorts plumbed in a couple of years back, to help with mucking out."

"What about Maria?"

The woman's pale face suddenly gained a blossoming of colour. "Erm, well, I needed to get the children out first, obviously. Maria's rooms are quite a way from ours. I was going to leave the children in the stable and then go back. But when I turned towards the house again, Maria was running out of the front door. As soon as I knew she was safe, I called 999 from the stable. We have an outside line in the barn we use as an office space." Mrs Golding suddenly succumbed to a fit of coughing. The paramedic came over, his face pinched with concern. "We need to get you all to the hospital for proper tests. Even a small amount of smoke inhalation can be dangerous."

"Sure," Alice agreed. "I'm finished here now."

The paramedic didn't seem to care either way whether the police had completed their questioning. He was already leading the children over to the waiting ambulance.

Chapter 4

The ambulance churned up a cloud of stone dust as it sped across the driveway and disappeared down the overgrown track.

Alice made her way back towards the front of what she now knew was 'Hill House'. As she got closer to the fire engines, she sensed an increased frenzy of activity. She upped her pace.

DS Falmer intercepted her path. His forehead and cheek were smeared black. He attempted to wipe the mixture of sweat and soot from his face, revealing that he only possessed three fingers on his left hand. His expression was grave. "You were right, Ma'am."

"Was I?" Alice was genuinely surprised and unsure what she may have been right about. Her instructions to this provincial officer had only been given to ensure the house had been systematically checked.

He nodded. "The men went back into the north wing, once the final flames had been extinguished. They found the remains of a body, in what appears to be a type of kitchenette on the ground floor. It was at the very centre of the blaze, they reckon."

Alice felt her stomach tighten. She hadn't really expected that the husband would have returned unexpectedly, but only wanted to be thorough. "Good God. Do you think it's Mr Golding?"

Falmer shrugged his shoulders. "The body is too damaged to be able to tell. I'm just glad the rest of the family have left for the hospital. It's not something they would want to see."

Alice strode purposefully towards the main door

of the house, one of the firefighters was leaning against the frame for balance, peeling off his breathing apparatus. "Did you find the body?"

"Yes, me and Robbie found it." He shook his head solemnly. "Far too late to save the poor soul."

"If DS Falmer is correct, and this person was at the epicentre of the fire, they wouldn't have lasted long. I'm sure they would have been dead before you even arrived."

"Aye, we reckon the same, but it still means someone died in there. That's a bad callout for us."

"Yes, of course." Alice peered over his shoulder. "We need to keep the body in situ. I'll call out the forensics team from Glasgow. Can I go in and take a look?"

He shook his damp hair vigorously. "Absolutely not. Some of the internal structure is still smouldering and we've no idea of the extent of the water damage yet. It will take us a few more hours to stabilise the scene."

Alice sighed. "Okay. It will probably take the forensics team that long to get here anyway."

"Our fire investigation officer is on her way. You can't disturb anything until she arrives."

"Fine. Could you give me her mobile number?" This was all new to Alice, she'd never investigated a fatal fire before.

"Sure, it's printed on the call out sheet we keep in the truck."

Alice left the men to complete their task. She walked slowly back towards Falmer, giving herself some time to think. If the body in the house was Roger Golding, why had he returned from a business trip without his wife's knowledge? Or had the woman with the anguished expression, clutching her children tightly and seemingly in shock, been lying about that fact?

Falmer was standing by the open door of his car. "This changes things, I suppose. I'll need to interview Mrs Golding properly and contact the hotel where the husband was meant to be staying."

Alice held up a hand. "I'd delay speaking further with the family until we have a proper ID on the body. We don't want to jump to any conclusions. Do you have a forensic team you use local to West Kilbride?"

Falmer grimaced. "No, Ma'am. If we require forensics, we send for a team from your neck of the woods. It's not something we need to do very often. Listen, I've only just gained my Sergeant's exam. I've got no experience of heading up an investigation like this."

Alice was impressed by the man's honesty. Usually, in a situation like this one, they would be sparring over whose jurisdiction the case fell under. If the fire was arson and someone was dead, it could very well be her team at Serious Crime that should take it on, but if it was merely a tragic accident, then West Kilbride were the station to deal with it.

Something about Mrs Golding's testimony had left her uneasy. The woman had made no attempt to find her young au pair in the north wing before exiting the house. Perhaps she was consumed by fear for the safety of her own children, but it seemed odd she had the instinct not to venture into the other side of the building, where the fire was at its worst. "Don't worry, DS Falmer. I will make a call to the lab we use in the city. If you don't have any objections, I'm going to request that my department take this case on."

Falmer showed no signs of resenting this incursion into his territory. In fact, he seemed mightily relieved.

Chapter 5

A structural expert, in a dark suit and hard-hat, who'd been called upon by the fire service, was completing an examination of the building. Grey water was dripping continually onto the exposed floorboards of the charred entrance hall and Alice could see that the roof had completely collapsed on the left-hand side of the house, leaving just a few blackened beams sticking up into the cloudy sky, like a birds' nest abandoned before completion.

The forensic team had just arrived and were unloading their equipment and suiting-up, waiting for the all-clear to enter the building. Beside the DI stood Eleanor Canning, the fire investigation officer for North Ayrshire. She gripped a clipboard in both hands.

"Do you need to go in first?" Alice asked the sensibly, but stylishly dressed woman. Her crop of ash-blond hair was mostly hidden beneath a canary yellow hard-hat.

"Yes, that is the usual procedure. I will take some preliminary photographs and identify the starting point of the fire. To be honest, I can work quite happily alongside the forensic team. They are the last people likely to contaminate my scene."

"True," Alice added dryly. "I'll inform them that you will be carrying out your own examination. I'm sure you will be sharing results anyway?"

"Absolutely so," the woman replied. "I always operate closely with the police investigation. It's my job to ascertain if this fire was deliberately set. In the case of fatalities from the blaze, my findings can contribute to a criminal case."

"I can see that." The DI stared at the devastating shell of half of what would once have been an impressive brick and timber Georgian manor house. "Is it common?"

Eleanor narrowed her sea-green eyes in puzzlement. "What?"

"Arson," Alice said without preamble.

"Oh yes, Detective Inspector. Very common indeed."

*

It took another couple of hours for the forensic team to emerge from the property with a sealed black bag on a stretcher, ready to be taken away to the mortuary. The forensic pathologist was following the solemn procession, tugging the mask from his face to breath in the fresh air.

He approached Alice. "We will take the body back to the lab to perform the *post mortem*. I would hope to get the results to you after the weekend."

"Thanks Dr Webb. Can you tell me anything about the body from what you've already seen? I will need to make a formal ID as soon as possible."

Webb mopped his brow with a handkerchief. "The body has suffered extensive burns. The fire at that location in the property would have been intense, but the skeleton seems intact. I imagine I'll be able to extract DNA and give you an idea of sex and height. The teeth were also extant. And surprisingly, the shoes seem to have survived. A sturdy pair of boots, I'd say. I never want to pre-empt, especially these days, when folk wear all kinds of clothing, but my guess from the size of the boots, this was a man. The rest of the clothes have burnt or melted into the flesh."

Alice nodded, suddenly relieved she'd not been able to view the body after all. "I wonder why whomever it was, wasn't able to flee the blaze? The body was found in a kitchen area, I believe, so they can't have been asleep?"

"No, with bodies that badly damaged by fire, we would usually conclude that smoke inhalation had rendered them unconscious in their beds so they couldn't get away when the fire reached them. In this case, the position of the corpse is unusual. But I should be able to tell after the *PM* whether or not the cause of death was due to the smoke or the fire itself. I'm hoping there is enough of the lungs and oesophagus remaining for me to test."

Alice felt the bile rising in her throat. She took a deep breath of the sea air. "Thank you, Dr Webb. Please contact me at Pitt Street as soon as your results are available."

"Of course," the pathologist dipped his head towards the exhausted looking firefighters who were packing their equipment into the back of one of the trucks. "We were lucky those fellas got here so quickly. The fire never fully took hold. Only about a third of the building is gone. If the fire had raged much longer, our body in there would simply be charcoal now."

The DI's breakfast was now dangerously close to making a second appearance. "Yes, we owe them a great deal," she managed. "And to the smoke detectors which were modern and had been recently serviced."

Webb grunted his agreement as he climbed into the front seat of his car and started up the engine, following the mortuary van as it crept along the drive.

DS Falmer was talking to Eleanor Canning whilst the fire trucks prepared to leave. Alice checked her phone. It was 2pm. She decided it was time for her to head for the Serious Crime Department in Glasgow and fully explain her morning's activities to

DCI Bevan.

The noise of a speeding vehicle, negotiating the steep entrance road, prevented the DI from contemplating her departure any further. Abruptly, a dark blue Land Rover careered around the bend and came to a sudden halt on the drive in front of the house. A chunk of gravel, whipped up by the spinning wheels, nearly struck Alice in the face.

A tall man with thinning hair, wearing a creased suit and appearing to be in his mid-forties jumped out of the driver's seat and stumbled backwards as he looked up at the house.

Alice marched towards him. "This is a crime scene, Sir. You need to keep well back. This building is unsafe."

He flashed anguished, bloodshot eyes at her. "What do you mean, a *crime scene*!? This is my bloody house!"

Alice staggered backwards herself, feeling oddly like she'd seen a ghost. "You're Roger Golding?"

"Of course I am! Rosaline called me from the hospital. I've been driving like a maniac to get back here!"

Alice looked across the driveway at DS Falmer. He was staring at the new arrival, his face pinched with concern. They were both clearly thinking the same thing. If this was Roger Golding, then who's dead body had they just removed from the house?

Chapter 6

The light was fading outside the bank of windows which overlooked Pitt Street from the fourth floor offices of Police Scotland. An overhead strip light had just flickered on. But Alice felt as if she'd only just arrived for work.

Once she'd negotiated the traffic on the M8 and filed a report on the fire, her own workload for the day was hardly dented.

DS Sharon Moffett looked up from her screen and stretched her fingers, creating a jarring series of bone clicks. "That's my paperwork up-do-date. Now, tell me about this mysterious fire."

Alice sighed. "Your work may well be done, Sharon, but some of us have catching up to do. Mum and Dad are happy to keep Charlie for an extra hour or so, but I can't start taking the piss."

"Surely the boss will give you extra time on your current tasks? This morning's shenanigans are a whole new case for you, aren't they?"

"I'm not sure yet. The forensics have all gone off to our usual lab and the *PM* is being performed by Dr Webb at the University Hospital mortuary. My name was given as the investigation lead. But the house is very definitely within the jurisdiction of West Kilbride."

"I thought they were happy to palm it off?" Sharon leant closer.

"Well, the DS at the scene was, which isn't exactly conclusive."

The detectives were interrupted by the sound of the DCI's office door creaking open. Dani Bevan strode through it and headed in the direction of Alice's workstation. "Sorry for the delay in getting back to you, Alice. I've been in meetings most of the day – just got off the phone from a conversation with DCS Douglas, in fact. He informs me that West Kilbride have no officers above the rank of Sergeant right now. So, he wants you to work from there for the duration of this fire investigation."

Alice's mouth dropped open. "You mean I've got to leave Pitt Street?"

Dani pulled up a chair. "Not forever. If you re-locate for a week or so, it will make it much easier to investigate this unidentified corpse. I also thought it might make life a lot easier for you, cut down the morning commute."

Alice gulped, not quite sure how she felt about this turn of events. "Well, it certainly would, but to be permanently posted to the West Kilbride station would feel like a demotion, Ma'am. I'm not comfortable with that."

Dani's brow creased. "I don't want you to feel that's what's happening here. I can completely understand your decision to move closer to your parents and your swift intervention in today's incident shows how valuable you are as an officer. You've already established yourself as the head of this investigation; co-ordinating the forensic team and the fire analyst. To be honest, since COP26, our job here in the city has quietened right down."

Sharon nodded her agreement, gesturing at her screen. "The DCI is right. I've spent the day chasing unpaid parking fines sent over by Traffic. Andy is giving talks on 'how to stay out of gang culture' at the local schools. We've not had a serious incident in the city since Quentin Lester was found dead in his hotel room."

Dani raised her eyebrows. "The DCS told me how helpful it would be to him personally if you took this case on. Apparently, the DI at West Kilbride is on indefinite leave, he wouldn't tell me why. The investigation department over there is completely lacking leadership right now. He really wants you in there to help him out, keep an eye on things."

Alice considered this. She didn't have much choice in the matter. The idea of taking a role at a new station, out in the sticks, felt like she was being side-lined. Yet, something about the case of the body in the fire had piqued her interest. "Okay. When does DCS Douglas want me there?"

"Tomorrow morning," Dani said brusquely, getting to her feet. "You'll have the whole of their detective team at your disposal."

"But if you need the help of an old, trusted colleague, don't hesitate to make a request for me," Sharon added with a grin. "Your unidentified body sounds much more intriguing than my caseload right now."

Alice managed a smile. "I might just take you up on that, Sharon."

*

Fergus plumped his pillow and rested a weighty hardback on his raised knees. "This is great news. It's a ten minute drive to West Kilbride. I wouldn't wish to rejoice in someone's ghastly death, but this investigation has cropped up at just the right time."

Alice cringed. "There's always an unpleasant clash of priorities in my job. There's nothing a senior detective relishes more than investigating a suspicious death, but on the other hand, someone has to have met a sticky end for the opportunity to arise. Although, I'm not quite so convinced by the virtues of this re-location."

Fergus shifted round to face her, his dark brown eyes searching hers. "Glasgow isn't the centre of the universe. It sounds like you'll practically be running things at West Kilbride." He cleared his throat, "it could even be a chance for you to move out of Bevan's shadow for a bit."

She lifted herself up on her elbows. "Do you think I'm in the DCI's shadow?"

He shrugged. "You all work really well together up there at Pitt Street, but you've been through a lot over the years. You're all fiercely loyal to Dani. None of you want to leave her command, even if it's quite obvious it would be in your own best interests." He took the edge off his words by placing a kiss on her lips.

Alice kissed him back, tasting the familiar mint of their toothpaste and nuzzling her head into the crook of his shoulder. Was Fergus right? A work move to Ayrshire would make life easier for her family. She would practically be in charge of the entire station. Wasn't this what she was working towards? If recent events had taught her anything, it was that life was precarious. Her child must now come first. Perhaps Pitt Street wasn't the centre of her universe any longer.

Chapter 7

The desk Alice had been assigned was covered in a thin layer of dust, only interrupted by a few A4 sized squares of clean wood, where she assumed piles of papers and files had very recently been removed. Likely for her benefit.

She wiped her hand across the surface and brushed away the grimy detritus. Alice had her own batch of files to replace the old ones, which she dropped onto the scratched wood with a thud. She pulled the first towards her and took a sip of strong coffee from her travel mug. She'd arrived early, hoping to get herself settled in before meeting the department.

Alice had requested the personnel files of all those officers who would be serving in her team. She wanted to gain a familiarity with each of them so they could hit the ground running with the investigation. The first file she opened was for Detective Sergeant Peter Falmer. A passport-sized photo showing his pale face and crop of sandy hair was secured to the corner with a paper clip. He was thirty four years old, and just as he'd told the DI at the scene of the house fire, had only been made a sergeant in May of that year.

She scanned the details. According to his medical notes, Peter had been born with severe Symbrachydactyly at birth, a genetic anomaly which had left him with only three fingers on his left hand. According to the medical exam he undertook during training, Peter had entirely compensated for this disability and it gave him no discernible disadvantage in the job. His active duties were unaffected, although he'd never taken firearms training.

Alice was relieved this information was provided by the file, it meant she wouldn't have to ask her colleague about it. Andy Calder was always telling her she lacked diplomacy in her interactions. She could be blunt, certainly, but never intended to cause offence, just to get on with her job as efficiently as possible. But she'd liked Falmer and had no wish to offend him, so was happy to be able to avoid the topic altogether.

It took her an hour to skim the remainder of the files. There were three DCs in the criminal investigation department at West Kilbride and one DS. None of the officers were over forty years old. Alice was herself only thirty-four, but her caseload background in serious crime was extensive. Nevertheless, none of her new team would be particularly experienced. She tucked a stray hair behind her ear, having decided to plait her mane of auburn hair and pin it into a sensible bun at the nape of her neck.

She heard the sound of voices travelling up the staircase. Her new colleagues were arriving. She got up from the desk and wheeled across a portable whiteboard which she was relieved to see had some chunky pens abandoned in the tray.

As the four men and one woman took their seats and turned expectant faces in the DI's direction. Alice took a deep breath.

"Good Morning. My name is Detective Inspector Alice Mann. I'm going to be heading up this team for the duration of the investigation into the fatal house fire at Hill House, Fairlie, in the early hours of yesterday morning." She paused to take another breath, noting how the room was quiet enough to hear a pin drop. "DS Falmer and I met at the scene, but I look forward to getting to know the rest of you in due course."

She picked up one of the pens and flicked off the lid, praying it had some ink left in it. Thankfully, her scribbles were leaving their mark on the melamine surface. "The family who own the property are called, Golding. The husband and wife are Roger and Rosaline." Alice was writing out a kind of basic family tree. "They have three children; Joseph, Jacob and Cassie. The family all had rooms in the south wing of the house. Then we have the au-pair, Maria Silva, twenty-five years old and originally from Valencia, Spain. She has worked for the Goldings for a year and a half and has rooms in the north wing of the house."

The female DC, who Alice knew to be called Holly Gadd, raised her hand. The DI nodded her permission to speak.

"Do we know yet how the fire started?" The young DC was in her late twenties and possessed a bob of shiny blond hair. Her features were small and pretty.

"DS Falmer is probably the best person to answer that question. He has been liaising with the fire investigation officer."

"Please, call me Pete," the man said amiably as he rose to his feet and addressed his fellow officers. "Eleanor Canning is the FIO for North Ayrshire. She has taken a look at the scene alongside the SOCOs from Glasgow who were primarily examining the unidentified body *in situ*. Ms Canning told me she doesn't provide preliminary findings and her report could take as long as four weeks to be published."

There were audible sighs and tuts of frustration echoing around the room. Alice raised her hand. "Bear in mind, that our forensic team will be looking at much the same questions and will be bringing me their conclusions within days. In the meantime, our priority is to identify the body found in the burnt out wreck of the north wing of Hill House. Any suggestions on how we proceed?" Alice knew this young team had almost no experience of working a serious crime. It was her job to train them as quickly as possible.

An officer sporting a neatly clipped beard and a dark blue turban, who Alice assumed was DC Matt Singh, raised his hand. "Hopefully, the forensic team will be able to extract some usable DNA from the corpse which we can run through the database, Ma'am. There may also be surviving teeth that can be compared to dental records. Enamel is tougher to burn than flesh."

Alice winced at the graphic detail. "Yes, forensic testing will be the way in which a final ID can be made, but what can we do in the meantime, whilst the *PM* is being carried out? The pathologist will have other cases that may take priority over ours."

The final member of the team raised his hand. The oldest of the detectives, DC Victor Novak was tall, pretty much bald, and with a bulky build to match. "The first thing is to question the family, Ma'am. If there was a person in their house during the night, they are the ones most likely to know about it. Particularly the au-pair. The body was found in the side of the house where her living quarters were, yes? Then, she is the first person I would ask."

"Following that," Holly Gadd chimed in, warming to the exercise. "We need to check if any missing persons have been reported in the area during the last twenty four hours. See if any of them have a connection to the Goldings."

Pete fell into the rhythm of the discussion, adding, "the house is very isolated on that hillside. They may well have some CCTV cameras installed, particularly for when they rent the place out. The FIO told me she was looking for evidence of cameras as part of her search routine. If any have survived the blaze, we may have some footage of people coming and going from the house. And, although the house has no real neighbours, I did spot a couple of cottages tucked away at the foot of the slope. Perhaps they share the entrance road? Someone there may have seen movement along the track on the night of the fire?"

Alice smiled, nodding encouragingly. "Well then, what are we waiting for?"

Chapter 8

The Cumbrae Hotel lay on the outskirts of Largs. It wasn't exactly the holiday season on the west coast of Scotland and the Victorian building looked a sad, gunmetal grey on this dull, October morning.

The interior was more inviting. The entrance hall was deeply carpeted and plush, velvet sofas were placed at various intervals to allow guests to relax at their leisure.

Alice and Pete Falmer had arranged to meet the Golding family in the guest lounge at the rear of the hotel, which overlooked a pretty, landscaped garden.

Rosaline Golding was wearing a ribbed cream jumper and slim-fitting trousers, a pair of brown leather boots were crossed at the heel. Her hair appeared freshly blown dry and she was looking far more composed than when the officers had last seen her.

Roger Golding was perched on the edge of his armchair, his hands clasped pensively in his lap. His handsome face was lined with worry. At another table, Maria Silva was seated with the three children; a complicated looking boardgame spread out before them.

Alice and Pete joined the couple who sat apart from the others. "Thank you for agreeing to speak with us again."

"Would you like to order tea? Or coffee, maybe?" Roger asked anxiously.

"No thank you. This shouldn't take long." Alice pulled an iPad out of her bag. "I'm afraid the forensic results on the," she cleared her throat, glancing across at the children, who seemed absorbed in their game, "*person*, we removed from your property after the fire aren't available yet. In the meantime, perhaps you have some idea who that individual may have been?"

Rosaline shook her head in frustration. "We've thought of nothing else since DS Falmer told us about the body at the hospital. We have no idea who it was. Do we even know if it was a man or a woman, Detective Inspector?"

"Not at this stage. As you can imagine, having been in the centre of the blaze, the remains were badly compromised."

Rosaline's cheeks blanched. It looked like she might be sick. Her husband reached across and squeezed her hand. "Is it possible, this was the person who started the fire? Perhaps they broke into our house, intending to steal something, and dropped a match or a cigarette which started a fire and then found themselves trapped?" Roger glanced between the two detectives with something like hope in his expression.

"We are examining all possible scenarios," Alice replied carefully. "Do you think the fire was started deliberately then?"

Roger shrugged. "Possibly, unless it was a burglar who started it by mistake. None of us smokes, but if someone were to drop a match, our house is full of old wooden furniture. It would have been like a tinderbox."

"We found no evidence of a burglary," Pete offered.

Roger whipped his head up. "I saw the aftermath of that fire. I don't imagine how you could possibly know if a window or door had been jemmied. It seems the only possible explanation for that *person* being in our house."

Alice sensed the man was only just holding onto his composure. She supposed it was no surprise, considering his property had almost been burnt to the ground and his entire family killed. She softened her tone. "It really doesn't help to speculate at this stage. If this person wasn't known to you or Mrs Golding, perhaps they were known to your au-pair? The body was found in the section of the house where she had her living quarters?"

Rosaline shifted uncomfortably in her seat. "It's something we've considered. I've asked Maria a dozen times, she says it was nothing to do with her."

"Okay, we will be asking *her* those questions ourselves." Alice took a deep breath. "Mr Golding, we are going to need to check your whereabouts during the night of the fire. Did you remain in your hotel in Aberdeen for the entire night?"

Roger's mouth fell open. "Do you think I might have set fire to my own house, with my wife and children inside!?"

It was Rosaline's turn to place a reassuring hand on his arm. "Keep your voice down, darling. They've got to ask that question. It's routine, I expect."

Alice nodded. "You were at a work conference, I believe? If you can supply us with the details, I'm sure we can establish your movements easily enough."

A thin sheen of sweat had broken out on his top lip. "I'm a Geochemist, based at the university on Clydebank. I also do survey work for a big oil and gas company in Aberdeen. That's why I was at the conference this week. I was giving a talk on the possibility of geothermal energy providing a future for oil companies in a post-fossil fuel world. The talk took place at 3.45 until 5.15, it was well attended."

"Ok, what about in the evening? Did you have dinner at the hotel?"

Roger began wringing his hands. "Actually, a few of us went out to a restaurant in the city, as it was our last night. I can, of course, give you their names?"

"Yes, we will need those. What time did you return to your hotel?"

"It would have been around 11pm. We had a nightcap in the bar and I retired to my room around midnight. I would have been over the limit to drive by then. We had a couple of bottles between us at the restaurant. I was down for breakfast around 8.30am."

"Thank you," Alice jotted some notes on her tablet. She knew Roger Golding was mentioning he was over the limit to suggest there was no way he could have driven back to the house in Fairlie that night, although Alice wasn't sure that if you were intending to set fire to your house with your family inside you would worry about a spot of drink driving. Besides, the man could easily have stuck to water all evening. Wishing to keep a clear head.

Roger eyed the DI quizzically, as if he could tell what she was thinking. It unnerved her. "Thank you for your help. We will need to have a word with Maria now. In private, if possible."

Chapter 9

Maria Silva sat on the edge of the single bed in her hotel room. She was small, with birdlike movements and a wavy crop of dark hair. She had a gold stud in her nose and a gash of scarlet lipstick defined her narrow mouth. She cradled a glass of water in both hands.

"How long have you worked for the Goldings, Maria?" Alice sat opposite her on an occasional chair. Pete leant against the window sill. The space felt cramped and airless.

"Since November of 2020. I'd flown over just after the New Year from Valencia. I spent a few months in Glasgow first." Her English was fluent, as far as Alice could tell.

"What sort of duties do you have?"

"I am mainly responsible for the children. I get them up in the mornings, make breakfast and get them ready for school. I use Mrs Golding's car to drive them to school."

"Which school do they go to?"

"Wemyss Academy. All three are in the prep school there. It is a long drive, the local primary is much closer, but the family wish for them to attend a private place." The final words were delivered with a moue of distaste.

Alice had come across Wemyss Academy before, in a previous case. "And when the children are at school? What do you do?"

"Plenty," the woman retorted, as if she'd been insulted. "I go to the supermarket, return to the house and tidy up. I must walk the dog and do the laundry. It is a large house and there are many jobs until I pick the children up again."

"Did you put the children to bed on the night of

the fire?"

An anguished look passed across her face, soon replaced by the guarded expression she seemed to permanently adopt. "Yes, I supervised bath time and made sure they were ready for their mother to come and read the younger ones a story. I retire to my room then. Mrs Golding likes that time with them alone."

"Did you notice anything odd that evening? Were there any visitors? Packages being delivered? That kind of thing?"

She shook her head fiercely. "No, I didn't receive any visitors that night. I've told the Goldings that."

"I don't mean the visitor was for you, necessarily. It could have been a tradesperson, perhaps?"

She shrugged exaggeratedly. "Not that night, that I remember. The post box is at the bottom of the driveway. Deliveries don't come to the door."

"What did you do after you retired to your rooms?"

She narrowed her eyes suspiciously, as if this question was an attempt to catch her out. "I watched some shows on my phone, took a shower and went to bed. I am exhausted after a day working in that house. I didn't light any candles, smoke any joints or start any fires. I have already told the Goldings this when they asked me."

Alice knew they would have more information on the cause of the fire when the forensics came back. There was no point pressing the girl now. "Did you hear anything during the night? Any movements downstairs?"

"I sleep with my earphones in, playing music. It helps me switch off."

Alice sighed, not thinking it was a very safe idea to cut off one of your senses so completely whilst at your most vulnerable. She didn't say so. "Okay, well, you must have heard the smoke alarms the following morning?"

"Of course, the noise would cut through anything. But I was already awake. My phone alarm had buzzed. I need to be up early to make the breakfast. I was brushing my teeth when the alarms started. I pulled on some clothes and ran into the corridor, smoke was filling the stairwell. The Goldings have put me on my own in the north wing. It hasn't been as nicely renovated as the rest of the house. I am aware my status is lower than that of the rest of the family, so I know I have to get myself out of there or I will be left to burn." She sniffed, as her brown eyes developed a glassy sheen. "I pulled my cardigan off and held it over my mouth. I ran down the stairs and out the front door. Mr Golding keeps the key in the lock. I didn't look back."

Pete had been listening quietly to the young woman's testimony. "It sounds as if you aren't very happy with the Goldings. Why do you stay?"

She glanced up at him. "I have my own rooms, plenty of privacy. The children are well behaved and Mr and Mrs Golding leave me alone most of the time. I am the staff, I don't expect to be treated like one of them. I will make some money and then move on. My life was worse in Spain."

He didn't pursue the reasons why. Alice got to her feet, sensing their conversation was over.

The two detectives left the hotel, emerging into a smirr of rain. "What did you make of that?" Alice asked as they approached the car.

"Maria Silva is extremely defensive and obviously doesn't care much for her employers. I sensed she wasn't telling us everything, that's for sure. Mr Golding looked mightily nervous when we asked about his trip to Aberdeen."

"Yep, I noticed that." Alice climbed behind the

wheel. "But it may have nothing to do with the fire. There could be another woman involved. We may get more out of him if we tackle him without his wife present."

Pete nodded. "But it means we have to check his alibi thoroughly. Is it possible to drive from Aberdeen to here and back between midnight and eight am?"

Alice pulled out of the driveway into the thickening traffic. "I'm not sure. But I'm certainly going to find out."

Chapter 10

It was Saturday morning and the autumn sunlight was dappling the bedsheets as Alice rolled over and shut her eyes, hoping to gain another ten minutes or so of rest. She could hear the muffled noises of Fergus and Charlie playing in the living room directly below. The echoing sound of plastic hitting plastic suggested they had the Duplo bricks out. She smiled contentedly, snuggling under the duvet.

The DI must have dozed off, because she awoke from a pleasant dream about oceans and white sand to the buzz of her phone on the bedside table.

She cursed as she swiped right on the screen, seeing it was the West Kilbride Station. "DI Mann," she barked.

"Sorry to bother you at home, Ma'am. It's DC Gadd here."

"Go ahead, Holly." Alice raised herself onto an elbow.

"We've had a walk-in at the station reception desk this morning. The desk sergeant processed the report and thought it might be of interest to us." The detective cleared her throat. "It was a woman who came in, aged in her late fifties, the sergeant reckoned. Her name was Victoria Braden. She lives in Seamill Road, we took her full address. Only, she wanted to report her nephew missing. He's twenty-four years old and is living with her right now. She's not seen him since Wednesday morning."

Alice was suddenly wide awake. "The morning before the fire at Hill House?"

"Aye, Ma'am. I thought you'd want to know right away, what with our unidentified body and everything."

Alice had already swung her legs round to rest on

the cool floorboards. "I'm coming into the station. Just give me half an hour."

*

Fergus hadn't been pleased about her rapid departure but he had understood. Alice had held Charlie in her arms for a long time and buried her face into the swirly crown of his thick hair. She'd barely seen him all week as it was. Her son was absolutely fine, of course. He'd been with his grandparents and would now have great fun with his dad who he'd also seen little of all week. But it didn't diminish the pang of separation that caused an ache akin to heartburn in her chest.

She pulled into the station car-park. She had to focus on the case, like she'd always been able to do in the past. Alice paused at the front desk. She gave the desk sergeant a friendly smile. "I'm DI Alice Mann. I'm not sure we've properly met."

"No, Ma'am. I'm on the weekend shift this week, not been in 'til now. Holly said you're interested in ma' walk-in from this morning?" Sergeant Armstrong wore a tight, short-sleeved uniform shirt which revealed a mass of intricate tattoos on the biceps of both arms. He stabbed his keyboard with an enthusiasm that suggested barely suppressed strength. "She came in at 8.30 am. Early for a Saturday. She looked quite distressed. I took down her details here."

"Could you send those to me, please?"

"Aye. I've already sent a copy to Holly. She's upstairs."

Alice nodded her thanks and made for the lift. The benefit of working out of a small station like this, was that walk-ins like Victoria Braden didn't get missed. At Pitt Street, such reports were one amongst dozens and an inexperienced officer taking down the details may not register a connection with one of the many on-going cases they dealt with all the time.

Holly was seated at her desk, sipping from a mug of tea. She lifted it up when she saw Alice approach. "Can I make you one, Ma'am?"

"No thank you. Let's look at what you've got." Alice wheeled over a chair.

"I've already looked up Mrs Braden's details on the DVLA database. Her address matches the one she gave Len this morning. She's 58 years old and drives a Hyundai. She told Len her nephew is called Leroy Torben. He's 24 and has lived with her since he finished studying at college. She said his mum, her sister, now lives abroad and his father is long off the scene."

"When did Mrs Braden last see her nephew? Does he have a job?"

Holly nodded vigorously and her glossy hair shimmered. "She last saw him at breakfast on Wednesday morning. He works as an apprentice at a garage in the town. She only called them on Thursday, when Leroy hadn't come home the previous night. The manager said he'd not shown up for work and they'd been trying to reach him on his mobile. The lady was quite cross they hadn't called his home number, then she would have known earlier that he was missing. She waited another day, getting increasingly frantic and then walked in here first thing."

"Mrs Braden obviously cares very much for her nephew," Alice rubbed her chin. "He's 24 years old and has been missing a couple of days. It's entirely possible he's off with a girlfriend somewhere."

"Yes, I expect that's what Len would have suggested if it hadn't been for the timescale matching with our arson in Fairlie." Holly sipped her tea.

"It's lucky he noticed. Did the woman give a description of her nephew?"

"Yep, and better than that, she left a photograph." Holly took a glossy print of a young man in a football kit, posing with a ball tucked under his arm from a file and passed it to the DI.

Alice examined the image carefully. The man was of medium height and lean build, obviously physically fit. He was of mixed ethnic heritage; she assumed Afro-Caribbean and Scottish.

As if Holly could tell what she was thinking she added, "his aunt gave us as much information as she could. Her nephew is 5'10" and skinny (in her words). He doesn't have a girlfriend right now, that she is aware of, which is why she is so concerned. The last time she saw him, he was dressed for work; which means old jeans and a sweatshirt, big work boots, which he puts overalls on top of when he gets to the garage."

Alice crinkled her brow in thought. "I'll chase up the pathologist and inform him we may have a possible missing person to compare with our corpse. I seem to recall him saying something about sturdy black boots surviving the fire, but I don't think we should jump the gun just yet. I suggest we check with his workplace and his mates; confirm this young lad really is missing before we make any suggestion to poor Mrs Braden that the burnt body in our morgue is her nephew."

Chapter 11

The officers on duty that weekend included Holly Gadd and DC Matt Singh. Alice decided to allow Pete to have his days off and instead, took Holly with her into the town, leaving Matt to hold the fort. It was the young DC's lead they were chasing up, after all.

The rain of the previous days had cleared and the sky was a powder blue; the sun highlighting the ever shifting auburns of the trees lining their route. Rossmore Garage was located at the end of the Main Street in West Kilbride. Alice pulled up to the kerb and parked a few yards from the entrance.

Five cars filled the forecourt, one of them was raised on a floor jack. Several mechanics were working on them, wearing the dark grey overalls and heavy boots Mrs Braden had described. The detectives walked past the men and entered a workshop. A desk was positioned in one corner and a portly man in overalls unzipped to the waist, exposing a grubby T-shirt, rested his weight on the corner of it.

"Mr Doyle?" Alice displayed her ID badge. "We spoke earlier on the phone. I'm DI Mann and this is DC Gadd."

He nodded. "Aye, that was me. Any word yet on Leroy?"

"No, he still hasn't returned home. When was the last time you saw him, exactly?"

Doyle reached out for a cloth and wiped his oily hands whilst he considered this. "He came in on Wednesday morning, 'till twelve. But he'd booked a half day. Said he had an appointment. I assumed it was at the docs. He doesn't ever ask for time off, so I was happy to agree. But then he didn't turn up on Thursday, which is really unusual for the lad. I kept calling his mobile, which went to voicemail, until his aunt called me in a state later that day to say he'd not been home."

Alice exchanged glances with Holly. "So Leroy left the premises at midday on Wednesday, and this was not a typical occurrence?"

"Nope, he finished at 5.30pm usually, like the rest of the lads. Unless we had a job on that needed completing for a deadline, then I offer time and a half. The boys are always keen, they're young mostly, with no ties."

"Did Leroy have any ties that you know of? Any girlfriends on the scene?"

"Not that he mentioned. He is a bit immature for his age. Those boys who've been to college always are. He's most friendly with Ewan Dawson. They play footie together in a local team, a few of the lads here are players, we've got a small sponsorship at the ground. But you're better off talking to Ewan. He's working on the Fiesta out front. The overalls have name badges on."

Alice made a note of this. "We will, thanks. Did Leroy change out of his overalls before he left on Wednesday lunchtime?"

Doyle creased his dirty brow. "I can't rightly remember. But the lads usually keep their overalls on until they get home. It's their job to keep them clean."

"Do you have any spares that I could take a look at? Ideally, I'd like to take one away for possible analysis."

Doyle eyed her suspiciously, wondering what this odd request could possibly mean. "I've got a few in weird sizes in the cupboard over there. You could take one of those."

"Thanks. Could you get it out for me?"

Holly clutched a carrier bag holding one of the spare overalls. The detectives approached a bright red Fiesta with its bonnet up. One of the mechanics was leaning into it, his top half obscured.

"Ewan Dawson?" She asked sharply.

The young man jumped, very nearly catching his head on the edge of the metal lid. "Aye? What's the problem?"

Alice immediately noticed the badge sewn onto the top pocket of the man's overalls, with DAWSON, printed in capitals. She noted how easily identifiable you'd be wandering about outside the garage in such a garment. She showed him her badge. "It's about Leroy Torben. He's not been seen since Wednesday lunchtime. His aunt has reported him missing. Mr Doyle says you were good mates?"

He slammed the bonnet shut and rested both hands on it. "We *are* good mates. Leroy and I play for a local team; the Seamill Shooters. We practise on a Friday evening at a ground near the Law Hill. A group of us go to the pub after."

"When did you last hear from him?"

Dawson eyes flashed with what looked like anger. "Not since I saw him here on Wednesday morning." He kicked one of his heavy boots against the front tyre of the car. "I've not had a message since, but I didn't think anything of it. I've been busy here and I thought I'd see him on Friday night. Catch-up then."

"So you would usually expect to have heard from him after this long."

The anger in his eyes had been replaced by sadness. "Yeah, I would. I just can't believe I didn't think to ring Victoria. I just thought he had a stomach bug or something and that's why he wasn't in work."

"Did Leroy have a girlfriend? A boyfriend?"

Dawson sighed. "He was really shy with girls. We chatted to lasses sometimes on nights out. He was decent looking and girls were interested, but he could be awkward with them."

"A bit immature for his age?" Alice repeated the garage manager's phrase.

"Yeah, that's right. He was a bit innocent, really. So that's why him going AWOL is really out of character."

Alice nodded solemnly. She handed him a card. "My number is on there and the number for the West Kilbride investigation department. Give us a call if Leroy gets in touch, or if you think of anything that might be useful, anything at all."

"Aye, I will." The young man's eyes misted as he stared at the card, as if all his fears had solidified in the dark formal letters printed there.

Chapter 12

Ten minutes later, they were back at the station. Alice was beginning to appreciate the benefits of provincial policing. You didn't have to spend a third of your day in city traffic.

This time when Holly offered to make teas, the DI didn't argue. Matt Singh was at his desk and Victor Novak had obviously now started his shift. Alice called them to gather around her desk, ensuring they were all furnished with a hot drink.

"Holly and I have just got back from Rossmore Garage, where our missing person, Leroy Torben, works. He was last seen at 12pm on Wednesday, the day of the fire at Hill House. We got a spare uniform, identical to the one Leroy was wearing on the day he disappeared. I'm having it biked over to the forensic lab this afternoon. They should be able to compare it to fibres extracted from our dead body."

"But we can't be certain he would have been wearing the overalls in the fire? Even if this man is our John Doe?" Victor sipped his coffee.

"No, and it would seem more likely he took them off soon after leaving the garage," Alice conceded. "The overalls would have been dirty and have a name badge on the top left pocket. I can't imagine anyone wishing to walk about town in them. It would make you very conspicuous."

"Then where are they?" Matt asked. "Does Leroy have a car?"

Alice shook her head. "No. He was saving up for one, according to his aunt's statement. He got the bus to work and when he was going out in town. I've requested the CCTV for his regular route for the Wednesday he disappeared."

"Might he have dumped them? How about the

nearby litter bins?" Holly offered.

"Yes, it's possible. But then finding them wouldn't be of any great use to us. It doesn't tell us where he was heading next."

"I think our priority should be to get a positive ID on the body. There's no point trying to track this lad down if he's already dead." Victor drained his mug.

"True. I wanted to be absolutely certain Leroy was missing and not just crashed out with a lassie somewhere before I requested a DNA swab from Mrs Braden." Alice sighed. "I think it's time we paid the poor lady a visit."

*

Holly Gabb's shift was over, so Alice asked Matt Singh to drive her to Victoria Braden's address. She needed to be gentle with the woman and sensed Matt may have a softer touch than Victor, although it was early days to be totally sure about the characters of her new team.

The house was a semi-detached property halfway along Seamill Road. The ten year old Hyundai that was registered to Mrs Braden was parked in the driveway. Matt slotted the squad car beside it.

"We need to tread carefully," Alice told her colleague before they climbed out of the vehicle. "I don't want to mention the dead body just yet. Follow my lead."

Matt released his seatbelt and trailed his superior to the door. Victoria Braden answered after one knock. Her grey streaked hair was neatly brushed to her shoulders but her face was lined with worry.

"Is there any news, detective?"

"No, I'm sorry. Can we come inside?"

The lady shuffled backwards into a dark hallway. "Of course. I just got off the phone from my sister. It wasn't an easy conversation, as you can imagine."

She led them into a small but pleasant sitting room facing a well-tended garden.

"Where is Leroy's mother living? We will need her address," Alice asked gently.

"Caroline is living in Almeria in Spain. She and her partner run a bar. I'll give you the number." She went to get an address book from a phone table in the hall and recited the digits carefully, including the international code.

"Thank you. Mrs Braden, I visited the garage where your nephew works this morning. According to the manager, Leroy had a half day on Wednesday. He left work at 12pm, saying he had an appointment."

The woman's eyes widened. "He didn't say a word to me. So he's been missing longer than I thought!" She fished a balled tissue from her cardigan pocket and dabbed at tears which had begun escaping onto her cheeks.

"I'm afraid that does seem to be the case. We would like to take a look around his room, if that's okay? There may be something in there which gives us a clue as to where he has gone."

"Yes, of course. Whatever you think would be helpful."

Alice cleared her throat. "And I would like to take a swab of DNA from you. This means that if we discover something we think may belong to Leroy, a piece of clothing perhaps, we can perform some tests to be sure."

Victoria looked at the DI with a puzzled expression. She blinked vigorously, the tears drying up as realisation seemed to dawn. "You mean if you find a *body*!"

Matt shuffled to the edge of his seat. "It's standard procedure, Mrs Braden. You are his closest blood relative here in the country. We want to do everything we can to find your nephew. Once these formalities are out of the way, we can concentrate on the search."

These words seemed to calm her down. "Yes, yes, I can see that. I'll give you the sample, certainly. I'm grateful you are taking my report seriously."

It always struck Alice as particularly tragic how, in the early days, families were grateful for any efforts the police made to find their missing loved ones. She also knew how quickly that gratitude switched to anger and recrimination when the case dragged on or the outcomes were bad. "That's okay, Mrs Braden. It's our job. Now, if you wouldn't mind, DC Singh and I will take a look upstairs."

Chapter 13

Alice sat on the edge of the neatly made single bed. The room was small but tidy. It overlooked an equally well-tended but bijou back garden. Matt Singh was examining the contents of the wardrobe.

"There's the usual selection of jeans, t-shirts and hoodies hanging here, along with his footie team kit and boots. I don't see any signs Leroy has packed to go away for a few days."

Alice sighed. "But his room is amazingly tidy, isn't it? It's got the look of somewhere somebody didn't just leave in a hurry to get to work."

Matt gazed around the small space. There were a couple of nondescript framed prints on the walls and a line of male moisturisers and aftershaves on top of the chest of drawers. "Aye, he was obviously a neat lad. Unless his aunt tidies up after him? Maybe she's been in here since Leroy disappeared?"

Alice crinkled her brow. If she had been, it was bad news for them. They needed the scene to be exactly the way the young man had left it, to get a sense of his frame of mind. She lifted the wicker bin by the bed. "It's empty. That's not a good sign. I hope Victoria hasn't been on a cleaning spree?"

The drawers were filled with underwear and more pairs of smart-casual clothes. "Well, his work overalls aren't here, or his black boots."

Alice dragged open the single drawer in the bedside table. She immediately spotted his driver's licence and an out of date student card. She picked them up and placed them in an evidence bag. "He certainly wasn't planning on hiring a car, or borrowing someone else's." She rummaged again, finding a few postcards from his mother in Spain; the messages short and sweet. "He must have his phone on him, wherever he is. What about a laptop?"

Matt shrugged. "There's not one in this room. We'll need to ask Mrs Braden. Perhaps he only uses a smart phone. You can do everything on those these days."

Alice nodded. "Yes, but Leroy had studied at college. I'd expect him to have had a laptop for that. I think we need to have another word with his aunt before we leave and see if we can get a copy of any of his phone bills. See if we can trace him that way."

Matt made sure the drawers were closed as neatly as when they entered. "Yes, Ma'am. Sounds like a good idea."

*

It was Sunday morning and the West Kilbride police station would usually have been as quiet as the grave. But the floor dedicated to the criminal investigation team was a hive of activity. Alice had requested the whole of her team come in. They all agreed without complaint.

The DI called her colleagues to gather around the flip-chart at the front of the open-plan space. She'd managed to find a café that was open and appeared to possess a decent Italian machine. She placed a tray of black coffees on the desk in front of her, ready for the officers to add their own milk and sugar.

"Help yourselves, folks. I appreciate you coming in on a Sunday morning when we aren't officially a murder investigation just yet. But a young man is missing and we have an unidentified body in the morgue, which to me suggests we need to crack on."

The detectives assembled before her all nodded and mumbled their agreement. Pete Falmer stepped forward. "How soon will we get the forensic results,

Ma'am?"

"Dr Webb has promised me his *PM* report first thing tomorrow morning. As of yesterday afternoon, he also has a sample of Victoria Braden's DNA, which I'm hoping he will have had time to compare with any DNA lifted from the body. That will make it clear once and for all if our missing man is the John Doe in the city morgue."

Matt Singh raised his hand. "Mrs Braden confirmed that Leroy Torben does have a laptop computer but she's got no idea where it is. I called the manager of Rossmore Garage and he's going to have a good look around the place tomorrow morning, but he's pretty certain Leroy didn't bring the device to work. He claims never to have seen it before and that the garage isn't the kind of place you'd bring your valuable possessions."

Alice nodded, taking up the narrative, "because Leroy didn't have much in the way of material possessions as it was. His room contained a meagre collection of inexpensive smart-casual clothing. He was saving to buy a car and his bank account indicates he wasn't very far along in that process. He had about £500 saved. He's not used his bank card since before he went missing. His phone company were very helpful and we are being sent a print-out of his call logs for the past year. Again, his number hasn't been used since Wednesday morning and is now switched off."

"It would be useful to see who he contacted on Wednesday morning though," Holly chipped in.

"Aye, we'll know that when the call logs come in," Matt said. "What wasn't so helpful is that Victoria Braden had tidied her nephew's room on the Wednesday afternoon, before she knew he was missing. She dusted and emptied his waste bin. She also took out any dirty clothing on the floor and washed them."

Victor Novak narrowed his eyes. "This Leroy is 24 years old, right? He is paying rent to his aunt for the use of the room. I know they are related and everything, but going into his room like that and tidying his stuff, it strikes me as weird. Our son is 16, I know it's a difficult age, but he doesn't let Lena anywhere near his room. Why would a grown man let his aunt have such open access to his private space?"

Alice thought about this. "Maybe he doesn't have a lot of choice? If Mrs Braden lets him stay on a peppercorn rent, he may feel obliged to let her have access? He doesn't have a dad on the scene and his mother is in another country. She's his only support network."

For some reason this made Matt Singh shudder. "The aunt clearly cares about Leroy and everything, but something about her place gave me the creeps. Just a bit *too* tidy, you know?"

Alice wasn't entirely convinced this was sinister in itself. She was a neat person and understood the compulsion. "Okay, we bear in mind that the aunt may have a little too much access to Leroy's personal space. That definitely gives the young man a motive to take off without telling her. He might have had enough of it. But he certainly wasn't planning to go very far, he'd not packed any clothing that we could see, or to hire a car, he left his drivers' licence. Mrs Braden told us he doesn't have a passport that she is aware of. He's never left the country before. It's not obvious he took anything much at all from his room." The DI ran a hand through her auburn hair. "Holly, could you look into Leroy Torben's digital footprint? Check his social media presence and if possible gain access from the main sites to view his private messaging?"

Holly drained her coffee cup and tossed it into a bin. "I'll get right on it, Ma'am."

"Victor, I'd like you and Matt to investigate the aunt a little further. What job does she do? Why isn't the husband on the scene? That kind of thing." She turned to the only DS on her team. "I don't want to pre-empt the forensic reports, but could you focus on the Golding family, Pete? I want to know if there could be any connection between them and Leroy Torben. Have they ever booked their car into Rossmore Garage for a service, for instance? Has Roger Golding ever drunk in the same pub as Leroy's footie team? Maria Silva is a similar age. Did they meet on a night out in town, maybe?"

Pete nodded sagely. He crushed his empty coffee cup with his good hand. "Sure thing. I'll get started right now."

Chapter 14

The fire had been lit, creating a gentle warmth. The aroma of a joint roasting in the oven floated from the kitchen at the rear of the ground floor. Both these sensations welcomed Alice as she stepped through the front door into the tiled hallway of her house.

Fergus's tall frame filled the kitchen doorway. An apron was tied around his waist. Alice dropped her briefcase and shrugged out of her raincoat. She took a few steps before folding herself into his arms. "Thank you. This is just what I needed."

"I could hardly encourage you to take on the leadership of a new department and then not try to smooth the way for you a little bit." He rested his chin on the top of her head. "But I have got this new case starting next week. I'm sorry, it couldn't be shifted. The timing is awful, I know."

Alice allowed her eyes to close and the softness of Fergus's woollen sweater to comfort her. He smelt faintly of coffee. "I know. It's your job and can't be helped. At least we've got my parents close to hand."

He pulled back from their embrace and motioned for her to take a seat at the table. "They've been great. Absolute lifesavers. Are you sure they're okay with all the childcare? My folks want the freedom to attend all their clubs and keep up with their hobbies. They'd do the occasional day, but wouldn't want to be tied down full-time."

Alice wriggled her toes in her black tights, getting the circulation moving. "They seem to love it. Having Charlie is giving them a purpose again. I don't think retirement ever suited them all that much."

"As long as it isn't an imposition." He placed a glass of wine on the table in front of Alice. Taking a long sip from his own. "We both have well-paid professional jobs. We could try childcare again. I know there are better places than the one we used before." The words hung in the air like an early morning autumn mist.

Despite the warmth of the kitchen, Alice felt a chill go through her body. She gulped a mouthful of the Malbec, which was smooth and subtly fruitful, and really should have been savoured more. "I can't consider that yet. Mum and Dad are fine with the situation for now. Charlie is so young yet. He needs to be with family. How has he been today, by the way? Was he upset that I had to go in to work?"

Fergus tried to hide the concern which was forming deeper lines on his handsome face. He knew that Alice's parents were perfectly happy to look after their son for as long as was needed, but he worried that Alice may never be comfortable about leaving Charlie with strangers again, which wouldn't be healthy for any of them. "He was grand. We went for a tramp through the forest. You know how he loves to stomp through leaves in his wellies. After his bath he was exhausted. He dropped off pretty quickly, even though he said he'd wait up for you."

Alice smiled, she'd go and check on him when she finished her wine. Tears prickled in the corners of her eyes. It was just the tiredness and missing a Sunday with her little boy. She swiftly wiped them away with the back of her hand.

Fergus was bending down to retrieve the roasting tray from the oven, so he didn't notice her sudden wave of emotion. The smell of the bubbling meat juices made Alice's mouth water.

The phone began ringing in the hallway.

"I'll get it," Alice said quickly.

"Thanks, darling," Fergus replied, the tray half way to the worktop.

The DI padded along the corridor and lifted the receiver. It wasn't her work phone so there was no need for formalities. "Hello?"

The line crackled in silence for several beats.

"Hello? This is Alice Mann. Can I help you?" She was about to lose her patience and hang up. They'd only recently been connected and had received a few wrong numbers.

"DI Mann?" A voice that was deep and gravelly enquired.

"Yes, who is this please?" Her tone was snappy and impatient.

"You need to go back to where you came from."

"I beg your pardon?"

"You are interfering where it's not wanted. Go back to the big city and take your little family with you."

The mention of Fergus and Charlie made her stomach constrict with dread. "How did you get this number?"

"Consider this your first warning. The next won't be so pleasant." The line went dead.

Alice was left holding the receiver limply in her hand, the comforting warmth of the house now making her feel hot and claustrophobic, as if she and the people she loved the most were at the centre of a mounting inferno, one that would very soon engulf them all.

Chapter 15

The criminal investigation department of West Kilbride police station was as deserted as the Marie-Celeste. Alice was the only officer at her desk. She sipped her takeout coffee. A double-espresso had seemed an appropriate choice at this early hour.

Alice hadn't mentioned the details of the previous night's phone call to Fergus. He had an important case he was defending at the Edinburgh High Court that week. There was no point in worrying him. She knew her parents took very good care of Charlie, watching him every second of the day. They also had CCTV cameras positioned on the front and back of their bungalow. She was confident he couldn't be any better protected.

The coffee was bitter but welcome. She drained the cup and dropped it in the bin. The DI had barely slept. She managed to eat the delicious meal Fergus had prepared for her, but, despite its succulence, the meat seemed to lodge in her throat. She'd had to wash it down with copious amounts of red wine. The voice on the phone was unrecognisable. The gravelly tone suggested some kind of voice distorter had been used. She rubbed at her tired eyes.

The door to the stairwell swung open. Alice started at the noise, angry with herself for being so jumpy. Pete Falmer strode across the floor and dropped his briefcase next to his desk. "Morning, Ma'am."

"Call me Alice, please." She stood up and moved across to his workstation. "I'm glad you're the first here."

Pete crinkled his brow, looking puzzled. Alice proceeded to describe the threatening phone call she'd received the previous night. The DS's brow furrowed more deeply as she went on.

"I'm assuming you checked the caller ID?"

"Withheld," Alice said with a sigh. "We've only recently been connected to the landline with BT. We nearly didn't bother, with us both having smartphones. But my parents like to use the telephone."

"Old school." Pete grinned, trying to ease the tension a little. "Do you want me to check with BT? See if they can locate the origin of the call?"

"Yes, please." She cleared her throat. "And could you keep this to yourself?"

He looked concerned again. "Of course. Any reason?"

Alice dropped into the seat beside him. "I got the sense that whoever made that call to me last night, isn't happy about me having joined the team here in West Kilbride. They told me to 'stop interfering where I'm not wanted'." She glanced around the empty office floor. "What if the threat came from someone here at the station? I've stepped in without notice and started bossing everyone around. I could have put a nose out of joint. A police officer would have a better chance of being able to find out my home number."

Pete shook his head with feeling. "I just can't see it. To be honest, we've been out of our depth since DI Mitchie took leave. I'm supposed to be in charge, but the others have all known me since I was in uniform. We muddled through, but now you've come along and we have a proper investigation to get our teeth into, it's been a bloody relief."

Alice nodded. "You may feel that way, but what about the others? Victor and Matt strike me as ambitious. Might they have wanted to take command after Mitchie left?"

Pete massaged his freshly shaven chin, which was still a little red. "They might have, but both need to pass their sergeants exams first. They're both due to sit them in the new year. Holly is over the moon she's got a female mentor, she told me as much yesterday morning."

"Good, I'm glad Holly's on side. She's got the makings of an excellent detective." Alice sighed. "It just strikes me that the phone call came on the evening after I'd called the entire team in on a Sunday. I could imagine that pissing someone off, especially if they have a family."

Pete shrugged. "Victor's kids are teenagers now, I don't reckon that's such an issue. Matt's little ones are much younger. But they're both police officers. We know the score when an investigation is on."

Alice took a deep breath. She hoped Pete was right. The last thing she needed was to have a team who weren't loyal to her. She thought about DCI Bevan and the loyalty her officers showed to her in all circumstances. Her cheeks began to flush. Self-doubt was creeping in. Was she really cut out for leadership? Andy Calder always said she was too blunt, lacking empathy.

As if he could sense what she was thinking, Pete leant forward conspiratorially. "If you give me your landline number, I will contact BT. But please don't worry about the team. Between you and me, DI Mitchie wasn't popular. He asked us to do stuff we weren't always comfortable with. That goes for us all. You arriving has been a breath of fresh air."

Alice accepted his words with a strained smile. She walked back to her desk just as the department doors flung open again and more officers streamed onto the floor to begin the working day.

Chapter 16

At every single desk, heads were bent over computer keyboards and officers hard at work. When Alice's extension rang at 11.30am she was feeling guilty for ever having doubted the loyalty of her team.

"DI Mann?" She answered in a clipped tone.

"It's Dr Webb here, Detective Inspector, from the Clydebank Laboratory. I have the results of the *post mortem* on our fire 'John Doe'. It should be in your inbox right now."

Alice logged into her mail account with her free hand. "Yep, got it. Thanks."

"Would you like me to give you a *precis*?"

"If you would."

"Firstly, as we suspected, the body was of a young male. The length of femur and fusion of the bone suggested the age of our victim to be between 18-25."

Alice felt her heart beat faster. It definitely fitted the description of Leroy Torben. She didn't interrupt.

"The young man was of roughly 5'10" in height. We cannot definitively suggest his ethnic origin due to damage to the skin and inconclusive ethnic comparisons on the skull shape. He wore a size 10 boot. More on the clothing recovered from the scene will follow from the forensics department."

"Did you manage to extract DNA? Have you got a cause of death?"

The doctor chuckled. "You want to skip to the exciting bits, eh? Well, the internal organs were still largely intact, thanks to the swift controlling of the fire by the emergency services. He had eaten a meal of burger and chips approximately 12 hours previously, a small amount of cola drink, some milky tea and nothing since then. Some toxins were found in the bloodstream. He hadn't taken any illegal drugs or alcohol in the hours leading up to his death, but there were traces of barbiturates in his system, of the type you might buy over the counter at a chemist. A mild sleeping pill, but in quite a high dose. Not enough to kill him, though. Most significant of all, his lungs and oesophagus were completely clear of smoke or heat damage." He allowed this information to settle between them.

Alice had been a detective long enough to understand what this meant. "He didn't die in the fire."

"Quite correct. Unfortunately, the body was too fire damaged to be able to give you an alternative cause of death. We weren't able to test for bruising or stab wounds, although his major organs and soft tissue bore no evidence of penetration. I can tell you he wasn't poisoned, nor was his skull bludgeoned in any way, but he may have been beaten in a superficial manner, but not strangled. His heart seemed healthy as did his kidneys and lungs. We simply cannot tell you any more, due to the extent of the burns."

Alice shook her head. "So, our John Doe was already dead when the fire started?"

"Yes. That I can tell you with absolute certainty. He did not take a single breath after that fire had begun."

"Then that makes the question of how he got there even more important."

"Yes. If our victim got to the house whilst he was alive, he was certainly dead by the time the fire started."

"Is it possible that the victim had an accident and died before the fire began? A fall, or cut that left him unconscious so he was unable to get out? What I'm asking, is whether there is any way this wasn't murder, Dr Webb?"

"The body wasn't found at the foot of a stairwell, or beneath a balcony of some sort, where he may have fallen and received a fatal injury. A cut in itself would not have prevented his escape that I can envisage, however nasty. If he'd fainted, he would have come to soon enough. Instead, the body was discovered in a small kitchenette at the centre of the blaze. That is where I would place a dead body if I wished to get rid of it, detective."

Alice grimaced. She'd come to the same conclusion. "Then someone else killed him. Or if he died by accident, the body was moved after death in an attempt to cover it up?"

"That would be my conclusion, yes."

"Okay, so how about the DNA swab I sent you? Were you able to compare it to our John Doe?" Alice actually found she had her fingers crossed under the desk and she'd never been superstitious in the slightest.

"Yes, I did. There was enough DNA extant on the body to perform the test. But you aren't going to believe what I found out there, either."

Chapter 17

Alice had gathered the team around her desk. The general mood was one of dedicated interest. The DI was determined to make the most of it. She briefly ran through the information Dr Webb had given her on the *PM* results, writing the key findings on her whiteboard with a pen rapidly losing its ink.

Matt Singh put up his hand. "So, our dead man didn't die in the fire?" He scratched his beard. "But the *PM* doesn't suggest an alternative cause of death?"

Alice shook her head despondently. "No. We are still waiting on the forensic results from the clothing and the scene, that may tell us more. The man was young and his organs suggest he was healthy. Whichever way we look at it, our John Doe did not die of natural causes. The barbiturates present suggest he may have been groggy at some point, but Dr Webb insists that by the time of the blaze, there wouldn't have been enough of the sedative in his system to render him unconscious."

Pete shifted in his seat. "Is he still a John Doe? What did Webb tell you about the DNA comparison?"

Alice took a breath, making sure each member of her team was fully engaged in what she was saying. "This is where it gets really interesting. Dr Webb compared the buccal swab we took from Victoria Braden with DNA extracted from the body." The DI looked closely at the notes she had taken, not wanting to get it wrong. "I had informed Webb that Braden was the maternal aunt of the man we believed to be our John Doe. If this was the case, he would have expected to see 19-33% shared DNA between Braden's sample and that taken from the body, which is typical between an aunt and nephew."

"Yes, I know about this because I took one of those ancestry DNA profile tests last year," Holly added eagerly. "My sister bought me the package for my birthday. A few of my relatives have already used the website and it matched me with them."

Alice nodded, pleased that someone was familiar with the science. "There was a definite match between the body in the morgue and Victoria Braden. There is no doubt they are related."

Victor let out a sigh of relief. "That's great news. We have an ID on our body. Something solid to build our investigation on."

Alice raised her hand. "Yes, it's definitely progress, but the match Webb discovered was not in the range of 19-33%. It was in the range of 33-50%."

Holly gasped. "That's like as close as you can get. It means the relation between the two is more like siblings, or mother and son."

Matt had furrowed his brow with confusion. "So what the hell does this mean? Is the body that of Leroy Torben or not?"

Pete tossed his pen onto the desk. "The lad has been missing without trace since the day of the fire. He shares 50% DNA with Mrs Braden, the woman who he was living with and is distraught at his absence. I'd say that body belongs to Leroy without a doubt. But regardless of what she's told everyone, Leroy was her *son*, not her nephew."

Alice nodded slowly, scanning the bullet points she'd printed on the board. "From what I've seen of these forensic results, Pete, I must say I entirely agree."

Chapter 18

The two DCs were eager to provide Alice and Pete with the information they'd so far gathered on Victoria Braden. Their body language was exuding enthusiasm, which Alice assumed was down to the fact they now knew for certain this was a murder investigation.

Matt opened his laptop so the screen was visible to his colleagues. "Victoria Braden, previously Torben, is 58 years old. She has no criminal convictions and has worked at the library in West Kilbride for over 20 years. She recently went part-time. Her colleagues say she is quiet and conscientious. Mrs Braden has never taken up a management position, but colleagues suggest she is very knowledgeable and well-liked by users."

Victor flipped open a notebook and continued the information flow. "She got married in 1990 to Greg Braden, a solicitor from Irvine. They had no children together. They were married for 6 years when he was killed in a car accident on the M77. A lorry ploughed into stationary traffic. Braden's car was one of the first it hit, he died instantly. The lorry driver was sentenced to 7 years for causing death by dangerous driving. A couple of others lost their lives too."

"So, she's been a widow for 26 years." Alice shook her head. "If she was Leroy's birth mother, why would she try to hide it? He would have been born a couple of years after the death of her husband. It would hardly have been scandalous?"

Pete considered this. "She seems like a very traditional sort of woman. Her habits are neat and controlled. Perhaps being a single-mother, with a child born out of wedlock, was something she couldn't countenance."

Matt let out a long breath. "Mrs Braden is certainly an up-tight sort of character. But we aren't living in a Brontë novel. I can't see her giving up her child just because of a few outdated values. And where does the sister fit in? She must have agreed to take on the baby as her own. Why would she do that?"

Alice lifted her jacket from the back of her chair. "You and Victor can find that out. I want the two of you to locate Caroline Torben in Almeria in Spain. She has a partner out there and they run a bar. Her sister claims they aren't married so hopefully she's kept her maiden name. Give her a call to inform her that her 'son' is confirmed dead. See what she's got to say about that."

"Do we let on we know she's not the mother, Ma'am?" Victor asked.

"See how the conversation progresses. I'd expect her to say she's coming over on the next plane. If we tell her what we know, it might spook her into staying put."

"Aye," Matt added sagely. "Once we've got her here in Scotland, we can question the lady a bit more closely."

*

There was no sign of life at the house on Seamill Road. Victoria Braden's Hyundai was parked in the driveway, so the officers were confident she must be at home.

Pete rang the doorbell. It took what seemed like an age for the woman to answer. The hallway behind her was in darkness. "Mrs Braden, may we come inside to talk to you?"

Her usually neat appearance was dishevelled.

Her hair was unbrushed and she wore a misshapen woollen jumper over old jeans. "Yes, come into the living room. I know it's bad news. I've felt it all day."

The officers followed her into the brighter room, which was lit by late afternoon sun and sat on the sofa, hoping their host would do the same. Mrs Braden hovered in the doorway. "Shall I make tea?"

"No, Mrs Braden, that isn't necessary. Please take a seat," Alice urged.

The woman dropped onto the armchair beside her, keeping her eyes fixed on the detectives, they were full of anguish and entreaty. "Please tell me. I have to know."

Pete cleared his throat. "We have now confirmed that a body removed from the scene of a serious house fire in Fairlie last Thursday morning was that of Leroy Torben. The DNA you supplied was a match for the body and the boots found with the body appear to correspond to a description given to us by Leroy's manager at Rossmore Garage of the boy's work boots."

Her body seemed to fold in half. Her head hung between her thin knees, as if she was trying not to faint.

"Are you okay?" Alice asked hastily. "Can I get you a glass of water?"

She shook her head. "There's no need. I've been trying to prepare myself, but you can't, not really. There's been no word for days and that's so unusual that of course I knew he was dead. But until you hear the words there's always hope." Tears were dripping onto the oatmeal carpet.

Pete took an unopened packet of tissues from his pocket, ripped it open and placed one in her limp hand. She dabbed at her face. "Can you tell me how he died?"

Alice shuffled closer in her seat. "We know that

Leroy was dead before the house fire started. He would not have known about any of that. Unfortunately, because of the damage to the body after death, the pathologist wasn't able to identify a precise cause of death. I'm sorry." Alice knew from experience there was no point trying to sugar coat the details of a *post mortem* to the family of a murder victim. If you didn't furnish them with the facts, they would only imagine far worse. "We believe Leroy must have died somewhere else and was placed close to the centre of the fire, perhaps to get rid of his body, or hide his cause of death."

Victoria had managed to lever herself back up to a sitting position but she was still trembling and holding the balled tissue in between darkly veined hands. "I don't understand. Why would someone want to do that to Leroy? He was a good boy; hardworking and sensible. He's never been in any trouble. What was he even doing at this house? Who set it on fire?" Her body jolted with a sudden thought. "I need to ring Caroline and tell her."

Alice took a deep breath. "We have an officer contacting your sister now. There's no need for you to do it, unless you wish to. But I think there's more you need to tell us about your relationship with Leroy, isn't there? The DNA comparison produced some results we weren't expecting."

"What do you mean?" Victoria glanced from one detective to the other, her expression questioning and panicky.

Alice continued in a gentle tone of voice, "the DNA results indicated that your relationship with Leroy was closer than that between aunt and nephew. You shared almost 50% DNA with him. That's more like the ratio we would expect between mother and son."

She licked her lips. "He must have inherited more

of Caroline's DNA than his father's. My sister and I are very alike in appearance, everyone has always said so. I'm not surprised Leroy took after me so much."

Alice shook her head. "That's not how genetics works, Mrs Braden. It's scientifically impossible for an aunt to share more than 33% of their DNA with a nephew."

Her voice lowered to a scratchy whisper. "I didn't know that."

"I realise you've had a terrible shock, but we need to find out what happened to Leroy. He lost his life at 24 years of age. We need to understand what happened to him, which means that we need to know *everything* about him. This is now a murder enquiry, Mrs Braden and there can be no more secrets."

The woman looked at Alice with an expression that could only be described as full of terror. "I think I'd like a solicitor with me," she said hoarsely. "the next time you come."

Chapter 19

In the grey drizzle, the house looked like something out of a horror film. Half of the building was still structurally sound. Floral curtains were visible behind several of the leaded windows. But when you allowed your vision to run along to the north side, you had to prevent yourself from gasping at the scene. The roof was semi-collapsed and the windows burnt out, like blackened, expressionless pits. The stonework was stained with soot and a few items of what would once have been expensive pieces of antique furniture lay in piles on the front driveway, either scorched from the flames or ruined from water damage.

Pete climbed out of the passenger door of the car. "I've no idea why they wanted to meet us here. I wouldn't have wished to return myself until the professionals had been in to sort it all out."

"It's still their home, I suppose," Alice replied.

They headed towards the southern end of the house, where a side door led them into a pleasant country kitchen which seemed utterly unaffected by the fire. Roger and Rosaline Golding sat at a large oak table, with papers spread out before them on the old, knotted wood.

Roger got to his feet. "Good afternoon, officers. Thanks for meeting us here. We were told by the North Ayrshire Fire Service we could begin the clean-up and we didn't want to waste any time."

"Yes," Pete said lightly. "The fire investigator has all the information she needs, although her report won't be ready for another few weeks."

Rosaline cleared a space on the tabletop. Please take a seat. We've got the Aga working so I can offer you tea?"

Alice pulled out a chair. "That would be lovely, thanks." She glanced about her. "Are the children with you?"

"No," Roger said hastily. "This isn't really the place for them. Maria is looking after them at the hotel. Rosaline's mother passed away a few years ago and my parents are down in England. I suppose we could all de-camp there for the time being, but we just wanted to be here, close to the house, so we could salvage something from this disaster." His face was pale and drawn, the worry clearly marked in chiselled lines around his eyes and mouth.

"I'm afraid you won't be able to leave the area for the time-being," Alice said firmly.

Rosaline spun round from her position at the stove. "Why? What's happened?"

"We have identified the body that was taken out of your property after the fire last Thursday. We know that the man who was killed was 24 years old. He was from West Kilbride and his name was Leroy Torben." Alice scanned both their faces for recognition. She saw nothing but shock.

Rosaline put a hand out to steady herself against the stone counter. "Now he's been named, it feels all the more real. He must have been the person who started the fire. Why would he do that?"

Pete cleared his throat. "We don't believe that is the case, Mrs Golding. We know from the *post mortem* findings that Leroy Torben was dead before the fire even started. His body was very badly damaged, but not enough to prevent the pathologist from finding this out."

Roger sprang to his feet, running a hand through his salt and pepper hair. "I don't understand! Do you mean there was a dead body in our house *before* the fire started? It doesn't make any sense!"

Rosaline seemed to have abandoned her attempt

to make drinks. Pete moved across to the stove and quietly took over. He found four mugs and waited until the water in the kettle had boiled. He then poured the steaming liquid over strong tea-bags and found an earthenware pot containing sugar, which he heaped into two of the cups, handing them carefully to each of their hosts.

Roger dropped back into his seat at the table. "Who was this man? What was he doing here?"

"Leroy lived with his aunt in West Kilbride. He was a college graduate who was an apprentice mechanic at the Rossmore Garage on the main street. He played football for the Seamill Shooters. They trained at the pitches below Law Hill and drank afterwards at The Law Bar on a Friday night. Might your paths have crossed in some way?"

Roger sipped from his mug, his expression one of bewilderment. "I've never heard of the football team or the bar. Maybe we've used the garage. We have my Land Rover and then the little runabout that Rosaline and Maria both use." He glanced over at his wife. "Have we ever used a garage in West Kilbride, darling?"

She shrugged her narrow shoulders, gripping the mug so tightly her knuckles were white. "I don't know. The Land Rover dealership do all the servicing for Roger's car. I suppose we could have used it for the Golf. It's ten years old, but pretty reliable."

Alice reached into her bag. She pulled out the photo of Leroy that Victoria Braden had given them. She handed it to Roger. "This is him. Take your time to have a good look. Perhaps he came to the house to visit your au-pair?"

Roger fished in the pocket of his plaid shirt for a pair of glasses which he slipped on. "He's very young. No, I don't think I've seen him before." He pushed the photo back towards the DI. "Do you think Maria knew him?"

Alice took the picture and moved across the room to hand it to Rosaline. She seemed to have to force herself to touch it. "We really don't know," Alice replied. "We will show the picture to Maria Silva and ask the same questions."

Rosaline stared at the photo. Her expression blank. "I've never seen him before. Certainly not here at the house." She handed it back. "Maria never brought friends here. She went into Glasgow maybe once a month. She had some friends from Spain who work over here and they'd meet up for drinks, but that was it, really."

Alice wasn't sure this woman would really know if their au-pair had visitors after the children had gone to bed. She lived in an entirely different wing of the house. But she didn't push it.

Pete sat back at the table, leaning his elbows on the wooden surface. "It doesn't make sense, you see? This man, Leroy Torben, was dead inside your house. Then, a terrible fire started in the exact spot his body had been. There's no evidence from the scene that he'd had an accident of any kind. So, the only conclusion we can come to, is that someone placed his body there deliberately."

Roger slumped forward, his head resting in his hands. "Oh God. I don't know how this happened. I'd been away since the Tuesday. Do you think that's why? This was planned for when I was away from the house?"

"It's a possibility we are investigating," Alice said levelly.

Rosaline took a step towards her husband, placing a hand on his shoulder. "I was in the house that whole time. I didn't hear a thing. Neither did the children. I can't speak for Maria, but she was certainly with us until the Wednesday evening. Apart from Roger not being here, it was just a normal day."

Alice couldn't help but sense this woman's statement felt almost rehearsed. Roger's shock seemed more genuine. "Obviously, we will need you to remain in the area for the foreseeable future. We will be questioning Maria Silva again and continuing to catalogue your movements in Aberdeen, Mr Golding. You will have to delay your clear-up as well I'm afraid."

Roger nodded with resignation. "Can I still submit a claim to our insurers?" He gestured towards the papers spread out before him.

"Certainly. Although, they will have to await the result of the fire investigation too."

The man's voice cracked. "What a bloody mess."

Alice moved towards the side door. "We'll see ourselves out."

The detectives crunched across the gravel to their parked car. "What did you think?" Pete asked.

Alice looked back towards the house. "She's hiding something," she said tersely, wrenching open the car door and getting behind the wheel.

Chapter 20

Fergus was staying at a friend's flat in Edinburgh for the duration of the trial. He'd asked repeatedly if this was still okay; whether he should drive back home in the evenings instead, before he'd departed that morning. Alice had assured him it was fine.

Now, returning to a dark, cold house after having collected Charlie from her parents' cosy bungalow, it didn't feel like such a good idea. Alice closed the front door firmly behind them and shot the deadbolt.

Her little boy had been given his tea at his grandparents' house so she proceeded to take him straight upstairs for his bath and bedtime routine. His head of dark, wavy hair was already resting heavily on her shoulder. Her mum had enthusiastically relayed how they'd been for a walk along the beach that afternoon and the sea air would have worn him out.

Alice sat on the closed toilet lid whilst Charlie splashed in the warm, fragrant suds. He filled a little plastic boat with blocks until it began to sink beneath the bubbles. She felt her own eyes becoming heavy. The warm, steamy atmosphere relaxing her tense muscles.

She found herself almost nodding off, when a noise from downstairs made her eyes snap open. She listened carefully, but there was now only silence. It had sounded like the bang of an open window, left to swing in the wind. But she knew the house was locked up tight. Alice lifted Charlie out of the water and patted him dry with a fluffy towel.

She swiftly put him into his pyjamas and carried him to his room, flicking on his nightlight and settling him under the covers more hastily than she might normally have done. Fortunately, his eyes were closing as she tucked the duvet around his shoulders. There was no demand for a story. She backed out of the room, pulling the door so it was left ajar.

Alice stood on the landing. The downstairs of the house was in darkness. They'd headed straight for Charlie's bedroom after arriving home, not lingering to turn on a light. Now she was away from the humid, soporific warmth of the bathroom, she felt a sudden chill. She began to slowly descend the stairs, allowing her eyes to adjust to the gloom.

It was most definitely colder on the ground floor of the house, more marked than the usual difference caused by the heat of the day gradually rising upwards. Alice picked up Fergus's golfing umbrella which was propped against the phone table in the hallway and stepped into the kitchen.

The cold air hit her like a slap. She flicked on the overhead light. The back door, leading to their modest garden patio was hanging loose on its hinges, but only just. It appeared, from the splintered wood around the handle, that it had been wrenched open and then battered with some kind of implement.

Alice took a couple of strides across the room. She stepped out onto the patio itself, holding the umbrella like a weapon in front of her. She turned on the outside light and scanned the small garden. There were thick bushes running along each boundary, the light casting strange shadows amongst the dense foliage.

For a moment, she thought there was a dark figure standing in the gap between the shed and the hedgerow. She took a few more steps forward, directing her gaze into the murkiness. The figure melted into the outlines of the dwarf conifers that guarded the edge of the plot like sentries on duty.

There was no sign of human life. As she stepped back inside, the DI noticed her hands were shaking. She had an almost unbearable urge to bolt up the stairs and hold her son in her arms. Instead, she dropped the umbrella to the floor and reached for her mobile phone.

Chapter 21

Pete was there in twenty minutes. He arrived dressed in a cable-knit jumper and jeans and had brought a large holdall with him. Alice led him into the kitchen, where she had already brewed a jug of strong coffee. She immediately poured him a cup. "Thanks so much for coming over. I could have called my parents, but they'd have insisted Charlie and I go and stay with them and I'm not sure that's what I want. This is my home."

Pete sipped the coffee thoughtfully. "Aye, I see your point. You want to stand your ground, not run away."

Alice slumped onto a chair, gripping her mug tightly. "But what am I standing my ground against?"

Pete sighed. "I tried to trace the call made to your number the other evening but the information BT gave me wasn't much help. They could retrieve the caller's number, even if it had been blocked, but in this case, the number they traced it to was a call box in the Highlands somewhere. A good seventy miles from here."

Alice crinkled her brow. She took a long sip of her coffee, grateful she'd laced it earlier with a slug of whisky. "Don't tell me, it's a box on a deserted road in the middle of nowhere, with a few sheep and Highland cattle as the only witnesses?"

Pete gave a thin smile. "Something like that. So whoever it was, probably supplied a voice recording to someone who they paid to call you from such a remote location. Which shows this individual certainly has some ingenuity."

"Do you think the same person beat my kitchen door in?" She dipped her head towards the damaged wood hanging askew on its old hinges.

"I couldn't make that assumption without more evidence. We should really be dusting for prints."

Alice shook her head despondently. "You know as well as I do that whoever did this was gloved up. They probably only made contact with a crowbar anyway. But I'll certainly question my neighbours. See if they noticed anything."

Pete glanced about him. "Is your husband not home?"

Alice drained her cup, feeling the sting of the spirit warm her throat and calm her tattered nerves. "He's in Edinburgh this week for a trial. Charlie is upstairs asleep."

Pete frowned deeply. "I've brought some slabs of wood I had in the garage and my toolbox. I should be able to make the door solid for tonight. But I don't recommend you and your son stay here alone for the rest of the week. Maybe your parents' place would be a better option?"

"I'm a detective inspector, Pete. This is my home. I'm not going to run away at the first sign of trouble."

The other detective sighed, not wishing to get into an argument with his new boss. Instead, he unzipped the bag and took out his tools.

Alice watched silently from her seat at the table whilst he secured the wooden panels to the damaged door and then to the surrounding frame. He did much of the work with his right hand, but the left one was adept at holding the wood and performing the less precise tasks. "You compensate for your disability extremely well, if you don't mind me saying?"

Pete continued to focus on his task, his face turned away from her, so she couldn't see his expression. "My hand has been this way since birth. I adapted very early on to my limitations. It hasn't held me back."

"I can see it hasn't. I wish Fergus was that useful with a screwdriver." To Alice's relief, Pete let out a laugh.

"To be honest, many of us who have disabilities, tend to over-compensate when we can. I've always wanted to do anything that my peers could, and better if possible."

Alice nodded. "I can understand that."

Pete hammered in the final nail. "All done. You're certainly secure for the time-being."

Alice felt her body sag with relief. "Thank you Pete. You've been a lifesaver."

He packed up his kit in silence, then slung the bag over one shoulder. "I just hope I don't regret this."

Alice wrinkled her brow in puzzlement. "Why?"

"Because if something happens to you and your wee boy upstairs when I didn't report these incidents properly, I'll never forgive myself."

Chapter 22

The team were busy at their desks by the time Alice entered the department. Despite knowing the house was thoroughly secured by Pete's handiwork, she hadn't slept well. The space in the bed beside her felt wider than it usually did when Fergus was away.

But Charlie had been entirely oblivious to her evening of trauma. He had slept through until dawn and trotted into her parents' kitchen twenty minutes earlier without a care in the world. Alice had almost told her mother to be extra vigilant, but then they would have asked her questions and she wasn't willing to tell them the whole story just yet.

The DI was shrugging out of her woollen coat when Matt approached her desk. "I've just got off the phone from the receptionist at the Banchory Hotel, Aberdeen."

"Ah, is this about Roger Golding's movements on the night of the fire?" Alice settled into her chair.

"Yep. According to their records, Roger attended every session of the conference. I spoke to one of his colleagues at his offices yesterday. She confirmed that Roger was present for all the group's activities, including his own talk, obviously. Like Mr Golding said, they went out for dinner in the city on the last evening and came back to the hotel and drank in the bar until late. She claims he was in no fit state to drive. He was seen at breakfast the next morning."

"How about his car? Was the licence caught on any ANPR cameras between here and Aberdeen that night?"

"Nope, no trace of his vehicle exists on the major routes. Although, if he avoided the A90 and took the cross country roads, he may have evaded the cameras. But if he did that, the chances of him making it to Fairlie, starting the fire and reaching

Aberdeen again by 8am are vanishingly small, Ma'am."

Alice sighed heavily. "I agree. I'd say that Roger Golding's alibi is solid. Good work, Matt."

Holly was hovering beside her colleague. "Morning, Ma'am. I've been looking into Leroy Torben's online presence. There's something I wanted to show you," she said tentatively. "I've not had much luck with WhatsApp, I could only access the conversations Leroy's friends allowed me to join, but that did throw up a few things."

Alice gestured to a spare seat, indicating the DC should take it. Holly sat down and laid her iPad on the desk between them. "Leroy wasn't active on Facebook or Instagram. According to his mate at the garage, he was part of a few WhatsApp groups with his co-workers and friends. Ewan Dawson allowed me to join each of the groups and I trawled back through all of the exchanges."

Alice raised her eyebrows. "Anything of interest?"

"Not on WhatsApp. It was general banter about nights out and times to meet up. Leroy contributed a few comments but not as much as others did. Dawson was correct. There'd been no comments from Leroy after Wednesday morning, when he'd messaged Dawson about whether he would be attending football training on the Friday night."

"He was planning ahead, then, beyond that day?"

Holly nodded. "It seems so." The younger woman knitted her brow. "Leroy didn't have his own accounts, but the Seamill Shooters have a very active Facebook and Instagram page. I saw pictures of the teams with Leroy amongst the players. He seemed smiley and happy."

"Everyone looks happy on social media posts. If we took those as evidence of the state of the nation nobody would believe the country's going to hell in a handcart."

Holly cracked a smile. "Very true. Without Leroy's laptop or phone, it's impossible to track what he'd been interested in during the weeks leading up to his death; what he was searching for and viewing, for instance. I couldn't find an email account for him, either. Victoria couldn't say if he'd had one. I don't think she's very technically savvy."

Alice sighed. "It could be that both those devices got incinerated in the fire. We'd never find a trace of them now. So what *did* you spot?"

Holly shuffled closer. "It may be nothing, but in the photos of Leroy's football team, posted on their Instagram page, you can see the pitch where they seem to play their home games. Around the edge, are billboards listing their sponsors; mostly local companies, including Rossmore Garage, which makes sense as some of their employees are on the team. But there were other names, so I checked them all out. I don't know why really."

Alice felt her interest mounting.

Holly continued, "one of the sponsors is an interior design company called 'Vintage Home'. It is registered to a woman named, Rosaline Crammond. The first name rang a bell, so I performed some searches on our Rosaline Golding." She slapped her hand down on the desk with excitement. "It was her, Ma'am! Rosaline Golding's maiden name was Crammond. The company has been registered to her for two years. I checked out the website. She offers personal consultations through to complete interior refurbs. There were lots of glossy photos of what they'd done in the south wing at Hill House. There's no doubt it's the same person."

Alice reached for her coat once more. "Excellent work, Holly. I think it's time we had another chat with the lady of Hill House."

Chapter 23

There was no sign of Roger Golding this time the detectives entered the side door of Hill House. Rosaline had asked them to meet her there. The kitchen felt dingy in the gloom of the damp afternoon. The aga wasn't lit for this visit.

Rosaline invited them to take a seat at the table. Holly kept her iPad gripped in her hands.

"Is there more news?" The woman asked nervously.

"Nothing more about the fire, I'm afraid," Alice said gently. "Are you on your own here?"

Rosaline nodded. Her cheeks were hollowed out and despite a covering of make-up, her features seemed drawn and pale. "The children are at school and Roger is at work at the university. I said Maria could go out for a ride on the pony, she finds it therapeutic."

"We only have a couple of questions for you," Alice continued. "It shouldn't take long."

Holly made a point of powering up her tablet. "Are you the director of a company by the name of 'Vintage Interiors'?"

The woman's cheeks reddened. It made her look better, even if she may not have felt it. "Yes, although I've not done much work for about six months. We've been too busy on this place. I have a diploma in Interior Design, I completed it online last year. When we decided to renovate this house, I thought I could use the building contacts we acquired to offer my services to other clients. I had quite a few projects in the beginning."

"Only, it seems that your company is one of the sponsors of a local football team. The Seamill Shooters? They are based at a ground in West

Kilbride."

Rosaline twisted towards a solid wood counter-top, busying herself putting clean mugs in a cupboard. "I gave them a few hundred pounds in return for some advertising at their ground. I'm amazed my name is still there. When I first started up the business, a friend of mine in marketing suggested some local sponsorship might be helpful, with advertising being so expensive. I think one of the parents at the kids' school mentioned this local football team needed sponsors, so I approached them. But that was months ago."

Alice took a breath. "When DS Falmer and I mentioned the Seamill Shooters and the football ground where they played to you the other day, you said you'd never heard of it."

Rosaline stopped rearranging the crockery. "To be honest, I'd completely forgotten. What with the shock of the fire and everything, plus you telling us this boy was dead before it even started. It slipped my mind. I'm not sure I took much notice of the team name, anyway."

Alice noted how the woman kept her back to them during this statement. She couldn't look the detectives in the face whilst she gave this explanation. "But you must admit it's a coincidence. This sponsorship creates a connection between you and the victim."

Now the woman spun to face them. "Hardly! I transferred a few pounds to the manager of the team and this young man played for them every so often. I'd hardly call that a *connection*, Detective Inspector. I really think you're clutching at straws. Someone tried to burn my house to the ground. My children could have been killed and you're worrying about an advertising billboard!"

Alice noted the flush of anger on the woman's

face and something else too. Fear, perhaps?

Holly kept her tone level. "Did you ever visit the football ground, Mrs Golding? Did you attend a local match on a Sunday, perhaps? It would have been nice to see your business name being displayed along the touchline. Perhaps you took the children, made a day of it?"

Rosaline clutched her hands together until the knuckles were straining at the translucent skin that covered them. She seemed to be conducting an internal battle over how to reply. "I don't think I want to speak with you again without my solicitor here."

Alice let out the breath she'd been holding in. She was starting to get tired of hearing that statement.

Chapter 24

As the detectives made their way back to the car, Alice noticed the petite figure of Maria Silva leading a chestnut pony along a path towards the stables, the russet autumn leaves on the oaks behind them creating an impressive backdrop. She nudged Holly's arm, indicating they should approach her.

As they got nearer, Alice noticed the mare had a coat a similar colour to her own flaming locks. She reached out a hand to pat its soft flank. It seemed to have a good temperament.

Maria looked up in surprise, recognition quickly settling on her striking features. "You are the detectives looking into the cause of the fire?"

"Yes." Alice walked alongside as the au-pair led her charge into the stable block and towards one of the stalls. "What a beautiful horse."

Maria smiled. "She is called Cinnamon. She's three years old. Jacob is learning to ride her. We are so relieved she wasn't hurt in the fire." Her brown eyes moistened at the very idea. She carefully removed the horse's bridle and saddle, gently stroking the animal's croup as she did so, keeping it calm.

The au-pair secured the gate and led them out into the fresh air. "You have identified the man who was killed in the fire? Mr and Mrs Golding told me?"

Alice nodded. "Yes, his name was Leroy Torben." She fished the photograph out of her bag. "Do you recognise him?"

Maria seemed to be making a real effort to examine the image. She shook her head sadly. "I don't really know anyone around here. I speak with some of the other au-pairs and nannies at the school gate. I have a few friends from back home who work around the area, but they are all women. I have not seen this man before."

Alice took the photo back, carefully placing it into its file. "But you are a young woman, Maria. Surely you are given time off from your job here? You must go out occasionally in the local area. You may have seen this man at one of the bars or clubs in West Kilbride?"

Maria made a scoffing sound. "I am here to make money and nothing else. It is cold and wet in this country and the Goldings keep me in the servants' wing of their damp old house which they think is so grand. I do not waste my precious earnings in the bars of West Kilbride, Detective." The final words were delivered with a sneer of distaste.

"Okay, Maria," Alice said in a deflated tone. "We'll leave you to get on with the rest of your day."

*

It was late afternoon and Victor Novak had just returned from a coffee run to the Italian café along the High Street. He doled out the cardboard cups from their moulded tray. Alice received hers with a grateful smile. She sipped the double espresso like it was water in a desert. The caffeine hit made her wince.

Matt Singh pushed back his chair and got to his feet. "I've just had an email from the duty officer at Prestwick Airport. Caroline Torben's plane from Valencia has just landed. She reported to one of the patrol officers like I'd instructed her."

Alice glanced at the drink in her hand. Despite the rush of stimulants she felt pulsating through her bloodstream, giving her a jolt of artificial energy, she knew a crucial part of her job was to give her team a chance to practise their skills. "Great news. Matt and Victor, can you take the squad car over to the airport now? You can bring her back here to be questioned before she gets dropped off at her hotel."

"Absolutely," Matt replied eagerly, obviously recognising himself that this was an important responsibility.

Chapter 25

The woman seated in front of detectives Novak and Singh, may once have been similar in looks to Victoria Braden, but now bore only a passing resemblance to her older sister. Caroline Torben had shoulder-length, dyed blonde hair and a deep tan that contrasted sharply with her neon pink blouse. She wore a diamond ring on her left hand and a number of gold chains were strung about her neck.

Matt had already furnished the lady with a coffee from the vending machine and chosen to interview her in one of the rarely used offices, rather than the airless interview room downstairs. They didn't have any real authority to coerce the woman to speak to them, she was hardly a suspect, having been over a thousand miles away when the young man she'd claimed was her son, died. "Ms Torben. I'm very sorry about your loss. I promise we are doing everything we can to find out why Leroy died."

She dabbed at her eyes with a tissue. "He was a lovely boy, so decent and hardworking. I can't believe this has happened."

Matt thought the woman was genuinely distressed, but perhaps not to the extent he might expect of a mother who'd lost their child in a shocking, violent way. "When did you last have any communication with Leroy?"

She shifted in her seat. "Well, he often rang me on a Sunday evening from Victoria's place. But I can't rightly remember whether we spoke this last Sunday, or the one before."

"When did you last see one another?"

Her awkwardness shifted to anger, a red flush sweeping across her bronzed cheeks. "I don't see what that's got to do with anything? My boy was found dead in some stranger's house – his body so burnt I can't even go and see him – and you're questioning *me*! Implying my parenting wasn't good enough!"

Matt waited a moment for her to calm down. "Leroy died in suspicious circumstances. We need to question everyone. We are aware you were out of the country when Leroy was killed, but in order to find out why he is dead, we need to know *everything* about him. Even the slightest evidence of something being out of the ordinary during the last few weeks and months could help point us in the right direction with our investigation."

The woman appeared to have composed herself again. "Yes, okay. I get it. Look, the truth is that Leroy hadn't been calling me as much these last few months as he usually would. I just thought he was busy with his apprenticeship and his footie and what have you. He was a young man getting on with his life. I thought it was about time, to be honest. "

Matt became more alert. "Since when had Leroy been less frequent in his phone calls?"

She shrugged. "Since the summer, I'd say. July, maybe. I knew he was being well looked after by my Vick, so I wasn't too worried."

Matt took a breath. "In order to identify Leroy, we needed to make a DNA comparison. We used a sample of your sister's DNA to perform the test."

Caroline narrowed her eyes shiftily. She took a long pull of the coffee, even though it must have been only lukewarm by this time. She set the cup down carefully on the desk, her vision suddenly fixed on examining the crimson polish of her nails.

"The results certainly showed a familial link, but they weren't exactly what we were expecting."

She glanced up. "What do you mean by that?"

Victor took over. "We mean that Leroy's DNA was

too closely matched to your sister's for him to have been her nephew." He allowed the words to hang between them.

Caroline sighed deeply. "*Christ.* I told Vick it was a mad idea, that one day the whole thing would come out, blow up in our faces. I suppose none of it matters anyway, not now that poor Leroy is dead."

Matt leant forward over the desk, knitting his fingers together. "I think you'd better tell us the whole story, Ms Torben."

Chapter 26

When they'd returned from dropping Caroline Torben and her luggage off at the local budget brand hotel, Matt and Victor marched straight up to the criminal investigation department where the rest of their colleagues were waiting.

Alice had pulled out a couple of chairs for the detectives. "Well? Did she admit to not being Leroy's biological mother?"

Matt Singh nodded slowly, making sure all his fellow detectives were paying attention. "It wasn't a formal interview, so nothing was being recorded. Ms Torben cannot in any way be treated as a suspect in the death of Leroy. Perhaps that was why she was so forthcoming in the end."

Alice felt her pulse rate rise with anticipation. They hadn't got anything solid out of Victoria Braden, they were in desperate need of a breakthrough.

"Caroline Torben admitted that she is Leroy's maternal aunt. It was Victoria who gave birth to the boy 24 years ago at the Glasgow Infirmary. The official records should all be in place. The birth certificate lists Victoria as his mother. But as Leroy hadn't ever applied for a passport he'd not had need to ever see it. They simply allowed him to believe Caroline was his mum."

"But that's a heck of a gamble, isn't it? The lad was bound to see his birth certificate one day?" Pete asked incredulously.

Matt nodded. "Aye, Caroline said she always felt it was a hair-brained scheme. Victoria came to her flat one evening in early 1998 in a terrible state. She'd been a couple of years widowed by this time and she informed Caroline she'd fallen pregnant. Apparently, the woman was hysterical, kept saying she couldn't keep the baby but it was all she'd ever wanted – to be a mum. She and her late husband hadn't been able to conceive together, apparently."

Alice crinkled her brow in confusion. "So, Victoria wanted the baby, but at the same time said she couldn't keep him? It doesn't make any sense?"

Matt smiled ruefully. "It didn't make much sense to Caroline either. She kept telling her it would be fine, nobody would care Victoria was unmarried and perhaps the father would help. This was when the woman became even more unhinged. She screamed that nobody could ever know who the father was."

Pete scratched his head. "I wonder who the father could've been? Victoria was working in the local library back then. She strikes me as an extremely conservative, traditional woman. She'd only relatively recently lost her husband in tragic circumstances. I can't see her sleeping around."

Victor answered, "she refused to tell her own sister, I can't see her telling us now. Victoria pleaded and begged Caroline to pretend the baby was hers when it came. She said her sister could move into the house for a while when the baby was born; Victoria would do all the nursing and care. But everyone else would believe the baby was hers. Their parents had both passed away by this time, Caroline was single, so there was nobody to question it."

Matt raised an eyebrow. "Plus, Victoria offered to put Caroline up rent free, giving her regular generous payments to look after the child when he was old enough to live with her. At this stage, Caroline had a low-paid shop job and no savings. After a sleepless night of hammering out a plan, she agreed."

Holly shook her head in disbelief. "Have they

broken any laws?"

Alice thought carefully about this. "They must have deceived the education authority as well as the child by claiming Caroline was his mother. It was a bit like an informal adoption, without the authorities being involved. I'm sure it's a criminal offence, but not one carrying a long prison sentence, I imagine."

Matt picked up the thread, "as Leroy got older, Victoria used to pick him up from school and give him his tea on a regular basis. This allowed Caroline to continue her social life. When the lad was eighteen, Caroline and her new partner moved to Spain. She said that her time being his mum was up, and besides, Leroy hadn't really bonded that well with her, or Victoria either, for that matter. When Victoria insisted Leroy lodge at her house after his studies, he'd been pretty reluctant."

Victor grunted. "I'm not surprised. Neither woman seemed fit to be a mother. Caroline is flighty and self-absorbed and Victoria Braden has a screw loose."

Alice wasn't sure about the terminology Victor had used, but his character assessments were fairly spot-on. She felt a pang of pity for the little boy who'd been raised by the Torben sisters; the aunt who was really his mother and the woman he must have called, 'mummy', who was out as often as she could be and had plenty of boyfriends over the years. It was hard to imagine how Victoria had thought this was a good upbringing for the child. "Does the birth certificate name the father?"

Matt shook his head. "No, they listed him as 'unknown'. But at the registry office, Victoria was adamant she wanted *her* name on the certificate, even if they kept it quiet after that point. Caroline thought it was odd, a contradiction."

"Well, if she hadn't done that, it would have been

a clear case of fraud," Pete added firmly. "An intelligent woman like Victoria would certainly know that much. She probably looked up the legal position at the library."

Alice grimaced. "We need to find out who Leroy's biological father was and why Victoria felt she couldn't acknowledge her son as her own when she was so desperate to have children. As it stands, the whole scenario makes no sense."

"I'll second that," Victor added in a steely tone.

Chapter 27

The clocks were about to go back in a few days. It was a murky grey outside now by six o'clock, but by next week it would be dusk even earlier. It would certainly be dark by the time Victoria Braden was driving home from the library on the days she worked. The woman tutted under her breath. She flicked on the kettle placed on the freshly wiped worktop and reached for a clean mug on autopilot.

The kitchen of her modest semi-detached house was lit by a neon strip across the artexed ceiling. Since she'd received the news her son was dead, every tatty detail of her house's interior was announcing itself to her; the chips in the plasterwork and the stains on the Axminster carpet they'd had fitted when they first moved into the place, newly married and filled with hope this would be a family home.

How could her life have been so full of tragedy? What had she really done to upset the universe so badly? She'd only ever acted in a way that seemed right. Was it the lies? The secrets? Was it time to tell that detective woman everything? What else did she have to lose now? She didn't much care about anyone else, not even Caroline. She gripped the mug with her left hand as she poured in the boiling water, not noticing that it was scalding her skin.

First, there was Greg's car accident. She could clearly recall the awful moment the police had come to inform her. They didn't have mobile phones then, but somehow she knew something had happened to him. He was on his way to visit his mother in Cumbernauld, where she'd retired. Her husband would always give her a quick ring when he got there, to put her mind at rest. But it had grown late and no phone call came. Perhaps she should have called Maureen to check if he was there, but they'd never got on, which was probably the reason why her mother-in-law hadn't rung her either, when Greg didn't show up at the time he was expected.

It seemed incredibly petty now. How neither of them picked up the phone to the other. Both loving Greg the way they did. Stubbornness, it must have been. Maureen resented her for not giving Greg children. Of course, she thought that was always the woman's fault. Victoria hated her for it. Having a child with Greg was all she'd ever wanted. She couldn't bear to listen to her mother-in-law nagging incessantly about when she'd become a grandmother, how she was giving up hope.

Victoria was aware the result of their obstinacy was that both women had to hear about Greg's death from a uniformed police officer at their front door. Which was quite as dreadful as everyone imagined.

Victoria felt tears pool in her eyes. She loosened her grip on the mug and noticed the skin of her palm was bright red and stinging badly. She took a tube of Savlon out of a drawer and rubbed it into the now blistering skin. Perhaps she should go to A&E, she wondered? Knowing she wouldn't bother.

Then, there was the baby. She'd shut that period of time firmly out of her mind for decades. Victoria recalled the baggy blouses she'd worn over work trousers with the waist button undone. Her colleagues hadn't noticed her blossoming pregnancy at all. She was a plain-looking widow in her thirties who quietly got on with her job. People didn't look too closely at someone like that.

She sipped the tea, managing to swallow past the lump in her throat. He'd been such a beautiful baby. Whatever the consequences, or the cause, that time in her life was her happiest. Her lovely, gentle Leroy. The tears fell in earnest now. She put down the mug on the counter and collapsed to the cold linoleum. Wrenching sobs were being released by her thin frame. The eruption of emotion was shocking to her. She'd kept it contained within her for such a long time.

Then she heard a noise. It was coming from the window in the dining room, she thought. A sound of splintering wood and the tinkling of broken glass. It was amazing how little she cared, as if she was viewing herself, slumped defenceless on the kitchen floor, from above, floating just below the Artex.

She quite liked the sensation. Perhaps carrying the burden of being herself had dragged on for too long anyway. It might not be such a bad thing if it finally came to an end.

Chapter 28

Holly Gadd got to her feet, the receiver of her phone extension still gripped in her hand. She searched out the waspish figure of the DI, that shock of red hair twisted in a plait down her back. The boss was deep in conversation with Matt Singh. "Ma'am, the switchboard have just had an emergency call diverted to them. A lady who lives on Seamill Road has reported a violent disturbance next door. Isn't that the road Mrs Braden lives on?"

Alice turned to face her colleague. "Do you have a house number?"

"Number 52."

"It certainly rings a bell." Alice moved swiftly towards her desk, scooping up her bag and mobile phone. "Pete, can you drive me there?"

"Sure," the DS replied, logging out of the computer system with haste.

*

As they pulled up at the kerb outside number 52 Seamill Road, Alice could see it was the property connected to Victoria Braden's house. The woman's red Hyundai was sitting in the drive. The officers approached the neighbour's front door first.

A woman in her early thirties with a thick, dark fringe and a small child balanced on her hip answered at their knock. "Are you the police?"

Pete produced his warrant card. "Yes, we're detectives. Are you the lady who made the 999 call?"

"Yes, I'm Donna Marshall. I've lived here for about five years. I don't make a habit of calling the emergency services, but I knew something was very wrong. Mrs Braden is usually as silent as the grave in there."

"Have you been round to check on her?" Alice asked without judgement.

The woman blushed anyway. "Look, I'm here with my little ones. It sounded like a nasty fight was going on next door. I wasn't going to leave them on their own to go and check, neither was I going to take them with me. So I called you lot."

"Very sensible," Pete added swiftly. "You don't have a spare key for next door, have you?"

The woman frowned in thought. "Actually, I think there's one on the hook in the kitchen. We exchanged them a couple of years ago when my husband locked himself out whilst taking down the bins." She rolled her eyes. "Idiot."

"Could we borrow it?"

"Oh, yes, of course." She lowered the child to the floor and he scuttled off ahead of his mum. She returned a few moments later with a Yale key on a Rossmore Garage leather fob. "Here you go." Her expression darkened, she lowered her voice, presumably so the children couldn't hear. "The sounds were really awful. I heard Victoria screaming and shouting and what sounded like a terrible struggle. I called you lot straight away, but I wonder if I should have gone and helped, you know? If Callum had been here, I would have sent him round."

Pete looked equally grave. "You were best to let us handle it, Ma'am."

She nodded, seemingly reassured by his words.

The officers walked across to the neighbouring driveway, with Alice thinking the poor husband next door was probably extremely lucky he was still at work.

Pete pressed the bell. The car on the drive indicated Victoria Braden should have been at home. They waited several minutes, banging on the wooden panel to be certain she wasn't coming. Finally, Pete fitted the key in the lock with a heavy heart.

Chapter 29

The door swung open onto a dimly lit hallway. As Pete stepped through, he felt the blast of a chill that seemed to permeate the ground floor. Something certainly wasn't right. When they'd been here previously, the place had been warm and inviting.

Alice slipped into the front sitting room whilst Pete continued to the rear of the property. He ducked into the dining room, where the draft seemed to have its origins. He immediately noted the source. The back window had been wrenched open and the glass was broken, leaving a pile of shards on the sill and the carpet beneath. "Ma'am, it looks like there's been an intruder," he called. "They may still be in the building!"

"Mrs Braden!" Alice cried from the hallway, making sure her voice carried upstairs. "Are you here? It's the police!"

There was no reply.

Pete then entered the kitchen, but his progress was abruptly halted. He felt some kind of liquid squelch beneath his right shoe. His stomach immediately constricted. It was gloomy in the small room but something made him reluctant to turn on the strip light. His gaze slid down to floor level and the bile simultaneously rose in his throat.

A figure was slumped against a kitchen cupboard. The head hanging forward so only the top of the scalp was visible. The grey hairs tufting from the crown were unmistakable. Spreading out beneath Victoria Braden's hunched form was a pool of thick, dark liquid, the aroma of which; faintly sweet and metallic, had finally reached Pete's nostrils.

The DS put a hand to his mouth and turned on his heels. He marched straight out of the house onto the sloping driveway, gulping fresh air like he'd been held underwater and was finally released.

Pete's vision was blurring and his legs felt weak. He heard Alice's voice beside him, barking instructions into her mobile phone. He was desperately trying to compose himself. Then, he felt a hand on his shoulder, guiding him down the slope to the low garden wall and gently manoeuvring him to a sitting position.

"Put your head between your legs," Alice said calmly. "I'll get the water bottle from the car."

As he gulped from the neck of the plastic bottle, he felt his body returning to normal. The waves of nausea had subsided. But he still felt woozy.

He felt Alice sit on the wall beside him. "You had a vasovagal reflex response," she said. "I take it that was your first dead body?"

Pete breathed deeply. "Yes. I've seen fatal casualties at the scene of road accidents, but that is my first violent death." He wiped his mouth with the back of his hand. "Sorry, Ma'am. I feel a total fool."

"Not at all. Sadly, I've seen my fair share of murder victims. You get used to it, which I'm not sure is such a good thing. I've seen officers joking together at the most horrific crime scenes imaginable. It's a way of coping, I think. But I prefer it when the response is shock and revulsion. It shows we still have our basic human values in place."

"Yeah, I see that. But I'm a police detective. People expect us to keep it together in the face of these things."

Alice sighed. "You'll get there. For what it's worth, I'm glad it was you I brought here and not Holly or Matt. They strike me as sensitive types."

"Aye, even more than me, you mean?" He managed a strained laugh.

"You won't get many in your career, as long as you stay out of the big cities. This one may well be the worst you encounter. Plus you knew her. That makes it tougher." She got to her feet. "I've called in the forensic team and the pathologist. There's some tape in the boot of the car. We can get busy securing the scene before they arrive."

Pete slowly rose to a standing position, waiting until the whooshing in his ears diminished. Hoping his senior officer was right.

Chapter 30

Charlie played happily on the mat by her feet whilst she gripped the glass of red wine in her hand like someone was threatening to take it from her. A local glazier was fitting a new back door. It was a chunky, UPVC affair with triple locks, not the usual style she would have chosen for their lovely period home. But what choice did she have? Her family's safety came first. Despite what she'd told Pete about being entirely used to violent crime scenes, the image of Victoria Braden's crumpled body, the front of her cotton blouse soaked in blood, kept flashing in her mind's eye.

She sipped the Malbec, trying not to down the remainder in one gulp. The glazier's bulky form suddenly filled the doorway. "All done, Madam. If you come through I'll show you how to use the lock. It's pretty straightforward."

Alice followed him, reluctantly putting down her glass to practise turning the key back and forth to the reassuring sound of steel bolts sliding into place. "It seems fine. Thanks."

He gathered up his equipment and made his way towards the front door. "I'll send the invoice through in an email. Any problems, just give me a call."

She closed the door firmly after him, padding back into the kitchen and being unable to resist the urge to double check the back door was locked, even though she knew the bolts had been thrown just a few moments before. Alice picked up her glass and took a long sup, hoping the broken door and threatening phone calls weren't going to turn her into a nervous wreck. She'd always been such a strong, resilient person. But having a family made you vulnerable. It gave you a weakness others could exploit.

As if on cue, she heard her little boy call her name from the next room. "Coming, darling," she called back in a cheerful, calming tone that belied her true state of mind.

*

Every single member of the crime department looked shell-shocked. Alice was reminded that this was the first time they'd handled a murder case, let alone one where the bodies started to pile up.

She was relieved to see Pete had a flush of colour in his cheeks and had clearly gotten over his initial trauma at seeing the dead body. He was already on his feet making notes on the white board.

Alice stood beside him. "The SOCOs spent most of yesterday afternoon and evening processing the scene at 53, Seamill Road. Dr Webb made the examination *in situ,* and he has removed the body to the Clydebank Laboratory where the *post mortem* will take place, hopefully later today."

Holly was shaking her head dolefully. "This can't be a coincidence, can it? That Victoria's birth son was found dead in suspicious circumstances last week and now she has been brutally killed in her home?"

Alice sighed. "We can't make any assumptions yet. The press will now take an interest, possibly even the Nationals. If a reporter approaches or calls you, it gets transferred straight to the Police Scotland media relations switchboard, who will give them information from a statement we will prepare and no more. I'll put a copy of the number on each desk."

Victor raised his hand. "But the press will draw their own connections, surely? We were about to question Mrs Braden again about who Leroy's father was and the circumstances of his birth, when she gets murdered. There's no way that's a coincidence. I reckon someone wanted to shut her up, keep their own secrets. The real father, maybe?"

Alice felt impatient. "Yes, we can all theorise about what has happened here, but we need to await the forensic results before we jump the gun. The press will be doing enough of that themselves. Now, it appeared to me, that Victoria was killed by an intruder who entered through her dining room window. This person then proceeded into the kitchen. A food preparation knife, with a roughly four inch blade, was discarded beside the body. There were sounds of screaming and a tussle, which was loud enough to be heard next door, but the victim must have been swiftly over-powered. On initial observation, I'd say her throat was cut."

Holly's face had drained of colour. "Might we get prints from the knife, Ma'am?"

Pete answered this question, "if the perpetrator dumped it, I'd say he was gloved up, so was unlikely to have left prints. The same will probably go for the window he broke in through. This attack was fast and efficient. We will be lucky if he left much of a forensic trace behind."

"Then we are assuming the perp is a man?" Matt asked.

Alice stepped in. "No. Victoria was a slight woman who could've easily been over-powered, especially if the perp brought the weapon with them. We keep an open mind on the sex of the attacker for now."

"What about the neighbour who reported the disturbance? What information did we get from her statement?" Victor asked.

"Good question," Alice replied. "Her statement suggests the shouting and screaming began at about 2pm and she had been about to put her baby down for a nap. It lasted only about 5-10 minutes before it fell quiet. This matches with our records, which show that the 999 call from Donna Marshall was made at 2.07pm yesterday."

"Did she see anything? A person coming or going from the house?" Victor persisted.

"It seems she stayed inside with the children. She was frightened, I think. There is a thick hedge between their property and Braden's back garden, so she wouldn't have been able to see much anyway. Even if she had gone outside." Alice made eye contact with the DCs. "But I'd like the three of you to perform house-to-house enquiries along the street this morning. We need to know about any suspicious activity in the last few days – unusual vehicles parked up, people hanging around number 53 or asking questions. Anything out of the ordinary needs to be recorded; with times and descriptions. Got it?"

The officers nodded obediently.

Alice sighed. "Meanwhile, Pete and I will pay a visit to Caroline Torben. It seems we have more bad news to deliver."

Chapter 31

They'd arranged to meet Caroline Torben in a café beside the budget hotel she was staying in. When Alice pushed open the door, she spotted the woman seated at a table pushed against a wall. Gone was the neon pink top. She was now wearing a grey Nike tracksuit and sky blue trainers. A mug of untouched coffee sat in front of her.

Alice told Pete to order them a couple of drinks at the counter. She went to join the woman at her table. "Caroline? I'm DI Alice Mann. I will be the chief investigating officer heading the inquiry into your sister's death. I'm so very sorry for your loss."

The woman gazed at her with red-rimmed eyes. She wore no make-up but her face had the look of one which usually sported plenty. "I can't believe it. I hadn't even gone to see her yet." Her eyes filled up, her voice wavering. "We spoke on the phone yesterday morning. To be honest, we had a blazing row. Now I feel bloody awful." She glanced about her. "Can I smoke in here?"

"No, Ms Torben, you cannot. What did you row about?" Alice asked gently.

Pete arrived and placed a couple of steaming mugs down on the Formica.

Caroline reached for a packet of tissues from her pocket. "About Leroy, of course. We were both upset about his death, naturally. But I was angry about the lies, why we'd had to deceive him all those years. He'd not had a proper relationship with either of us because of it. It pained me to think he'd gone to the grave not knowing who his real parents were." The tears were falling bountifully now.

Alice sipped the weak coffee with a grimace of distaste, giving the woman time to compose herself.

She snuffled loudly, mopping up the tears with her crumpled tissue. "I suppose I can bury them together. That might mean something."

Pete cleared his throat. "Your sister was killed in her own home, by an intruder. But coming so soon after the death of Leroy and on the back of these revelations about his parentage, we can't help but wonder if Victoria's death wasn't just a random event. We can't find any evidence that the intruder intended to burgle the property. Nothing of value was missing."

Her eyes widened. A flash of fear crossed her tanned face. "I just imagined it was some terrible tragedy. You know, like bad things happening in threes? It didn't cross my mind they could be linked. How could I be such an idiot?"

"What we're asking," Alice continued, beginning to feel frustrated with this woman, who had agreed to pretend to be the mother of a new born baby without having asked nearly enough questions about why and carried out the task with little dedication. But she tried to keep the feeling out of her tone. "Is if you know of anyone who would have wanted your sister out of the way? We had begun asking questions about the circumstances of Leroy's birth. The young man himself was likely murdered, or certainly an attempt was made to cover up his death. Who would want to do this?"

She strained her features, as if trying to force a piece of information to present itself. "Victoria *never* told me who the father was, or even how the conception occurred. She was working at the library then and Greg had been dead a couple of years. There was no question of her dating again. She was still in mourning for him. Occasionally, she visited Greg's mother. They didn't get on but had their grief in common. She may have socialised with some of her colleagues, but none she'd ever mentioned to me of any great significance. I'm really sorry, I can't give you any clue as to who got her pregnant. She'd become hysterical if I ever raised the subject, so I learnt not to."

"Okay," Alice replied despondently. "We will speak with her work colleagues in due course. Perhaps there is somebody at the library who knew Victoria back in 1997."

"Please don't return to Spain until we give you permission," Pete added, as the detectives rose to their feet.

Caroline glanced up. "Can I just ask you something? I know this is a murder and everything, so you can't release the bodies for the funeral just yet, but I was wondering about Victoria's will? How do I go about finding what was in it?" Her bloodshot eyes, looking up through long dark lashes, gave the inquiry an innocent appearance, but the firmness of her gaze suggested to Alice that she actually cared a great deal about the answer.

Chapter 32

The traffic heading into the town centre was heavy, but it gave Alice time to think. Pete was driving and the DI noted how he gripped the wheel more tightly with his right hand, leaving the left free to slot into an attachment on the gear lever which allowed him to shift its position with relative ease.

"That's a good gizmo," she commented idly.

"Yep, I struggled without one for years. I managed the gears okay, but it was awkward. Apart from reverse, when I had to use both hands. But now I can do it all without letting go of the wheel. In recent years a lot more stuff has been developed for people with disabilities. Mostly because of the aftermath of the Afghanistan war. The demand has increased and the issues have been in the public eye more."

Alice nodded. She wondered why it had taken so long for designers to come up with what were basically fairly simple gadgets that made people's lives infinitely easier. Because none of them were disabled themselves, she surmised.

Pete was stopping and starting through one of the side streets in West Kilbride, looking for a space to park. "I suppose we should have Caroline Torben down as a chief suspect in the murder of Victoria Braden. She returns from Spain and within hours, her sister is dead. Plus, if it turns out she does benefit from the will, that gives her a serious motive."

"Yeah, we're certainly going to have to consider her as a possible perp. I'll get Matt to check her whereabouts yesterday afternoon. But I think it's a stretch. She was genuinely upset about her sister. The break-in at Seamill Road was neat and professional. Could Caroline really have slit her sister's throat with such ease?"

"But that comment about the will as we were leaving. It gave me chills. Maybe she paid someone to do it? We'll have to check her finances too." Pete involuntarily shuddered.

"Yes, a part of her is probably revelling in the thought that with Victoria and Leroy dead, she is probably now the sole beneficiary of her sister's will. Which means she'll very likely inherit the house. But people are complicated, she may be happy to receive the money, but desperately upset they're dead. I can't see her bumping either of them off simply in order to create the situation."

"We can take her prints for comparison with the scene, just in case. She did say she hadn't actually visited the house yet, so there shouldn't be any on the property legitimately. Not the way Victoria used to clean the place."

"Absolutely, it should be a priority."

Pete finally found a gap in the line of parked vehicles and skilfully manoeuvred their car into it.

*

The library in West Kilbride was much the same as every other she'd visited in the medium-sized towns of provincial Scotland. At the centre of the open-plan space, a labyrinth of steel bookcases, sat a wide wooden counter behind which a couple of neatly dressed middle-aged ladies in lanyards stood guard over their domain.

Alice approached the desk, showing her ID card to the lady wearing a lanyard which declared her to be the manager. "If you wouldn't mind," she added in a lowered voice, once she'd introduced herself, unable to shake the ingrained habits of a lifetime, "it might be better to speak in an office, perhaps?"

The woman, called Janice, silently led the officers through a door and into a communal break area. It was deserted, so Alice thought it would do the job fine. "Would you mind taking a seat? We have some difficult news."

Janice's expression revealed confusion but she dutifully sat on the edge of a chair, clasping her hands together in her lap. "This is all very 'cloak and dagger'. Should I be worried?" She smiled nervously.

"I'm afraid that one of your employees, a Mrs Victoria Braden, who works here part-time, I believe, was found dead at her property yesterday afternoon."

The manager's face slackened and her jaw dropped. "What?! I can't believe it. She's due in tomorrow. Victoria has worked here for nearly 30 years!"

Alice could tell the news was a shock. It hadn't yet been processed. "I'm really sorry, but it's true. We believe she was killed by an intruder to her house."

A hand flew up to the neck of Janice's blouse. Alice imagined if there'd been a string of pearls there, she would have clutched them. "Good God. But that's a very respectable area! Full of young families! This doesn't make any sense!"

"No, it really doesn't. Which is why we are here asking questions. The details of your colleague's murder will be all over the press and TV soon. But we would appreciate it if you kept any information we give you to yourself, if they ask."

Janice looked about her desperately. "The journalists are going to come here, aren't they? To the library? They'll be forming a mob outside!"

Pete thought this reaction was a little hysterical. "You may get one or two, but no more than that. The press aren't going to imagine Mrs Braden's death has anything to do with her job here. They'll just be looking for a few quotes about what she was like as a person, that kind of thing."

She nodded stiffly, appearing to be calmed by this. "How could her death have anything to do with the *library*?" Her tone was hushed and almost reverent.

"I'm sure it hasn't, but Mrs Braden had been widowed a long time, and according to her sister, she didn't have many friends. She'd worked here for three decades. You were amongst the people who knew her best."

Janice relaxed a little and crossed her arms over her narrow chest. "Well, that's true enough. Her sister was a bit of a 'fly-by-night', as my mother used to say. As soon as her son turned eighteen, she was off to run a bar in Benidorm or somewhere similar. Before that, there had been a stream of different boyfriends too. Victoria was the only stable influence in that poor lad's life."

"You know he was found dead last week?" Pete ventured.

"Yes, awful news. I told Victoria to take as much time off as she needed, but she'd insisted on coming back in tomorrow. Said she needed to keep busy." The woman tutted loudly. "What a terrible tragedy to have struck that family. It beggars belief."

Alice leant forward. "This next piece of information I'm going to give you, I'd like to remain confidential if possible. We don't want the press to find out."

Janice puffed her chest up, like a bird pluming its feathers. "You won't find me gossiping about poor Victoria to the press. I've always treated this library a bit like a church. Whatever I see or hear within these walls; *avant garde* internet searches and unusual book withdrawals, I treat like a priest would a confession." She mimed the sealing of her lips.

Alice tried not to laugh at the pomposity of the remark. "Fine, well the truth is, we now know that Victoria Braden was, in fact, the biological mother of Leroy Torben. Not his aunt at all."

Chapter 33

Janice sat stock still. Her face turning the same shade of grey as the sky beyond the room's tiny window. "That's a mistake. It can't possibly be the case."

Pete recognised the beginnings of a genuine, physical reaction to shock and offered to get her a cup of water. He returned a few seconds later and placed it in her trembling hands, encouraging her to take a sip.

"I'm afraid we have DNA proof this was most certainly the case. It's irrefutable. Caroline Torben has now admitted to us that in 1998, her sister told her she was pregnant and begged her to take on the child as her own. To make everyone believe Leroy was *her* son."

Janice gulped a mouthful of water. "But I knew Victoria back then. She was never pregnant. I recall her taking some time off to help her sister after the baby was born, but she was back soon enough. I can't believe it."

"Some women are extremely skilled at hiding a pregnancy. Victoria must have worn baggy tops or jackets to cloak her changing figure. She may never have shown very obviously in the first place. There's no doubt. It was Victoria Braden who gave birth to Leroy in the November of 1998 at the Glasgow Infirmary. The records are clear."

Janice let out a rush of air from her lungs. "Well, I'll be damned. We never had the slightest clue. Not any of us."

"Who else worked with Victoria back then?" Pete asked, flipping open his notepad.

"Debbie outside has only been here a couple of years. Back then, Donny Jones was the manager. He retired in 2012, but I've got an address for him. There were some younger staff, folk who came and went. Of course, Victoria and I were much younger then too. I'll have to check if our personnel records stretch back that far."

"If you wouldn't mind checking, we'd most appreciate it," Pete said.

Alice continued to probe, "the question we're struggling with, is that knowing Victoria was widowed back in '96 and according to her sister, she hadn't been dating anyone since, who could Leroy's father have been? Did you know of a boyfriend back then? Did she go out to any particular bars or clubs? Did you socialise together?"

Janice looked at the DI like she'd just landed from another planet. "Victoria, much like her royal namesake, went into a long period of mourning after her Greg died so suddenly. The very *idea* of her having boyfriends back then, or visiting pubs and clubs, is simply ludicrous. I really can't stress that fact strongly enough."

Alice returned the library manager's steely gaze, suspecting this lady was absolutely right.

Chapter 34

"Are we any further forward?" Alice asked philosophically, as they climbed the stairs to their department on the second floor. She felt uncharacteristically weary.

"I'm going to check those personnel records the manager promised to email. Perhaps Victoria confided in another of her workmates from back then?"

Alice pushed open the door to the department, which was buzzing with activity. "But from what Janice told us, Victoria wasn't the type to open up to her colleagues. They seemed more like acquaintances than friends."

Pete reached his desk and tossed down his notebook. "I can't believe she never told *anyone* about her pregnancy other than Caroline. What about antenatal visits and scans? Did she attend all those alone?" He was thinking of his own sister's pregnancies when his brother-in-law had to take endless days off work to attend such appointments.

"She was determined to keep it quiet. Caroline described Victoria as 'terrified' about the pregnancy. I don't think she'd have trusted anyone else with the secret."

Pete sighed. He wasn't sure he entirely believed that. But their victim's list of friends and family was vanishingly small. He dropped into his chair and logged onto the system, hoping to find the information he wanted waiting in his inbox.

Alice weaved around the desks until she reached her own, where a tall figure was standing by her chair, his hand on the pile of papers resting in her tray, his vision apparently trained on their contents. When he sensed someone approach, his head whipped up. "Ah, Ma'am, you're back. I was just trying to find the statement from the neighbour, to double check the timings. I got some information from the house-to-house enquiries that could be important," Victor Novak explained.

Alice placed her bag down carefully and shrugged out of her coat. She watched Victor's face. His expression was a blank, but beads of sweat had broken out across his brow and a fresh sheen glowed on his upper lip. "Well, that statement is in the case file. There's a copy on the shared document area."

"I know, I just wanted to check the times quickly, that was all."

Alice didn't push it any further. "What have you got?" She asked instead.

Victor paced back to his own desk, as if happy to put some space between them and picked up his notebook. "I was knocking on the doors of numbers 20-40. The lady at no. 37 claimed she saw a green-grey hatchback parked opposite her house on the street on the afternoon Victoria Braden was killed. It's a quiet road so she thought it was odd. Didn't belong to any of the neighbours. She said it'd parked up there at about half one and left at just before three. I wanted to compare that with the time the neighbour reported the break-in."

"It was between 2pm and ten past," Alice added, without needing to consult the file.

"Okay, so that might fit, don't you think?"

The DI felt her heart increase its tempo. "She didn't by any chance take a note of the registration?"

He grimaced. "I'm afraid not. She said it was a light grey colour, possibly green, and it was a small hatchback, like a Fiesta or a Corsa."

Alice rolled her eyes. "It's hardly very specific. There must be hundreds of cars fitting that description in Ayrshire."

Victor's expression hardened. "We can check whether our suspects own a similar vehicle."

Pete called across from his desk a few metres away, "the Goldings have a ten year old Golf. It's a sort of muddy green colour. They keep it parked in one of those old disused stables. Perhaps Victor could show this neighbour a picture of it, see if it rings a bell?"

Alice considered this. "Yeah, sure, it's worth a try. But why the hell would any of the Goldings want to murder Victoria Braden?"

Pete shrugged, looking a little offended.

"Okay, good work," Alice conceded. "Victor, liaise with Pete to find a picture online of the model of car the Goldings use as their 'runabout'. Then, take a copy round to number 37 and see if it rings any bells. We will need a proper witness statement from the resident anyway." She raised her voice to encompass the room. "Any other developments come out of the house-to-house enquiries?"

Matt and Holly both muttered a negative.

"Okay then, we work with what we have. Let's hope the *post mortem* and forensic results give us something more solid to go on."

Chapter 35

The new kitchen door was certainly cutting out the drafts better than their previous one had. Perhaps that's how Alice could explain the replacement to Fergus when he returned? That she was improving their insulation? She'd still not mentioned the vandalism of the old one during their nightly phone calls. He'd be angry that she'd kept it from him.

The thought created a knot in her stomach, but she smiled cheerfully as she placed a plate of buttered toast and marmite on the table in front of Charlie. He picked up a soldier and chewed it with deep concentration.

When the doorbell rang, Alice nearly tipped over her son's beaker of juice. "For God's sake, pull yourself together," she muttered under her breath.

She looked through the peephole and twisted the deadlock. The door swung open and DS Sharon Moffett, wearing jeans and a pink fluffy jumper, a wheelie case standing to attention beside her, was positioned on the doorstep. Alice pulled her old colleague into a firm embrace.

"Good grief! You've never hugged me before, in all these years. What on earth is wrong?"

Alice ushered her inside and closed the front door firmly behind them, making sure the bolt and chain were fixed into place.

"Calm down, Alice. This is Fairlie, not Easterhouse," Sharon chuckled, then she saw the look on her friend's face and her smile faded. "Bloody hell, you really *are* spooked."

Alice led her into the kitchen. Charlie clambered down from his seat and bowled towards their visitor. "Shazza!" He exclaimed, his mouth full of toast.

Sharon scooped him up in her arms. "How's my favourite wee man?" She asked enthusiastically. Much to her surprise, the DS proceeded to get an answer, which involved a detailed description of his gran and grandad's house in Largs and all the activities they'd been doing. "Wow!" She responded, when he'd finally run out of steam. "Someone's loving his Ayrshire life!"

Alice made Charlie finish up his tea and took him to bed. When she returned to the kitchen, Sharon had found a bottle of Malbec which she was opening with one of Fergus's corkscrews. "I hope you don't mind? You looked like you needed a bevvy. Lovely house, by the way."

Alice collected a pair of crystal glasses from a cupboard. "Aye, you've got that right. And thanks. We fell in love with it the moment we saw it."

She pulled out a chair and sat down, allowing Sharon to fill her glass almost to the brim. "cheers," she said without much enthusiasm.

Sharon put her own glass to her lips and sipped. "So, much as I love coming to visit you, why am I really here?"

"You must know my case at West Kilbride has developed into a double murder?"

Sharon nodded. "Yep, the most we've got to deal with at Pitt Street right now are overenthusiastic 'guisers'. Bevan and the DCS had been discussing whether to send some officers over to assist you. So when I said you'd invited me to stay, the boss jumped at the chance of seconding me to your team."

"Good, I'm glad DCI Bevan was okay with losing you for a few days. I wouldn't want to step on her toes, not her of all people."

"She's totally cool with it." Sharon leant forward, resting her head in her hands. "Now, tell me what's been going on."

Alice relayed the details of the murder cases and the vandalism of her own property. She finished by describing how she found DC Novak reading the files on her desk that afternoon.

Sharon took a long sup of wine, mulling over the information she'd been told. "There must be a connection between your two deaths. Which means a lot of digging needs to be done into the lives of everyone connected to both cases. You're going to need your team to work hard, and be trusted."

"Exactly. It's the trust thing I'm struggling with. My DS, Pete Falmer, is totally legit. I trust him, but the others, I'm not so sure. Someone threatened me on my home number, telling me I was muscling in where I didn't belong. I can't help but feel only someone in the department would hold that kind of grudge."

"Okay, well this Victor Novak fella certainly seems dodgy for a start. What do you know about your predecessor? He's on indefinite gardening leave, isn't he?"

"DI Mitchie. Pete said he wasn't always an easy man to work with. I'd like to know what he was up to whilst he was running West Kilbride CID. That's where you come in." She tipped her glass in the direction of her friend.

"You want me to find out why Mitchie had to leave and what his methods were when he still ran the department? But you don't want the rest of your team to find out?"

"Got it in one." Alice felt the wine start to loosen the tension in her body. A warmth spread through to her bones knowing she had an ally with her.

Someone in the house alongside her and Charlie on the long, dark nights.

"I'll need a pretext to be in the department, though. Otherwise my presence will arouse suspicion."

"I'll say you're coming it to assist with the investigation, now we have two bodies on our hands. You're right, this case is going to involve a lot of legwork from now on. I will probably need your help with that too."

"Sounds like a plan." Sharon grinned.

Alice felt a stab of awkwardness. "I hope you're okay with the foldaway bed? We haven't got a great deal of space."

Sharon waved her hand dismissively. "Not a problem. It seems so peaceful here. The noise of the M8 from my flat makes the windows rattle."

Alice laughed. "Well, I'm glad I can offer a decent incentive to make you stay."

Sharon got to her feet. "Keep the wine flowing and you've got me for as long as you want me."

Chapter 36

It was decided that Sharon would share a desk with Pete Falmer. He cheerfully cleared her a space opposite him. "We've never investigated a suspicious death before and now we've got two," he commented. "The DI has been great at telling us what to do, but we'd certainly value having someone with a bit more experience amongst us in the rank and file."

Sharon had arrived laden with goodies, as was her trademark. She'd got Alice to drop her at a nearby bakery where she stocked up on pastries and doughnuts before walking the final few yards to the station. She'd already offered them around the desks whilst introducing herself. Now, she sat down and took a large bite from an almond croissant. "We've certainly handled plenty of murders at Pitt Street," she replied, puffs of icing sugar spraying from her mouth in an incongruous contrast to her words. "I tend to handle the research side of things. From what I've read about your cases, we need to track down anyone who knew Victoria Braden around the time she was pregnant with Leroy. Which means focussing on her work colleagues at the time, any health professionals she was in contact with at the infirmary during her pregnancy and trying the sister again. She may know more than she's letting on."

Pete nodded enthusiastically. "Yep, I agree. Let's start with the employment records from the library."

*

Alice was happy to leave her pair of detective sergeants to it. She trusted both of them to do a thorough job. The rest of the team she felt might require a little more guidance. Holly Gadd was driving the DI to the Law Road, on the far side of town, where Leroy had been an active member of the Seamill Shooters football team. They had an appointment with the team manager at the ground where they trained.

The car park formed a gravelled area beside a large pitch surrounded by tall fences. Alice had only seen it on the photos she'd been shown from the team's Instagram page. It was modest, but well kept, and the billboards running around the touchlines were bright and professional looking. The DI immediately noticed the advert for Vintage Interiors. It didn't seem to the detective that the sign was more than a couple of months old.

A man in a red and white tracksuit with heavily gelled hair emerged from a pre-fab office. He was mid-thirties and good looking. He offered both officers his hand to shake. "I'm Martin Quinlan, the manager of the Seamill Shooters. The whole team have been devastated to hear what happened to Leroy. He was a very popular and talented young man."

Alice nodded in recognition of his words. "Can you give us the names of those team mates Leroy was closest to?"

"Of course. Ewan Dawson is the most obvious, they were great mates and worked together at the garage in town. A couple of other lads went to the Law Bar with them on a Friday night. I can give you the contact details for them. Everyone's devastated, I can assure you of that."

"Did you socialise much with the team, Mr Quinlan?"

He gave a thin smile. "The lads are all a decade younger than me. I've got small kiddies at home. We've run some fundraising events over the last few years where we all join in, but I never go drinking with the boys. Those days are over for me." His tone was wistful.

Alice felt he seemed genuine enough. Close up, she could see the puffiness under his eyes and the dark shadows which suggested the man didn't get a great deal of sleep. His body was fit and strong, nonetheless. "Okay, I'll give you a card with my email address on, so you can send me those player details."

Holly cleared her throat. "There was something else I wanted to ask you about, sir," she said uncertainly. "We noticed that you have a number of local sponsors? One company in particular, Vintage Interiors, is of interest to us. The managing director is called Rosaline Crammond? Her married name is Golding. Do you know her?"

Quinlan furrowed his brow. "The sponsorship is handled by the club chairman, Tony Stubbs. I can add his details to my email to the detective inspector. I know that Tony puts out feelers at meetings for the West Kilbride Chamber of Commerce to encourage advertising and sponsorship. We also get some businesses approaching us, if they are savvy about their marketing. We get a few hundred spectators through our gates on match days. But I can't say her name rings any bells with me."

Holly looked disappointed. "Okay, thanks. I will contact the chairman." She took a breath and said, "she's a few years older than you, Rosaline Golding. She's slim and attractive, with chestnut hair and has three young children. They go to a private school out of town. There's usually an au-pair with them, a dark-haired, petite young woman called Maria. Perhaps they've been to the ground on a match day?"

Martin considered this for a moment. "You know, that description does actually ring a bell. I recall my wife commenting on a woman who was sitting in the stands glued to her phone whilst her little ones were being entertained by what looked like a nanny. She made a joke about fancying one for herself." He grimaced. "Our two can be a bit of a handful."

Holly's expression brightened. "If I sent you a photo of the lady, would you be able to see if you recognised her? Show it to your wife perhaps?"

He shrugged his broad shoulders. "Sure, I'll take a look. But there's no way I'll be able to tell you for certain. We weren't that close to them or anything. It's not like we recognised her as another school mum."

"That's fine, I'd appreciate it if you just took the time to look."

Alice shook the manager's hand, thanking him for his cooperation. She glanced about her once again, at the oval of green nestled against the slate grey scree of the hillside. "Do you have CCTV at the ground?"

"Yeah, there's a camera by the entrance and one outside the clubhouse, then another pointing at the stands. We need them to deter rowdiness. We do have a licence to serve alcohol."

"How long do you keep the footage?"

"I don't believe anyone deletes it. The digital files go onto our database, organised by date."

"So, if we had a particular date we wanted to look at, that wouldn't be a problem?"

"I'd have to get permission from Tony, but I don't think that would be a problem, no."

Chapter 37

A couple occupied a table in the corner. They were leaning towards one another, separated by a bottle of prosecco. The bubbly suggested an anniversary of some sort. Apart from them, the pub was empty as the officers from the West Kilbride station pushed noisily through the double-doors.

Alice offered to buy a round. It was Sharon's idea they go for a drink after their shift. It hadn't occurred to Alice to do so earlier, since her arrival in the department, she was always rushing to get away and pick up Charlie. But this evening, she'd asked her parents to keep him for a while longer.

Sharon joined her at the bar, her thick curls escaping from a large, tortoiseshell clip, as if only allowing themselves to be contained for the duration of the working day. "Matt had to go home to his family," she said matter-of-factly. "His youngest has got tonsillitis."

Alice placed the orders and handed over a couple of crisp twenty pound notes. "How come you now know more about my team than I do and you've only been here five minutes?"

Sharon grinned. "We've got different information gathering styles, that's all. Besides, you're the big boss and I'm one of the guys. It makes all the difference."

The DI glanced across at her colleagues settling themselves into one of the wooden booths, shrugging out of their coats and chatting comfortably together. She knew Sharon was only partly correct. Andy Calder was always telling her she was too cold with people, too distant, that they would never open up to her properly unless she loosened up. But she reckoned she had other strengths. "So, what other gossip have you picked up?"

Sharon perched on a bar stool and watched as the barman prepared their order. "Victor's teenagers are playing up at home but seem to be keeping their heads down at school, so he's not too worried. Holly is having doubts about her boyfriend. He keeps complaining about her work schedule and has no ambition."

Alice laughed. "Bloody hell, you've certainly been busy!"

"Pete is single and has just bought his own house. He's been doing it up, as it was in a bit of a state when he moved in."

Alice noticed a blush creeping up Sharon's cheeks. Her friend was useless at hiding her feelings. She nudged her arm. "He's quite dishy, don't you think?"

Sharon tried a nonchalant lift of her shoulder. "Yeah, he's okay. Definitely a nice guy."

Alice started placing glasses on a tray, ready to join the rest of the group. "He's lovely. But I thought you and Dermot were an item?"

Sharon raised an eyebrow, putting in a last minute order for crisps and nuts. "I wouldn't let him hear you say that. I don't think he'd be impressed."

Alice rested the tray on the counter. "How do you mean? I thought the two of you got on really well. I sensed something romantic between you two after that trip to Africa you took last year?"

"Actually, it was during that trip I really saw myself through his eyes. It wasn't terribly flattering, what I saw. I'd been trying so hard to build something with Dermot and then, out there under the stars, amongst the sounds of the savannah, thousands of miles away, it suddenly became crystal clear."

Alice shook her head. "What did?"

Sharon cradled her armful of snacks. "It shouldn't *be* that hard. *I* don't deserve for it to be that hard."

Alice let her colleague walk ahead, joining her new team mates with a smile and a ready joke, thinking there was more to her old friend than she'd realised.

Chapter 38

The autumn sun was hanging low in the sky. The glare was almost blinding, but there was only a weak warmth to accompany it. Maria Silva gripped Cinnamon's lead rope, walking a few feet ahead of the animal as Jacob sat a little uncertainly in its saddle, clutching the reins and trotting gently behind.

Maria guided the pony down the slope of the garden, towards the line of trees which created a natural border to the lawn. She was hoping to take the pair through the woods to the tiny shingle shore which met the banks of the Clyde. The view widened out there, to encompass the Isle of Cumbrae and the Arran peaks beyond. She felt she could breathe better down there, under the broad skies. The sense of claustrophobia she'd been gripped by since the fire was given some temporary relief.

Her aim was only partly selfish. She'd been instructed to get Jacob more confident on his horse, to take them further afield. But the au-pair was also desperate to get away from the house. Rosaline seemed to want to keep coming back there, despite the terrible fire damage to a great swathe of the building. Maria would rather have remained at the hotel, where it was warm and comfortable.

But it was Saturday and the Goldings were determined to come back to see their property, regardless of the state it was in. Maria thought it was no place for the little ones. She had to constantly tell them off for venturing too close to the north wing, which was structurally unsound. Not to mention that a young man had lain dead inside its scorched walls.

She shook her head and tutted. It was no place for children, that was for certain. And whenever they returned to the place, her employers sat at the old kitchen table with piles of documents spread out before them, arguing in subdued voices. She knew they must be in financial trouble. Her employment was probably set to expire pretty soon. But she'd continue until the bitter end. Then she would move on to better things. The children deserved that much. If the Goldings could no longer afford an au-pair, their lives would get much worse, she was sure of this.

Her thoughts were interrupted when Cinnamon abruptly came to a standstill. Jacob was so unprepared for the action that he lurched violently forwards, having to grasp the horse's bridle to remain in the saddle. "What's wrong with her?" The boy shouted down to his companion.

They'd reached the line of old oak trees that marked the edge of the small copse beyond. There was a path running between two of the wide trunks which took them most directly to the shore. The tree at the end of the line was particularly old and gnarled. It's trunk had twisted under the weight of thick, knobbly branches so that it resembled a wizened old man reaching out with unnaturally long, spindly arms. It was particularly creepy, she had to admit.

Maria tugged on the rope. "Come on Cinnamon, it's okay. We're going to the beach. You can trot along by the sea, you like that," she kept her tone soft and cajoling. When a horse was spooked, there was no point in getting frustrated. It only made things worse.

But the pony stood her ground. Her hooves remained firmly positioned on the soft ground. Her head swung from side to side in a clear indication of a stubborn unwillingness to cooperate.

"What's wrong with her?" Jacob asked, in a tone which conveyed both concern and impatience.

"She doesn't want to pass between the trees," Maria replied. "I usually take her on the path straight from the stables. She's not used to this one. Perhaps she thinks it's too narrow for her."

"But it's plenty big enough for us to get through." Jacob's voice was becoming a whine.

Maria sighed inwardly, giving the lead another futile tug. To her surprise, Cinnamon took a couple of reluctant steps forward, but when they reached the trees, she reared upwards, lifting her front legs off the ground. Maria turned in panic, hoping her ward hadn't been thrown from the animal's back. To her great relief, the boy was still clinging on, but he'd started sobbing and calling loudly for help.

Maria moved forward swiftly, patting the horse's flank and encouraging her to lower her front legs back down to the soft grass. The last thing she wanted was for Cinnamon to make a bolt back up the hill, with the boy still clinging to her back. She placed her face close to the animal's muzzle, making soothing noises. She felt her gradually start to settle.

When the horse's heart rate had lowered sufficiently, she moved round to the flank and helped Jacob down from the saddle. They both then slowly led the pony back up the hill towards the stables.

"But I wanted to ride along the shore," Jacob sobbed quietly, as he walked by his nanny's side.

"We'll go another day," Maria replied gently. "Next time we'll take a different path. But for now, Cinnamon needs to rest. Horses are nervous animals, she will have to recover from whatever it was that spooked her."

Jacob nodded, seeming to understand, despite his disappointment. "Poor Cinnamon," he said through his tears. "She was terribly frightened."

"Yes," Maria replied, shivering beneath her padded gilet as she gazed back up at the ruined outline of Hill House, beginning to understand herself how the animal had felt.

Chapter 39

Victor tried to straighten his jacket as he took the seat beside Pete Falmer. It was creased from where he'd fallen asleep in it on the sofa the previous night. Lena had shaken him awake at about midnight, worried he'd not come home at all.

Pete had printed off a copy of some images of 2009 registration Volkswagen Golfs in a Seagull Grey. He showed them to his colleague, trying not to turn his nose up at the stale smell that hung about him like an unwelcome cologne. "This looks like the model of car the Goldings own. Although the paint colour is described as grey, it looks more green to me."

"Yeah," Victor added. "Looks like the tone of my skin after a night out, do you know what I mean?" He nudged Pete's arm and laughed.

Pete managed a chuckle, but he thought the joke was probably a bit close to the bone with Victor right now to be funny. He'd noticed his colleague coming into work a few minutes late most days that week and looking like he may have slept in his clothes. He wondered if everything was okay with Lena. He didn't know the man well enough to ask. "Can you drive over to Seamill Road and show these pictures to your witness? See if she can identify this as the car parked opposite her house on Tuesday afternoon."

Victor didn't get a chance to answer.

Alice was pushing back her chair and addressing the room. "We've had the *PM* and forensic results back from the Clydebank lab. Could you take a break from whatever you're doing and come and hear them?"

The officers responded swiftly. The results were their best chance of picking up a meaningful lead.

Alice was still skimming through the report Dr Webb had just sent through to her email, she scooped up a pen and began scribbling on the white board. "Okay, as we suspected, Victoria Braden died of a massive haemorrhage of blood due to the severing of the carotid artery. The neck was cut from right to left with a sharp, steel blade which matches with the knife left at the scene."

Sharon raised her hand. "If the cut was made right to left, does that suggest a right-handed attacker?"

Alice nodded. "Yes, we would usually say so, but it has been known for left-handed perpetrators to switch to their less dominant hand in order to throw doubt on their guilt, so we can't rule out anything here."

"But that would be a tactic used by an experienced killer, wouldn't you say?" Sharon persisted.

"Yes, but we can't rule out that possibility in this case. The killer of Mrs Braden acted swiftly and without being seen. We aren't talking about a complete amateur. The perp was, at least, someone who has killed before."

Sharon nodded, accepting this information.

Alice turned back to her board of notes. "Webb noted defensive wounds on the victim's hands and forearms. There was a minor scald to the left palm but he thinks it's unrelated to the attack. She definitely tried to fight back, as the neighbour's testimony corroborates. But once the neck had been sliced open, death would have occurred within minutes. The blood would have been pumped out by the artery, hence the stains on the woman's shirt front and kitchen floor."

Holly Gadd's features had drained of colour. She was glad the boss hadn't decided to pin the crime scene photos to the board as well. She'd already seen those and had no desire to look at them again.

"A few fingerprints were picked up by the forensic team on the door frames and handles around the house. There were a couple on the dining room window and sill, but none were a match for anyone on the criminal database."

A sigh went up from the gathered officers. If a forensic connection could be made to a known offender at a crime scene it made their lives a whole lot easier.

Alice continued, "neither were those prints a match for Caroline Torben. Most belonged to Victoria herself and one other individual we must assume was Leroy, as he had lived there for several months before his death. Unfortunately, his body is too badly burnt to be able to lift any prints for comparison."

Holly felt her stomach churn once again, but was desperate not to show her discomfort.

"Any prints on the knife?" Pete asked hopefully.

Alice shook her head. "Sorry, the handle of the knife was clean, either wiped or handled with gloves. The shaft was soaked in Victoria's blood and nobody else's. Apparently, there were kitchen knives in one of the drawers but it's not possible to confirm whether the murder weapon was taken from there. The forensic team identified it as a cheap implement stocked in several budget home stores. My theory is the perpetrator bought it new and purely for the purpose of killing Mrs Braden."

"Could we check local stores to see who they sold a similar model to?" Matt asked.

Alice shrugged. "It's worth a try. We may pick up the customer on CCTV. But if I was carrying out the crime, I'd make sure I bought the knife well away from this area. I wouldn't want to waste too much investigation time on it. I think it's a dead end."

Victor let out of huff of frustration. "Did the forensic reports provide nothing useful at all?"

Alice tried to hide her annoyance at his tone. All evidence was useful in a murder case, even the absence of forensics, which suggested the perpetrator knew what they were doing and was either a career criminal or the act was carefully pre-planned. This was not a spontaneous killing they were dealing with. "Well, we now know that Victoria had certainly given birth at some point. Which confirms our belief that Leroy was her son. According to the *PM* she was very healthy for her age and without having her throat cut, would likely have lived for many more years, decades perhaps."

Pete shook his head solemnly. "Mrs Braden may have deceived everyone about the parentage of her child, but she didn't deserve this."

"No," Alice said firmly. "She did not."

"Are we still thinking the birth father may have a connection to the two deaths?" Matt asked.

"Yes," Alice replied. "If Victoria was so terrified of him finding out about the baby, it means she was scared of him. We have to assume he was of Afro-Caribbean origin, based on Leroy's ethnicity. He would be around Victoria's age, I imagine, possibly older. So in his sixties perhaps?"

Matt crinkled his brow. "Caroline Torben told us that Leroy had stopped calling her around July of this year and withdrew himself from both her and Victoria. Do you think the lad may have had suspicions himself that Caroline wasn't his real mother?"

Alice stopped writing on the board and turned to face the detective. "It's possible, I suppose. But why now? I know Caroline wasn't particularly maternal towards him, but that had always been the case. Why would he start to question his parentage at this stage of his life?"

"He must have found something out," Holly offered.

"Or someone told him something," Sharon added. "Something that got him thinking about his mother and his aunt and the odd relationship they'd always had."

Alice tapped the lid of the pen on her lower lip. "I think we're onto something here. Leroy started asking questions about who he was, where he came from, around about the summer of this year."

Pete got to his feet. "Then I suggest we find out just exactly *who* he asked."

Chapter 40

Sharon was behind the wheel of one of the pool cars. Pete was in the passenger seat beside her. He was navigating from a printout they'd generated from an internet search. They were driving up the coast to Wemyss Bay. It was a pleasant journey with the Clyde islands rising out of the water into the sunshine to the west.

"The Goldings' kiddies go to school up here somewhere," Pete commented. "Wemyss Academy, it's called."

"They make this journey every day?" Sharon thought it would be a great inconvenience to them.

Pete chuckled. "The au-pair takes them, in that runabout of theirs. She's not too happy about it. But I expect there must be a bus they could take, once the wains get a bit older."

"The au-pair – Maria, isn't it? She is used to driving that car then? Did the neighbour of Mrs Braden identify it as the one parked outside her house on the afternoon of the murder?"

Pete sighed. "She told Victor she couldn't be certain it was the same one. I suppose we were lucky she noticed it at all."

"Yeah, don't be discouraged. Now we can check the registration on ANPR cameras around the area on the day of the murder. You'd be surprised how much that kind of circumstantial evidence can help build a case."

Pete spotted the contours of the art deco pier pointing out from the headland which indicated they were entering the pretty seaside town of Wemyss Bay. "Take the right turn up here," he instructed. "The house is on the left, number 14."

They crept up the hilly road until they noticed the number they were looking for on a plaque to the side of an entrance gate. Fortunately, it was open and Sharon edged the car onto a narrow driveway.

Pete got out and surveyed the property. It was a neat, whitewashed bungalow with a fantastic view over the bay towards Dunoon. This was the address that the manager of West Kilbride library had given them for the man who had run the place back in 1998.

Sharon followed her colleague to the front door. He pressed the bell. A pair of sculpted conifers in pots stood guard on either side.

The door opened after several minutes. A man in his early sixties stood behind it. He wore a mustard jumper and smart jeans, his head was bald and patched with moles. "Can I help you?"

"Donald Jones? We are DS Falmer and DS Moffett from West Kilbride police, sir. May we come in? We have a few questions relating to a current investigation."

He took a step backwards, allowing them to enter. "I suppose so, although I've no idea what this is all about."

They walked along a hallway lined with photographs of snow-capped mountains and smiling men in climbing gear to a living room with a bank of windows making the most of the view.

"What a lovely outlook," Sharon commented genuinely.

"I'm lucky," he added. "My late partner Anton found this place. It's an absolute gem. Can I make you tea or coffee?"

"No thanks," Pete responded, perching on the edge of a patterned sofa. "This shouldn't take long."

The man shrugged his shoulders. "Suit yourselves. Now, how can I help you?" He sat in an old captain's chair that was positioned beside what looked like an antique telescope on a stand, which was pointing out to sea.

"Mr Jones, we are interested in the period when you were the manager of the library in West Kilbride. The year 1998, to be exact," Pete continued.

"Call me Donny, please." He narrowed his brow in thought. "That's a long time ago. May I ask why you're looking into that period in particular?"

"A lady who worked for you back then, Mrs Victoria Braden, was killed in her home a few days ago. We believe she may have been murdered to keep secret something that occurred during that time."

Donny's eyes widened like saucers. "Good God. I remember Victoria very well. She was a quiet, mousy type. Lost her husband in some awful road accident. I gave her a few weeks off when it happened but she was back sooner. A stoical character, I seem to recall, stiff upper lip."

Sharon leant forward in her chair. "We believe, that during the beginning of 1998, Victoria Braden was pregnant with a child. She gave birth to this baby in the November of 1998 at the Glasgow Infirmary. Were you aware of this fact?"

The man's face turned white. He gripped the arms of the chair as if trying to keep himself upright. "You can't be correct. Victoria didn't have a baby back then. You must be thinking of her sister. She got pregnant by some boyfriend who'd buggered off. Victoria wanted to help her, so she'd asked me for some leave after the bairn was born. She even had the sister live with her for a while, I think."

Pete nodded patiently. "Yes, that was the story they told everyone. But it was *Victoria* who gave birth to the baby boy. We want to know who she socialised with that year. Who she was close to and may have confided in. We are particularly keen to find out the identity of the father. We think it connects to her murder."

Donny Jones looked suddenly sick to the gills. Sharon thought he might faint. "Can I get you a glass of water?"

He nodded, a sheen of sweat spreading across his top lip. "Yes, please. I'm not sure why this news has affected me so much. My mother died around that time and I'm re-living the whole period, I suppose."

Sharon returned with a glass of cold water. He sipped it delicately. "Are you okay to carry on?"

"Sure, I'm sorry. It's just life is very quiet for me these days. First, you tell me Victoria Braden was murdered and now that she had a secret baby under all of our noses."

"Yes," Pete said wryly. "It's certainly a lot of information to take in. But please think carefully for us. Janice Kirk is adamant Victoria didn't have any boyfriends after the death of her husband. But we have biological proof she gave birth around that time."

Donny took a deep breath. "Janice's quite right. Victoria wasn't the type for casual flings. She took her husband's death very badly, which wasn't surprising, he was only in his thirties. I'm afraid I can't recall her being particularly close to anyone who worked there. We had a few assistants come and go around that time, but none I'd link to Victoria. She was closer to myself and Janice if I'm honest."

"And you never had any suspicion about her pregnancy?" Sharon asked gently.

"Not at all. As I say, she barely missed a day of work, even when her husband died. She did take a week or so of leave to help her sister, but that was *after* the baby was born. Or so I thought."

Pete got to his feet. "Thank you for speaking with us. Please take my card, in case you do remember anything from back then, however trivial it may seem."

Donny took the card and stared at it. "Yes, of course."

They proceeded towards the front door. Sharon paused for a moment. "You said your mother passed away during that year? Did you by any chance take some compassionate leave at any point?"

The man considered this. "Yes, I believe I did. She died in the February of 1998. I took a few days off to organise the funeral and everything. It did hit me very hard, I'll admit."

"Thank you sir," Sharon replied. "You've been very helpful."

As they reached the door and Pete was stepping over the threshold, Donny suddenly exclaimed. "Wasn't the baby mixed race?"

The detectives stopped in their tracks. "Yes, the young man who was brought up by Victoria and her sister was of Scots and Afro-Caribbean heritage."

Donny looked flustered. "I've just recalled that. Because the sister brought him into the library one day, in his pram. I commented on how dark skinned he was, his tufts of hair were an inky black. Victoria said he had African blood. It stuck in my mind, for some reason. So, the father you're looking for. He must have been black, mustn't he?"

"Yes, that is our assumption," Pete answered.

The detectives climbed back into the car and shut the doors. Sharon put the key into the ignition. "Now, why on earth would Donny Jones have remembered *that*?"

Chapter 41

They took a walk along the Law Brae, in the direction of the football ground. Ewan Dawson ate a bacon roll as they strolled along. It was his lunch hour and Mr Doyle wasn't prepared to give him any extra time off to speak to the police.

Holly and Alice flanked the young man as they crossed the main road and found a bench to sit on. "Thanks for letting me view your WhatsApp group messages," Holly commented. "We've now got a good idea when Leroy stopped communicating with his friends and therefore when he disappeared."

"No problem. It's the least I could do," Ewan said through a mouthful of bacon and red sauce. "Now his aunt's dead too. It's a total head trip."

"We are wondering if there might have been a connection between Leroy's death and the murder of Mrs Braden," Alice said.

The younger man screwed up his face. "I can't see what that could be? Leroy died a couple of weeks ago now?"

Alice concluded that this lad probably wasn't the most adept at lateral thinking. "We've been given some information that Leroy began acting out of character around the summer of this year? He stopped ringing his mum in Spain and withdrew from his family. Do you know why this might have been? You were probably his best mate."

Ewan puffed himself up at this last comment. "Yeah, I was really. Cause I've got a motor, we went round everywhere together. When Leroy got his, we were still going to share rides, to reduce petrol costs and that."

"What make of car do you have?" Holly asked innocently.

"A Ford Fiesta ST, Mars red. I've lowered the springs on the wheels. It looks sick. Doyle lets us modify our own cars out of hours. He's not so bad, bit of a petrol head himself." He grinned.

Alice noted it most certainly wasn't Dawson's car that was seen parked up on Seamill Road when Mrs Braden was killed. His vehicle would be highly conspicuous. "So what about Leroy? Did something happen this summer to change his attitude towards his family?"

Dawson chewed the final mouthful of his roll. "His relationship with his mum was always weird. My mam still makes my dinners and that. Leroy's shoved off to the Costas as soon as he turned 18. It must've hurt him, although he never said so. But he did ring her regular, like you said." He wiped a smudge of sauce from the corner of his mouth. "He never told me he'd stopped."

Alice was beginning to feel frustrated. This lad didn't seem to grasp the significance of his best friend dying in horrific circumstances and his aunt soon after. Perhaps he just saw the two events as simply a run of bad luck. "Try to cast your mind back, Ewan. Did anything happen this past summer, around July, maybe, that seemed in any way out of the ordinary for Leroy. It doesn't matter how insignificant it seems, we still want to know."

He screwed his face again, as if trying with all his might to dredge something up from his brain. "The only thing I can think of, is that bird at the footie."

The detectives exchanged glances. "There was a woman at the football ground?"

"Yeah," he nodded, more confidently now. "She was at one of our matches at home. It was a busy turnout because we were in the semis of our league finals. At the end of the game, we'd won, so we were lording it about the stands and that, high-fiving with our families, getting bought pints of 70 shilling. This woman was there, sitting in the east stand with her kids and a girl about my age who I thought was their nanny."

"Did she approach Leroy?"

"No, he approached *her*. I was with my family and didn't notice he'd broken away from us. Then, I looked across and saw him talking to her. She was older, but nice looking. A yummy mummy type." He glanced at Alice. "No offence," he swiftly added, indicating he'd put her in a similar category.

"None taken. Did you hear what they were saying?"

"No, I was too far away and the crowd was rowdy, what with us having had a home win. They both looked serious, though. She was shaking her head. Then he walked off, back to the changing rooms. We went to the Law Bar afterwards to celebrate, but Leroy was a bit subdued, I reckon. I took the piss out of him about it. Like, he was hitting on an old bird and maybe he should've gone for the nanny, cause she was quite fit too." Ewan had the good grace to blush at this admission of unsavoury banter. "But he got annoyed about it, which made me wonder if he did really fancy her."

"Did you see this woman at the football ground again? Did Leroy ever mention her?"

He shook his head. "No, I didn't. And I reckon I would have noticed her at the footie, cause we never had such a big crowd again for a match. The league final was played in Irvine."

"If you saw this woman again, would you recognise her?" Alice felt her heart rate rise.

"I dunno, to be honest. But if you put her in an identity parade, I'd have a go at picking her out."

Alice had to suppress a smile. "I was thinking more of a photograph."

"Yeah, I'll take a look." He frowned. "Hey, you don't think that woman had anything to do with Leroy's death do you?"

"We don't know yet, Ewan. But every piece of information you can give us will help us to find out what happened to your friend."

For a moment, his expression was melancholy. Then, he glanced at his phone. "Shit! I'm gonna be late back from my lunchbreak! Doyle's gonna fuckin' kill me!"

The detectives remained seated on the bench, watching the young man sprint off in a whirlwind of expletives.

Chapter 42

The semi-final match Ewan Dawson had mentioned during their conversation took place on the 22nd July that year. It wasn't difficult to find this out after they contacted Martin Quinlan again.

Holly was seated beside the man right at that moment, in his unheated pre-fab office at the football ground, looking through the CCTV footage saved from that date.

"I've got a description from Ewan Dawson, which isn't particularly detailed. But you and your wife saw this woman too, didn't you?"

Quinlan nodded as he tapped open various files from the day. "Aye, we did. But, like Ewan, I'm not sure I could give you much of a description. There were lots of folk there that day; the families and friends of the players, plus all our big sponsors and the chairman, of course. Not to mention the supporters of the opposition team."

Holly scanned the images on the screen in front of her. Quinlan was right, the ground had been very busy that afternoon in July. It looked like it had been a warm day. Most of the spectators were in shorts and T-shirts or summer dresses. The queue for the bar stretched right out into the stands during half-time. The detective sighed, she couldn't make out Rosaline Golding at all.

Martin pushed back his seat. "Fancy a cuppa?"

Holly nodded. "Yeah, I would thanks. Milk, no sugar please."

The man moved off into a kitchen area, with a small sink and preparation area. He banged about with the kettle and cups. "It's a terrible business with Leroy's aunt, too. We were watching the reports on BBC Scotland last night. She only lived a few streets from us. It's just not the kind of thing you expect in West Kilbride. We've got our trouble wi' kids hanging about and thieving and that. It's one of the reasons I wanted to get into youth football. Keeps the young 'uns off the street and out of trouble."

Holly had stopped listening to the man's distant chat. She had found a file which contained footage of what she assumed to be the east stand. She scoured the scene with her nose almost touching the screen. Then she pressed pause.

Quinlan returned with two steaming mugs in his hands. "Have you spotted something?"

Holly pointed at a group of people in the blurred, freeze-frame. "There's a woman there, on the fourth row back. She's seated with some children and a dark haired young woman in a floral sundress. Is that the woman you and your wife commented on?" The detective was pretty certain it was Rosaline Golding and Maria Silva, but she didn't want to lead him in any way.

He squinted at the screen. "Aye, it certainly looks like it. But I couldnae swear to it in a court of law, sorry." He shrugged his broad shoulders.

"Is there a way of printing off this image?"

"You could take a screen shot, but it's not a very clear image. I'll email you the whole file and I bet your techies could do a better job of creating a still from it."

Holly took a gulp of her tea, suddenly parched. "Thanks, I'll do that. You've been a brilliant help Mr Quinlan."

*

Holly showed the printed-off image to Alice, who sat back in her chair and examined it closely.

"Pete has some software on his PC that cleaned up the still and made it a bit clearer. The tech department have the video now and said they could probably sharpen it up even further."

"I think it's pretty good as it is. This is definitely Rosaline Golding and her family. Excellent work, Holly. We've got something solid here to present to the woman which contradicts her previous testimony."

"I've emailed the screen shot to Ewan Dawson too. I'm hoping he can identify her as the woman Leroy spoke to that day."

"If he could, that would provide a link between Leroy and the Goldings we don't now have." She let the paper drop to her desk. "What does it mean, Holly? Why did Leroy approach Rosaline? How did he know her and what did they talk about?"

"From what Dawson said, it sounded more like an argument than a conversation. Rosaline has lied to us about it and Maria has too. Her employer must have told her to keep her mouth shut about having been there that day."

"Then, this young man who Rosaline had an altercation with at the football match, ends up dead in her house three months later." Alice drummed her fingers on the table. "We're missing a big piece of the puzzle here."

"I thought I might contact Tony Stubbs, the club chairman. He may know why Rosaline decided to sponsor that particular team." Holly's expression was open and eager.

"Good idea. We need to know what brought Leroy and Rosaline Golding together."

Chapter 43

A bound plastic file lay in the centre of the oak table in Alice's kitchen. She'd made sure the remnants of Charlie's dinner were thoroughly cleared away before she placed the document there.

Sharon trudged down the stairs, finding her friend seated at the table with a large glass of red wine in her hand.

"Help yourself," Alice urged. "The bottle's open."

"Cheers. It's amazing how much reading about Hey Duggee's adventures brings a thirst on." She reached for a glass and filled it generously. Taking the seat opposite.

"Thanks for putting him to bed. Charlie loves you reading him a story so much he's almost forgotten his dad isn't here."

"No worries. I've always felt a character called Duggee should have a Scottish accent anyway."

Alice laughed, raising a glass and taking a long sup. "Agreed. Although I'm not sure he ever does much more than woof."

Sharon gestured towards the chunky document placed between them. "What's that?"

"It's the preliminary fire investigation report on Hill House. Eleanor Canning, the fire investigation officer, brought it to the department in person this afternoon. I've not had chance to read it yet. It's going to be a long night."

Sharon was wide-eyed. "I thought it was going to take weeks? Months even?"

"Apparently, DCS Douglas gave the chief of the Scottish Fire and Rescue service a call. He asked them to put a rush on the report as the fire was now linked to two suspected homicides."

"It seems we have much to thank 'Dour Douglas' for."

Alice sighed. "I hope he's not giving me special treatment because this is my first SIO assignment."

Sharon gulped her mouthful noisily. "It's not that, I can assure you. Both Dani and the DCS are watching this case with keen interest." She leant forwards, cradling her glass in both hands. "I think I may know why."

Alice's interest was growing. "What have you found out?"

Sharon's expression was conspiratorial. "I didn't want to talk to you in the department about it. You never know whose listening. You asked me to find out why your predecessor has been put out to pasture for the foreseeable?"

Alice nodded. She'd put her glass down, wanting a clear head to process this information.

"I asked Andy Calder to do some digging for me. He's got some contacts at the IOPC. According to his sources, DI John Mitchie is still under investigation. He'd worked at the West Kilbride station for over ten years. There'd been a couple of complaints against him during that time; mostly for bullying behaviour. In fact, one of the complainants was a 22 year old PC Gadd."

Alice gasped. "That must have been Holly, when she was in uniform."

"Mitchie had shouted at her in front of members of the public. He was given a slap on the wrist and Holly didn't take it any further."

"Sounds like a real gent," Alice said sarcastically.

"Aye, we both know the sort. Pick on the young, pretty girl in uniform when you're having a bad day. Easy target."

"Not so easy these days. This younger generation of recruits won't put up with it."

"Aye, it seems like Mitchie's methods finally caught up with him. In November last year, the criminal investigation team were looking into a gang who were receiving cocaine and cannabis smuggled on freight lorries into Irvine Harbour. One night, a team led by Mitchie, some officers from the National Crime Agency and DCs Falmer, Novak and Singh intercepted two trucks leaving the docks."

Alice hid her surprise and allowed her friend to continue.

"One of the trucks was secured and the drivers arrested. The other, for reasons that are still unclear, managed to get away. It was found four hours later abandoned on an industrial estate on the outskirts of Irvine. The drivers had scarpered and the drugs were gone. They estimate it had been carrying £1.2m worth of cocaine and £2m worth of cannabis."

Alice let out a long breath. "What the hell happened? How did the second truck evade the officers?"

"Mitchie claimed there was a diversion. A group of men came out of the docks, dressed in balaclavas, charging at his team of officers and attacking them with iron bars. Whilst this was happening, the truck got away."

"There must have been evidence to support this? CCTV images? The testimony of the other officers? Injuries to the team from the assault?"

Sharon smiled wryly. "There was no CCTV in that area of the docks. A couple of officers had cuts and bruises, including John Mitchie, but the extent of injuries was inconclusive to prove the attack took place. In the end, they could only produce the sworn testimony of those men who'd been in Mitchie's team. The IOPC think Mitchie let the truck go and took a cut of the drug money. They've been all over his bank accounts, but there's no money trail. Andy says they reckon he's got other accounts overseas they can't access. Or he's playing the long game. Waiting until the heat's off for him to receive his payoff."

Alice forgot about her good intentions and reached for her glass, draining nearly half of it. "Bloody hell! That was bigger than I thought it would be. Over three million went missing that night."

"Yup. Whoever was involved in that truck evading capture, would have a great deal riding on it."

"So who was in the team DI Mitchie was leading that night? The ones that let the truck get away?"

Sharon raised her eyebrows. "Mitchie himself, a guy from the NCA, and Falmer, Novak and Singh."

Alice whistled. "Well, that *is* interesting. Very interesting indeed."

"That's why Douglas and Bevan are watching this case so closely. Nothing's been proven yet, but they are wondering if one or more of your officers is as bent as the Clyde Arc."

Chapter 44

Despite switching to water as soon as Sharon had gone to bed the previous night, Alice still had a pounding headache. She'd finished reading the fire report at nearly 2am, but with the information swirling around her head and the wine from earlier in the evening lying heavily in her stomach, she'd hardly slept at all.

She'd been distracted as she kissed Charlie goodbye that morning, but he hadn't noticed, running straight to his grandad who'd set up a new configuration of his favourite train tracks. Her parents certainly knew the route to her little boy's affections.

Alice would need to relay the fire department's findings to the rest of her team. She found a packet of ibuprofen in a drawer and swallowed a couple of pills along with a big gulp of coffee. Currently, she wasn't sure if she could trust any of her team, apart from Sharon and Holly. Now, even Pete was tainted by suspicion, although she was struggling to believe his guilt.

She'd need to read the statements her officers had made about the night last November they'd intercepted the drug traffickers. But right now, she was up to her eyes in a double murder investigation and all her focus needed to be on that.

Alice took a deep breath and summoned the team to her desk. "Okay, everyone. I received the preliminary fire investigation report last night."

A few surprised glances were exchanged between the officers but she wasn't in the mood to explain its early arrival.

"It is a very detailed and thorough document, but I've tried to summarize the key findings for you.

According to Eleanor Canning, the fire was started deliberately. We are looking at a case of arson, and with Leroy's body having been placed at the centre of the blaze, we are also looking at murder, or at the very least an attempt to unlawfully conceal a body."

Her audience nodded their understanding.

"The evidence gathered from the scene indicated the blaze was started in the ground floor kitchenette of the north wing of Hill House. Remains of a gas cooker were recovered from the scene and it appeared the appliance had been left on. When firefighters first attended, they smelt the presence of lingering gas on the air. It appears the cooker was fuelled by a cylinder of propane gas which was ignited by a pile of papers and wood left burning in a wire litter bin. When the gas volume had risen significantly, there would have been a small explosion which triggered the fire which swept through the rest of the northern side of the house. They predict the cylinder exploded at around 5.30am."

This information was met with a moment of silent contemplation. Pete finally raised his hand. "Would this explosion have been heard by the family who were in the house? Especially Maria, who was closest to the source of the fire?"

"The report suggests the canister explosion would have sounded like a door slamming, or a crack of thunder. It's possible that Rosaline and her children, in the south wing of the house weren't woken by it and were roused instead by the smoke alarms going off."

Pete looked sceptical. "But Maria Silva must have heard the explosion, surely? Does that mean she's been lying to us? That she is the arsonist?"

Holly Gadd shook her head. "It strikes me that Maria is interested purely in self-preservation. She doesn't want to upset her employers. My sense is that she doesn't have much to return to in Spain and wants to stay with the Goldings until she has enough money saved to set herself up somewhere else. I believe she'd lie about what she heard or saw that night in order to protect her future. It's not necessarily a sign of guilt."

Alice sighed. "I agree. It seems all the incendiary devices used to start the fire at Hill House originated on the property; the gas canister, the paper and kindling and we have to assume the matches used to light the makeshift brazier in the litter bin, although traces of them are now completely obliterated. This was an inside job. Once set up, it would have been possible for the residents to return to bed before the fire really took hold. Yet Roger Golding was 150 miles away and Rosaline and Maria deny all knowledge of how it started or how Leroy's body got there."

Sharon crossed her arms over her ample chest. "And they were all dressed in night gear when you attended the scene at around 8am?"

Pete nodded. "All of the householders looked shocked and as if they'd been woken from their beds by the alarms."

"It's a hell of a risk," Sharon continued. "To initiate a gas explosion when your own small children are in the house, however far away you would be from the blast."

Victor tutted loudly. "I've been thinking the same. Setting a fire like that, you could never be certain it wouldn't spread too quickly and prevent you getting out. If the mother did this, she was taking a terrible gamble with the lives of her children."

Alice considered this. "But it would certainly point the blame elsewhere, wouldn't it? We would hardly suspect a mother who was asleep on the premises with her young children of setting the fire herself."

"There's still a chance someone else did it," Pete added. "The house is completely secluded. There are neighbours down at the bottom of the approach road but they saw and heard nothing that night until the fire engines arrived. Another individual could have come to the house."

"But could they have placed Leroy's body there and set that fire without Maria and Rosaline knowing about it? My gut says they must have known something, been involved somehow, at least one of them. Does anyone disagree?" Alice eyed her team's reactions carefully, but not a single officer present contradicted her.

Chapter 45

The impressive aspect from the bay window of the pub was obscured by a drizzly front of rain passing across the Clyde towards the Isle of Bute. But Sharon was savouring it regardless. If she was back at her desk at Pitt Street, the view would have been of the thinning pate of her colleague Andy Calder, leaning intently over the lunchtime roll Carol would have filled lovingly for him before choking it in clingfilm to sustain him for his day protecting the people of Glasgow.

She smiled at the thought, realising she was missing her old colleagues after all.

Pete approached the table with a couple of glasses of coke, deftly balanced between his hands. "Here you go. Our sandwiches should be along in a few minutes."

"Thanks." Sharon sipped her drink gratefully. "You're very capable with your left hand. Can I ask why you only have three fingers there?" She felt unsure asking the question. Sharon knew she could be overly blunt, but at the same time, she wanted to get to know Pete better. There was no point ignoring his disability.

Luckily, the detective gave a wry smile. "It was a birth defect, although I'm not fond of that term. My parents were very positive and I've never felt there was anything I couldn't do like anybody else."

Sharon nodded earnestly. "They were quite right." She decided to move onto other topics, sensing he wasn't a man to dwell on this side of himself. "I invited you out for lunch so we could chat in private, away from the rest of the department."

Pete raised his eyebrow playfully. "Oh, aye?"

Sharon found herself blushing. "I wanted to know about how things were before Alice arrived. Not when you had no commanding officer, but back when DI Mitchie was in charge."

Pete's expression clouded. The barman arrived with two plates of sandwiches, garnished with a small green salad and a smattering of crisps. He set them down silently, sensing the tension in the air. "Why do you want to know about that?"

Sharon picked up one of the crisps, popping it into her mouth. "I'll level with you. Alice wanted my help with your murder cases, but she also wanted to know why she'd received a threatening phone call. She reckoned someone in the department, someone loyal to DI Mitchie, might be pissed off at her being there."

Pete sipped his drink and took a bite from the sandwich, as if giving him time to digest her words. "Have you been spying on us?" His tone was almost hurt.

Sharon felt her stomach turn with unease. It seemed she didn't want to upset this man. She really liked him. "Look, I wouldn't be telling you this if I didn't trust you. But Alice and I do know that your old boss is still under investigation by the IOPC. I wanted to hear your side of it, not just the official line."

Pete laid down his food and crossed his arms over his chest. "I suppose Alice was going ask at some point. Up to now, I've been relieved that bloody awful episode seemed to be put to bed. I should've known that would never be the case."

"Tell me what happened, in November last year. How did that truck get away during your operation?"

Pete glanced about him, as if there might be spies in this old-fashioned pub halfway along the Largs Road on a quiet Wednesday lunchtime. He lowered his voice. "Have you read our statements about that night?"

Sharon shook her head, continuing to munch on the ham and mustard sandwich, which she had to admit was very good. "I've asked my contact at the Office for Police Conduct, but he says all the paperwork is confidential, until they finish the investigation."

Pete's cheeks flushed with anger. "Which means that a cloud of suspicion hangs over all of us who were in that operational team, until they finally come to a decision."

"But you are still working, along with DC Singh and DC Novak?"

"Yeah, we've never really been under serious suspicion. It was Mitchie that the suits in Glasgow had their doubts about."

Sharon raised an eyebrow. "How come?"

"John Mitchie was a DI when I arrived at West Kilbride, straight from training at Tulliallan. He wasn't much of a mentor, not to any of us. Matt and Victor joined soon after and Holly about six months later. Mitchie seemed more pally with the local petty criminals than he was with us."

Sharon drained her coke. She knew the type. Mitchie was of the school of thought that if you kept the local criminals sweet, they'd cooperate with you on the bigger cases, keep you in the loop. It wasn't an approach much favoured in the Force these days.

"Mitchie never encouraged us to go for promotion, but I was studying for my sergeants exams in the autumn of last year. Then, we got the tip-off about the drug consignment coming into the docks at Irvine. The information came from a long running investigation that the National Crime Agency were leading. But they needed more men for the interception of the lorries. They'd been working on busting this particular gang for months."

"So they asked Mitchie to put together a team?"

Pete nodded. "I wonder now if it wasn't some kind of test, from somewhere on high. Because our team only consisted of Mitchie, Matt, Victor and myself. Plus a NCA officer called Tom who we never heard from again after that night."

"You think it was a set up to see if DI Mitchie was bent? Would the NCA really risk botching a massive drugs bust for that reason?"

Pete shrugged. "I've heard so little since, that I wonder if that drug gang ever existed at all. I've had nearly a year to form crazy theories in my head at night. There was £3million in cocaine and cannabis in our truck alone. It's silly money, especially for round here. It feels like pure fantasy, the figment of a dream."

Chapter 46

Sharon narrowed her brow, so fine lines pillowed the soft skin. "Could Mitchie really have been set up in such a calculated way?" She was as cynical as the next person, but she couldn't imagine this.

He sighed heavily. "I just don't know. The whole thing feels so surreal now." He leant forward, holding her gaze. "Mitchie got confirmation that the operation was taking place that evening. The trucks were due off the freight ship at 8pm. He gave us a perfunctory briefing about how we should intercept. We dressed in black and were given anti-stab vests. We had no other weapons, not even a baton. It was the first task of this kind Matt, Victor or I had ever been involved in. I'll be honest, we were bricking it."

Sharon smiled. "I can imagine."

"We arrived at 7pm. It was pitch dark except for a few lights dotted around the dock area. Mitchie was very jumpy, which I assumed was because of what was at stake." He shifted uncomfortably in his seat, as if the events he was recalling were distressing for him. "At about quarter to eight, we started to see movement from our positions between the containers. I thought it was the consignment arriving and that there were gang members on the ground, ready to assist. But then these guys, dressed in black with balaclavas, carrying coshes and lengths of lead pipe, came at us." He dropped his head and examined the hands clenched in his lap. "They seemed to know where we were hiding. I got shoved to the ground but managed to twist out of the way as a length of pipe was brought down, narrowly missing my head." He looked up again, his eyes shiny with moisture. "Then I ran, Sharon. I was a bloody police officer, a *detective*, and I ran for my life. I didn't even catch sight of the sodding lorry. I've no idea where the others were either, they could have been injured or dead for all I knew. I may not be corrupt, but in the face of danger, I'm a pathetic little coward."

Chapter 47

Holly put down the phone on her desk feeling dissatisfied. She'd made scribbled notes during her brief conversation with Tony Stubbs, the chairman of the football club where Leroy Torben had played.

She pushed back her seat and made her way to Alice's desk, taking her notepad. This had been her lead, finding the connection between Rosaline's business and the football ground and she desperately wanted it to come to something. "I've just spoken to Tony Stubbs, Ma'am."

"Ah yes," Alice replied. "What did he have to say for himself?"

She screwed up her pretty face. "Not a lot, unfortunately. He did look through his database of sponsors for us though. It seems Rosaline Golding approached the club to become a sponsor in January this year. Like she claimed, a friend of hers in marketing had suggested she try local sports clubs to sponsor. Rosaline told Stubbs she'd seen the team's successes in the local paper and wanted to support them specifically. She donated £250 in January and then the same amount in August. This meant she gets her banner up at the ground for the entire year. All sponsors get invited to attend home matches. That must be why she was at the game in July, where she spoke with Leroy."

Alice considered this. "The club certainly didn't approach Rosaline, she went to them. There must be plenty of youth footie teams in Fairlie? So why choose that particular club in West Kilbride? In fact, I'd say the family were more the horsey types. I could see her sponsoring a horse stables rather than the football." Her mind wandered to the beautiful chestnut pony Maria was so fond of.

Holly nodded, thinking perhaps she'd gleaned more from her conversation with the chairman than she'd realised. "And not wanting to be critical, but the footie ground on the Law Road feels a little *downmarket* for someone like Rosaline. I'm sure the clientele for her interior design business wouldn't necessary be found naturally in the stands there?"

"I agree. It feels like Rosaline had another reason to want to associate herself with that particular club."

"It must have had something to do with Leroy being a player there," Holly continued. "Should we bring her and Maria in for questioning again? We know they lied to us?"

Alice chewed the end of her pen. "The Goldings have got themselves a very expensive lawyer. I don't think we're going to get any more out of them in a formal interview. If Maria has been told to keep quiet, I bet they'll get her a brief too. No, we need more evidence before we confront them. This meeting with Leroy is circumstantial. We need something more concrete to prove there was a connection."

Sharon had been listening to their conversation from her position at the next desk. "I hope you don't mind me butting in? But I think you should pull out all the stops investigating this Rosaline Golding. It's her house that burnt down, wasn't it? Pete told me she'd inherited it from her family. So, what's her story? How many businesses has she run before this interior design one? Has her path crossed with Leroy Torben's in the past? While we're at it, we should take a closer look at Maria Silva too. What was her life like in Spain before she came here? Why did she chose to work in Fairlie when she says all her mates are in Glasgow?"

Alice's mouth broadened into a smile. "It's what Sharon's best at," she said to her young DC.

"Nosying about in people's pasts, finding out their secrets. Why don't you two work together on this? Sharon can show you all the ways we have to dig the dirt on a person's private life."

Holly nodded enthusiastically. She was always keen to learn.

Chapter 48

The sun was setting behind the Arran hills to the west as Alice pulled up the driveway of her house. She'd not collected Charlie yet, as her parents were taking him trick or treating around their estate. The DI sighed heavily, hoping there'd be no 'guisers' on her doorstep this year. Her cupboards contained only jars of peanut butter and packets of rusks.

She climbed out of the driving seat, her limbs feeling heavy. She unlocked the front door, abruptly aware of the ridiculous number of deadbolts she added since the back door was beaten in. Were they really necessary? Like Sharon said, this was Fairlie, not the southside of Glasgow.

She removed her shoes and collapsed into the armchair, not even taking off her coat. Sharon was out for drinks with Pete and Holly. They'd asked her to join them but she made her apologies. She was dead on her feet. Her parents would give Charlie a lift back when he was tired of cadging sweeties off the neighbours, which could actually take some time.

She wriggled her toes, feeling the warmth returning to her extremities. Maybe she'd just close her eyes right there in the comfy seat and allow her exhaustion to swallow her up. Alice's eyelids were closing when a sound outside jerked her body awake.

A surge of adrenaline dissipated as she realised it must be trick or treaters pushing open the creaky gate at the front. "Shit," she muttered under her breath, wondering what on earth she could give them that wouldn't warrant her car getting a pounding with eggs later on.

She hauled herself to her feet, intending to rummage in some kitchen cupboards when she heard another noise, like a kind of scuffling on the front step. This was followed by a bright, multi-coloured flare lighting up her entire hallway, accompanied by a wild whizzing sound, like a kid's toy on steroids. The scene was so bizarre she was frozen to the spot for a moment. Then, she realised what had happened. Someone had let off a firework on her front step. The small explosion had been clearly visible through the glass panes of her front door.

If Charlie had been at home with her, she'd have thrown the bolts and called for immediate assistance, but as she didn't have to worry about his safety, the DI was suddenly gripped with a blind fury.

She slipped her shoes back on and opened the front door. The shell of the firework was burning itself out in a final blaze of smoke and sparks on her step. She kicked it onto the gravel and stamped out the last of the embers. Then, she took to her heels and sprinted out of the gate into the quiet road. She predicted that a group of kids having just committed such a prank would most likely make a run for the fields that were reached through a narrow passageway between the houses where the road ended. It wasn't well lit beyond the close and they could easily then blend into the trees and bushes and not be found. She couldn't be sure that's the direction they'd go, but it was her best chance.

Alice ran flat out down the centre of her road, noting how a number of her neighbours had gone all out with their Halloween decorations. Had she been targeted for being a killjoy and not even placing a pumpkin in her window? She passed a few groups of parents and small kids, carrying buckets full of sweets and lollipops. They gaped at her as if she was mad, streaking past them, her coat open and flapping in the wind.

She reached the passageway and stopped to catch her breath. It was dark up ahead. There wasn't a streetlight beyond this point. She wished she'd taken time to bring a flashlight, but it was too late now. Her breaths were heavy and ragged, her blood pumping loudly in her ears, but even so, she heard the crunching of footsteps up ahead.

"Stop!" She cried. "I'm DI Alice Mann, make yourself known!"

The footsteps were pounding the gravel path, moving away from her towards the fields, where whomever it was would be quickly lost. "Bloody hell," she muttered again and set off at another sprint.

This time, she could hear the stomping footfalls ahead getting louder. She was gaining on her quarry. The pathway suddenly curved to the right and she ran straight into the solid bulk of a tall figure, in padded jacket and balaclava. This was no group of kids. Abruptly, Alice regretted her decision to go in pursuit. They were alone in a dark alley. She didn't even have her phone on her, she'd been in such a hurry to catch the person who'd attacked her house.

There was no time to think about that, she shoved the figure to the wall of the passageway and twisted his arm around to his back, feeling him wince in pain. "I'm arresting you on suspicion of causing criminal damage, with an intent to commit arson. You do not have to say anything, but it may harm your defence if you do not mention when questioned something which you later rely on in court. Anything you do say may be given in evidence." She tugged his arm higher.

"Arson?" His voice was muffled, but oddly familiar. "It was only a little fire-cracker."

Alice felt the anger burn in her chest. "Just a *firecracker*? My son could have been near that door. If it had exploded in the wrong direction it would've burnt my bloody house down!"

The man's body seemed to go limp. "I'm sorry," the words were delivered in a defeated tone.

Alice wrenched his body around to face her. "Do I know you?" She demanded.

The man raised his free hand and lifted off the balaclava. Visibility was poor, the only light being provided by the upstairs windows of the houses the passageway ran between, but Alice could still identify the reddened features, the bald head and sweating brow. "*Victor Novak*. What the *hell* do you think you're doing?"

Chapter 49

When Sharon arrived back from the pub, she encountered the unexpected sight of DC Victor Novak sitting slumped at Alice's kitchen table with a glass of amber liquid placed in front of him.

She removed her coat and tentatively approached the kitchen, raising her eyebrows at Alice when she found her leaning against a counter, the bottle of whisky in her hand.

Alice's expression was steely. "I think we'd all better take a seat. Victor's got some explaining to do." She poured two more measures of the peaty spirit, not even bothering to ask if anyone wanted water with it.

Sharon had already downed a couple of glasses of wine with Holly and Pete, but was up for a chaser. This seemed serious. "Is someone going to tell me what's going on?" She suddenly sensed the quiet emptiness of the house. "Where's Charlie? Is he okay?"

"He's fine. I've asked my mum and dad to keep him overnight." She tipped her glass towards the man slouched in front of them. "I thought it was best after Victor here set a firework off on my front doorstep and tried to run away, like a wee Halloween scallywag."

Sharon gasped, taking a slug of her whisky. "What the hell?"

Victor raised his head. "I'm sorry. It was only meant to scare you. I made sure it wouldn't hit the house."

Alice shook her head in disbelief. "My little boy could have been inside. Did you want to scare a three year old too?"

A red flush crept up Victor's thick neck. "I didn't want to do it. The idea was to make you nervous enough to abandon your command and return to Glasgow."

"Did you bash my back door in? That's criminal damage, very possibly with breaking and entering. That holds a potential prison sentence of one year. If convicted, you'd be off the Force. As an ex-copper with a criminal record, you may never work again."

Victor's eye's flashed with fear. "I didn't want to do it! He made me! Said it would be easy to put you off. You had a young family and had recently had a fright with your little boy. We never thought you'd stay this long."

Sharon could feel the anger building in her chest, but she said nothing, letting her friend deal with the situation first.

"You thought you'd use the recent kidnapping of my son to intimidate me into abandoning my command?" Alice almost hissed the words. "You underestimated me."

"Yes, we did." Victor's eyes dropped to the tabletop.

"I assume the person who put you up to this was John Mitchie?"

He nodded. "John is staying up in the Highlands right now with his missus. He was worried when you took over command of our team. He thinks you're there to dig into his activities as DI."

Alice sighed heavily. "The IOPC are doing a pretty good job of that already. Mitchie must have made that anonymous phone call warning me to keep my nose out. We traced it to a phone box in the Highlands. But when it was clear I was staying put, he told you to up the ante." She shook her head in disappointment. "Are you on the take too, Victor? Were you in the employ of those drug dealers?"

The man sat up with a jolt, nearly knocking over the thick tumblers placed between them. "No! I swear! That isn't the reason I'm doing this stuff for Mitchie." He shuddered. "About two years ago, Lena got a cancer diagnosis. She had to give up work for the treatment. The kids were still only young and I was struggling to make the bills. So, I started working nights as a bouncer. Cash in hand. But Mitchie has connections all over the area. He found out what I was doing from one of the nightclub owners in Ayr, where I'd been working. The DI said I could continue, as long as I did some tasks for him if and when he needed them."

"Was one of these tasks to let a truck evade capture that was carrying a consignment of 3million pounds worth of drugs in November last year?" Alice tried to keep her tone level.

Victor gripped his glass with both hands. "He told me nothing about it beforehand. But on the night of the operation at the docks, we were waiting in the shadows of the containers for the target truck to arrive. Before it did, a group of masked men appeared out of the darkness and attacked us. I got a metal pole to the side of the face, but I'm a big bloke, I fought my assailant off. Mitchie was suddenly by my side. He told me to keep quiet and when the truck came, we were to let it go."

"So you did as he said?"

"He had information about me. I thought I'd lose my job. I couldn't afford to have that happen." His eyes glistened in the low light.

Alice sighed. "You're in this up to your neck now Victor. I should have called in the team from Glasgow already." She downed the remainder of her drink.

"How is Lena now?" Sharon asked levelly.

Victor's voice had choked up. "She's been in remission for three months. I've been so grateful she's better. She doesn't know anything about what I've done, not even the moonlighting. She just thinks I had to work extra shifts, that's all."

Alice and Sharon exchanged looks.

It was the DI who finally spoke. "I'm going to have to take you in, Victor. This is too serious for me to ignore. But if you offer to testify against Mitchie, especially his role in aiding a major drugs gang, you may stay out of prison. You'll lose your job, though. There's no doubt about that."

The big man's frame sagged. He put his hands up to cover his face as the silent tears stained his cheeks.

Chapter 50

A sombre atmosphere seemed to hang over the department like a funeral pall. Only Holly appeared unaffected by the news that her colleague had been arrested in the night by officers from the IOPC and remanded in custody in Glasgow.

Matt Singh looked like he was reeling from a punch. Alice decided she needed to address the issue. She called her team to gather around her desk, sending Sharon out for coffees to the Turkish café on the high street.

"As you will already know, from the email I sent round this morning, Victor Novak has been arrested and will not be returning to his job here at the station. As the case is still under investigation, I can't give you any further details than that. But at some point, officers from the IOPC will be questioning each of you about Victor's actions in recent months."

Matt put up a hand. "Is this something to do with DI Mitchie, Ma'am? Our previous boss was under suspicion over that drug bust that went south last year. Victor was always thick as thieves with him."

Alice sighed. "I can't give you that information, Matt. But if I were you, I'd go back over the statement you originally gave the internal investigation into what happened that night at Irvine docks. I'm sure they'll want to go over it again in detail following Novak's arrest."

Pete's face drained of colour. "Did John Mitchie and Victor Novak really have something to do with the thugs who attacked us that night?" He ran a hand through his hair. "I can't believe it. We were his colleagues, his friends."

Matt looked similarly sickened. "I had to accept counselling after that night. I didn't sleep properly for weeks. I hope the blood money they both got from the drug barons was worth it."

Alice could understand their anger and disbelief. The most important characteristic a police officer could possess was loyalty. They often relied on one another for their lives. Mitchie and Novak had breached this code in the worst possible way. "I could request that this team is disbanded whilst the investigation proceeds, considering you all worked with Novak, but I'd like us to continue working on the murders of Leroy Torben and Victoria Braden." She rested both hands flat on her desk and met the gaze of each officer. "I need to know I can trust you all. I'm your SIO and I'm not going anywhere. Does anyone here have a problem with that?"

"No, absolutely not, Ma'am," Holly said decisively.

Pete and Matt both shook their heads.

Pete said, "I'm pleased you're here, and grateful you've not bunched us together with Novak. I promise we had no idea what he was up to."

Matt sighed deeply. "I'm afraid I counted Victor as a mate. We worked closely together, but I had no idea he was in Mitchie's pocket. I swear to it."

Alice took her time to respond. "I believe you, but there will be others in the Force, those higher up than me and with more power, who think you must have known something, maybe turned a blind eye. So if you want to remain detectives, you're going to have to prove the doubters wrong."

The doors swung open and Sharon barged onto the office floor with a cardboard tray full of cups. "Come and help yourselves, folks. Hamit persuaded me to buy a tray of Baklava, straight from the oven, so I'd get in there quick, if I were you."

The heavy atmosphere was lightened as the officers broke away from their huddle and rushed to claim their share of Sharon's goodies.

Chapter 51

Alice cradled the mobile phone in her lap. She'd just ended a difficult call with Fergus. Finally, she'd admitted to the incidents when Novak had attacked their home, but effusively assured her partner he was now locked away in Barlinnie on remand and could do no more harm.

This didn't seem to reassure Fergus all that much. He was determined to return home the next day, even if it meant getting a delay on his trial. She'd tried to persuade him she and Charlie would be fine, but it was no use. Alice didn't blame him, of course. She'd have done exactly the same.

Charlie was snuggled beside her on the sofa, a board book resting on his knees and his eyelids drooping over his big brown eyes. She smiled, he was worn out from another busy day. But despite the lecture she'd just received from Fergus, this was the first time she'd felt safe in her home since the anonymous call from John Mitchie.

It did worry her, what her predecessor might still be able to do from his hideaway in the Highlands, how many other bent officers he had under his control. But DCS Douglas had set her mind largely at rest when she spoke with him that afternoon. Due to the information Novak had so far volunteered, a team were ready to arrest Mitchie. The charge would be of corruption on a grand scale. He was an accessory to a huge drug trafficking operation. It was unlikely the man would ever see the outside of a prison cell again.

Sharon entered the living room with two mugs of tea. She glanced at the little boy, nodding off on the seat beside his mother. "Aww, bless his wee heart. Do you want me to carry him upstairs for you?"

"No thanks," Alice whispered. "I'll take him up myself in a minute." She accepted the mug and blew across the steaming rim. "This is awkward, Sharon, but I've just been speaking to Fergus. What with everything that's been going on, he wants to come back tomorrow. To check we're all okay. The thing is, accommodation here is a bit tight." She cringed as she spoke the words. Her friend had been such a great support to her these past few days. She certainly still needed her help running the investigation.

Sharon dropped into the armchair. A fresh bloom of colour made her cheeks glow. "Actually, I was planning to go and stay with Pete this weekend. His house has plenty of space and he's asked me to help decorate the dining room, in return for a nice home cooked meal. After that, I can book into a hotel. DCS Douglas has given me expenses."

Alice beamed. "That sounds perfect. Does this mean you two are an item?"

Sharon's blush expanded, so that her neck and chest were a rosy hue. "Since he spoke to me about the night of the drug raid, we've just grown closer. He gave me a lift home after the pub closed last night and we may have shared a wee kiss."

Neither woman had noticed Charlie's eyes were now wide open. "Have you got a *boyfriend*, Aunty Sharon?" He exclaimed loudly.

Both women burst into gales of laughter.

*

The office floor was busy but subdued the following morning. Pete had got to his desk early. Victor's fall from grace had been swift and unsettling. He was determined to prove he was nothing like the two men he'd previously shared a team with.

Pete cradled the mug of tea he'd just made. Should he have blown the whistle on DI Mitchie when they worked here together? The thought had been circling around his brain all night, as he tossed and turned. Yet, there was never enough solid evidence to have approached a DCI about, just the rumours of friendships with local dodgy characters. In fact, he'd never even met a DCI. Their little team felt remote and isolated out there on the Ayrshire coast. Besides, when you were first recruited as a detective, it was drummed into you that loyalty to your senior officers was crucial.

"Penny for them?" Sharon said gently, as she dropped into the chair opposite.

Pete shook the troubling thoughts from his head and smiled. "Just mentally running through the case notes we've got so far." He dipped his head towards the computer screen. "I've been re-reading my interview notes, hoping something jumps out at me."

Sharon nodded, knowing that wasn't the only thing on the mind of her colleague. "I'm going to do some in-depth research on our Mrs Golding today. I'm certain she had some kind of connection to Leroy."

"Aye, it looks that way. She's been increasingly jumpy too, whenever Alice and I have spoken with her. She's hiding something from us." Pete sipped his tea, glad he'd heaped a few spoonful's of sugar in there to pep him up a bit. He'd not managed much sleep. "You know, I keep thinking about that visit we made to the retired library manager up in Wemyss Bay."

"Donny Jones?"

"Aye, it just seemed unusual how much he remembered about Leroy as a wee bairn. It's odd if he thought the baby was simply Victoria's nephew."

Sharon wrinkled her brow. "Yes, the fact he recalled the baby looked dark-skinned. It struck me as odd too."

Pete leant forward. "It's just that I was glancing at all the photos he had on the walls, as we walked through the house to the sitting room. It looks like Donny was a keen mountain climber, possibly still is. Only, in a few of the shots, another man featured. In a couple of pictures, it was just the two of them, with their arms around one another."

"He mentioned an ex-partner. Didn't he say he'd passed away?"

"Yes, that's who I thought it might be. Only, this man, he appeared to be Afro-Caribbean in origin. I mean, it wouldn't have made me think much, except that passing comment that Donny made as we left, about the baby having a father who was Afro-Caribbean?"

Sharon absorbed this piece of information. "Perhaps Rosaline Golding isn't the only person who's background we should be digging into," she said finally. "Let's add Donny Jones to that list."

Chapter 52

Roger Golding marched down the garden path in his Hunter wellies and waxed jacket, looking every bit the lord of the manor. Their little black and white spaniel dashed ahead of him, as impetuous and energetic as ever. The puppy stage seemed never-ending. Roger kept his vision fixed ahead of him, towards the copse of trees leading to the small shingle beach which was still a part of their property and finally, the sea.

From this distance, if he turned and looked behind him, he would see the house in its entirety. With the fire damage making one wing appear sunken and jagged, like a scar that mars one side of a beautiful face.

He actually felt tears sting his eyes at the thought. When he'd first met Rosaline, at a dinner and dance at the golf club in Largs where both he and her late father were members, he'd not been particularly taken with her.

Rosaline had seemed pretty enough to him. She wore a narrow sheath dress that shimmered gold and her hair was twisted into a chignon which fell down her smooth, creamy back. He'd found her attractive, certainly. That's why he asked her to dance that night. Made light conversation and invited her out for dinner the following week.

But it wasn't until their fourth date, when Rosaline had brought him here to Hill House, on a lovely, unseasonably warm June day for Scotland, to have tea with her parents, that Roger had fallen in love. Rosaline had been rosy cheeked in designer jeans and a Ralph Lauren shirt. She'd looked lovely, he couldn't deny. But it was the house he fell in love with. Compared with the smart Victorian villa he'd grown up in, Hill House represented a considerable step up the social ladder. Here, they could keep horses in the stables, employ a cook and a maid, even. For Roger, who was perfectly comfortably off and assuredly middle class, this was another level entirely.

Billy had disappeared into the trees. He'd probably spotted a poor squirrel to chase. Roger increased his pace to keep up with the young dog. Recalling a walk he'd taken in these very woods with Rosaline's father fifteen years before. He'd been there to ask for Stephen Crammond's permission to propose to his daughter. The humiliation of that conversation still flared painfully in Roger's chest.

Stephen had taken his time to answer, poking his bone-handled walking stick into the undergrowth, as if looking for a solution in the tangled earth. Roger knew the man didn't think he was quite good enough to marry his daughter. But Rosaline had been approaching thirty by this time, and the man was obviously having an internal debate about which was worse; an unmarried daughter, the only heir to Hill House, or a boring middle-class academic like Roger as his son-in-law.

He must have decided the former was the least desirable option as Stephen eventually reached out a tweed clad arm and patted him heavily on the back. "Welcome to the Crammond clan!" He'd boomed, raising the jackdaws from the branches of the oaks in a cacophony of screeching caws.

Roger called Billy back to heel as they emerged onto the grassy path leading to the shingle beach. Perhaps the fire had been his penance for wanting this lifestyle too much. The police had now informed them that the cause was most definitely arson and the young man who was found dead in their property had been placed into the north wing before the fire was started around him. Without question to destroy the evidence of his body. Someone had opened a gas canister from the old stove and set a fire near it so a delayed explosion would take place, but give them time to get away. This was a pre-planned event. He wondered if the canister was one of the ones they'd kept in the garage for camping trips? He was pretty sure that stove hadn't been connected to fuel the last time he'd checked. Nobody ever used the bloody thing.

Hadn't his wife used gas canisters when she ran that homemade goat's cheese business at food fayres? She'd provided teas and coffees too, he seemed to remember. Another of her hobby-businesses that cost more than they made. His chest constricted at the thought. It wouldn't be long until the police had the same thought and came searching their property again. But if it was *their* canister that caused the fire, what the hell did it mean?

He shuddered in the onshore breeze. Rosaline had been acting very strangely since the fire. Roger knew it wasn't just because of the damage to her childhood home. She seemed less bothered about that than he did. No, his wife was distracted and anxious. Something was wrong. Roger was certain it wasn't because she knew he'd spent the last night of his conference in Aberdeen in the bed of his colleague, Anne Benton. The police didn't seem to have discovered that fact. Yet. His occasional lover had been extremely discreet.

It was something else. Roger watched as Billy splashed into the shallows of the gently ebbing water, leaping like a fish amongst the tiny waves. Rosaline was deeply worried about something. Roger knew it was related to the fire and that young man. Had his wife known him? Had she invited him there, knowing Roger would be away overnight? He shook his head violently, as if to banish these unpleasant thoughts.

He knew he should be asking *her* these questions, setting his mind at rest, rather than torturing himself with doubts. But something was holding him back. Because in his heart, he knew he didn't really want to hear the answers.

Chapter 53

Fergus examined the back door closely, running his hand down the smooth composite plastic where it met the wooden frame. "They've done a decent job. It's as solid as a rock." He screwed up his face. "I just wish it didn't look so out of place compared to the age of the building."

Alice lifted the full glass jug from the coffee-maker and poured out two cups. "I didn't have time to shop around and get a more sympathetic design. Besides, it would have cost the earth to get one with those kinds of security features in a Victorian style."

Fergus moved across the room and placed an arm around her waist, he gave her a squeeze. "I'm sorry I wasn't here. You must have been frightened on your own."

She turned and relaxed into his firm body. "I'm a senior police woman. I knew I could manage on my own. Charlie was at my parents' house when Victor placed the rocket on our doorstep. He meant to scare us, nothing more."

Fergus wasn't convinced his partner had been as blasé about these events as she was claiming. "Still, it's not often police detectives get targeted personally, let alone by a fellow officer." He thought about Charlie's abduction the previous year and the troubled young woman who took him, Kirsty Turner, still being treated in a secure psychiatric unit. "It's happened to you twice."

Alice twisted away and lifted her cup, downing the nutty, bitter brew. She was more aware of this fact than anyone. But she'd never wanted to be anything other than a police officer. Were the events of the last year really going to force her out of the career she loved?

Sensing it would be a good time to change the subject, Fergus said, "so Pete Falmer came over to secure the back door, when it was initially broken in? That was good of him."

"He's going to be an excellent officer. It's been unfortunate that those young officers' first experience of working as detectives was under DI Mitchie. They haven't been trained properly. Falmer, Gadd and Singh all have the potential to be top class."

Fergus sipped his coffee. "They've got you now. I bet you'll whip them into shape soon enough." He gave a wry smile.

"I hope so. Sharon's been a great help. I feel bad about kicking her out of our place."

"Sounds like Sharon has got herself nicely sorted." He raised an eyebrow playfully. "What do you reckon to her and Pete Falmer? Are they a good match?"

"Yeah, I really think they are. I thought she was totally into Dermot Muir, but she said something interesting; that she'd realised it wasn't worth the effort she was putting in, that he'd never feel the same way about her that she did about him."

Fergus reached out for Alice's hand. "That sounds a bit deep for Sharon. But she's probably right. None of us are getting any younger. Sharon deserves to be with someone who really loves her and appreciates how far she goes out on a limb for a mate and for what she believes in."

Alice considered this, surprised at how accurately Fergus had assessed Sharon's character. She supposed he was a trial lawyer and reading people was an important part of the job. "You're right. Even if it just proves to be a brief fling whilst she's on secondment, then good for her. She deserves a bit of fun for once." The DI glanced at the clock. "I need to go into the department in an hour. Sharon and Holly are already there, researching our key suspects."

"Don't worry, I understand. There's a local petting farm I found online that looks suitable for Charlie. I'll take him after lunch if the weather holds. We've got some quality boy-time to catch up on."

Alice smiled, leaning forward to kiss him gently on the lips, tasting coffee and something sweet, more relieved to have Fergus back home than she'd have liked to admit.

Chapter 54

As it was a Saturday, and as they were mainly doing paperwork, Alice had told her team to dress casually if they liked. There needed to be some perks to being asked to come into the department during the weekend, regardless of the shift rota.

Sharon wore a woollen jumper with a couple of sheep frolicking on the front. Pete approached her wearing a more conservative roll-neck and cords. "Are you still okay to come over for dinner this evening? You won't be sick of me after us working together all day?"

Sharon smiled. "'Course I am. I've got an old shirt in my bag, so we can crack on with the painting."

Pete shifted awkwardly from one foot to the other. "I would have made you dinner anyway, even without you having to do some decorating for me."

Sharon nudged him playfully on the arm. "I know you would. But I don't mind helping out. My flat has a strict 'no decorating' rule, so I'm looking forward to being let loose with a roller and some Dulux."

Holly interrupted their banter. The young DC wore a ribbed top and jeans which showed off her athletic figure. "Hey, guys. I've been doing some digging into the background of Maria Silva. Something of interest has come up."

Both officers reverted to their professional roles and listened to her with curiosity.

Holly summoned up a map on Sharon's computer screen. "I used an online genealogy site to trace Maria Silva's family history. She grew up in the city of Valencia, being born in the Valencia General Hospital in 1997 to Alessandro and Bettina Silva. Her father's occupation was listed as a '*trabajador portuario*', or dock worker. Maria told me and the DI she'd had a difficult childhood. I suspect her family didn't have much money. I got in touch with a colleague in the Valencia Polica." She gave a wry smile. "My Spanish Higher finally came in useful. He gave me a print out of Maria's tax history in Spain. She didn't pay much after leaving her *escuela secundaria* and there were years when her employment must have been sporadic. But what caught my attention, was this." She pointed a neatly manicured finger at the screen. "Maria had paid tax for six months in a new location in 2017, listing her occupation as a *'camarera'*."

Sharon furrowed her brow in thought. "Like a waitress or barmaid?" She smiled at their surprised expressions, Holly wasn't the only one with some language skills.

"Yep, that's right, and her address was in the city of Almeria in Andalusia." Holly made eye contact with Pete. "Isn't that where Caroline Torben and her partner have their bar? I mean, I know Spain is a big place, but it struck me as a coincidence, nonetheless."

Pete scratched his head. "Do you think Maria Silva and Leroy's aunt may have known one another in Spain, before the au pair came to the UK?"

Sharon's heart was pumping faster. "Did anyone show Caroline a photo of Maria, to see if she recognised her?"

Pete shook his head. "Victor and Matt were the ones who interviewed her. I wouldn't have thought so, as we had no idea there might be a connection. Caroline was in Spain on the day Leroy died."

Sharon got to her feet. "Then I suggest someone gets over there and speaks to this Torben woman again. Does Maria Silva have a UK driving licence? Can we get a photo from the database?"

"Yes," Pete replied eagerly. "Maria drives the Golding children to and from school."

"Then let's inform the boss and get that picture over to Ms Torben, right now."

Chapter 55

The last time Pete had been at the house on Seamill Road, he'd been overcome by the horrific murder scene they'd encountered there. In the meantime, the forensic cleaners had been into the property and Caroline Torben given permission to return. Victoria's sister possessed a key and was considered the victim's closest relative.

Pete recalled Caroline's unseemly haste in wishing to know the details of her sister's will and felt the same chill run down the back of his neck, making the tiny hairs there stand on end. It seemed as if the woman had already installed herself in the house she hoped to inherit.

Matt Singh pressed on the bell. Caroline opened up, wearing a face full of make-up and a lounge suit of dusky pink. She stood back and allowed the detectives to enter. Pete could already pick up the scent of stale cigarette smoke. He suspected Victoria would never have allowed smoking in the house whilst she was alive.

They were led into the front sitting room. As predicted, Caroline dropped onto the sofa and reached for a cigarette from a packet on the table. It sat beside an already bulging ashtray. "I would offer you a drink, but I can't go near the kitchen yet. I ripped up the lino yesterday and there are *stains* on the concrete below. I don't expect they'll ever come out."

Pete tried to look sympathetic but he was struggling. It was a bit premature for re-decoration. The woman seated before them didn't know for sure she owned the place yet.

It was Matt who changed the subject. "Ms Torben, last time we spoke, I asked you about your relationship with Leroy. Can I just confirm that he never travelled to Spain to visit you since you've lived there?"

Caroline narrowed her eyes suspiciously. "Where's that Polish chap you usually work with?"

Pete cleared his throat. "He's busy on other enquiries, Madam."

She raised her prominent eyebrows and sucked hard on her Marlborough, her knowing expression indicating she understood exactly what that euphemism meant, although there was no reason why she would. "I told you before. Leroy never applied for a passport. It's one of the reasons why he never clocked on Vick was his real mother. So no, he never visited me and Rick at the bar."

Matt fished the copy of Maria Silva's photo-driving licence from his pocket. The young woman's personal details had been blacked out. "We wondered if you'd ever seen this woman before. She worked in Almeria as a barmaid five years ago. She may have come to your bar looking for work, perhaps?"

Caroline leant forward and balanced her cigarette on the side of the ashtray in order to take the printout and look at it more closely. "People always look weird in these pictures, don't they?"

Pete got the sense she was actually examining the image intently.

"I'm not sure," she offered. "We have a lot of staff who come and go at the bar, especially in the summer season. We tend to employ local people as they're better workers than ex-pats or kids on a gap year." She squinted hard at the page. "I think I might recognise her. What did you say she was called?"

"Maria Silva," Pete said. "She's twenty five years old now and works as an au-pair at the house where Leroy's body was found."

Caroline shuddered at receiving this information. She glanced up at Pete. "Do you reckon she had something to do with his death?"

Pete shrugged. He decided full disclosure would get him the best results. "We really don't know, but when we found out she'd spent six months in the same town as you were living, it felt like a coincidence we needed to follow up on."

She nodded slowly. "Yeah, I can see what you mean." She glanced at a shiny watch on her wrist. "I'm due to Facetime Rick when he comes off his shift in half an hour. Can I show him this picture when I do? He does all the hiring for the bar. Plus he's better with names and faces. He might be able to remember her more clearly than me?"

Pete felt heartened by her cooperation. "I think that's a very good idea, Ms Torben." He turned to his colleague. "Matt, could you nip over to the garage on the corner and get us three coffees? They've got a Costa machine in there."

Matt got to his feet seeming less than pleased. Caroline sank back into the sofa, with the cigarette raised in the air, a spiral of smoke twisting up to the Artex ceiling, looking delighted at the suggestion.

Chapter 56

Sharon wrinkled her nose theatrically, as Pete joined her in the spartan dining room of his house. The carpet was covered in dust sheets and all the furniture had been moved out into the corridor. "You smell like an ashtray," she chuckled.

"I know. Caroline Torben must have puffed her way through ten fags in the time we were with her. I'm not used to it. Our witnesses don't smoke like they used to." He looked embarrassed. "Would you like me to shower now? I was going to do it after we'd painted?"

Sharon shook her head. "Don't worry, do it after if you'd like. Let's get some tins of paint open. The smell of solvent will overpower it."

Pete laughed. "I'm not sure which is worse."

She got down onto her haunches and levered open a tin with the end of a pallet knife. The colour was a tasteful, milky green. "At least you got a decent result out of exposing yourselves to all that second-hand smoke."

"Yeah, Alice was really chuffed when we reported back to her. Rick Portman swore he recognised Maria as a girl who'd worked behind the bar for them in August 2017. Better than that, he has a spreadsheet of employees for their company records. Her name was on it. He emailed it to me within the hour."

Sharon poured the gunky liquid onto a tray. "It's great news. It provides another connection between the family at Hill House and Leroy Torben. The link with Rosaline and the football club was a bit tenuous, I thought; difficult to prove, but Maria Silva having worked for the woman Leroy thought was his mother for his entire life is something else entirely. There's no way it's a coincidence."

"Yep, we'll have to interview Maria again now, with or without her expensive lawyer in tow."

Sharon guided the roller rhythmically up and down the wall. It was satisfying the way the historic stains and blemishes were covered so comprehensively by the paint. "I looked a bit deeper into the history of our friend Donny Jones this afternoon."

Pete lowered his brush. "Oh yes?"

"It seems Donny married a man called Anton Campbell at the registry office in Ayr in 2016. But they could have been together for much longer than that. Same sex marriage was only made legal in 2014. Anton's dad was from Jamaica and his mother was Scottish. Sadly, he died of an undiagnosed heart defect in late 2017. He was only fifty-eight."

Pete went back to applying paint to the edges of the window frame. "We can't ask Donny Jones if his late husband may have been the father of Victoria Braden's baby purely on the basis that he was of mixed heritage. I can visualise the complaint to the IOPC right now."

Sharon laughed. "Aye, me too. But it was Donny himself that brought the issue up, of Leroy having appeared mixed race as a baby. It must have lingered in his mind for a reason."

"I totally agree. But I don't think we've got enough to warrant us interviewing him again."

"No," Sharon added wistfully.

"Come on," Pete added in an enthusiastic tone. "Let's get this first coat on the walls. Then I'll fetch my culinary masterpiece out of the oven. Prepare to be wowed."

Sharon winked at him. "A man who can do DIY *and* cooks. You're really spoiling me."

*

The meal Pete lifted out of his oven, in a heavy casserole dish, was a fragrant tagine of lamb and vegetables. He set it down on his pine kitchen table, dishing out generous portions onto their plates. After a long day of police work and grafting in Pete's dining room, Sharon was famished.

Pete poured the wine. "Thanks so much for your help. Refurbishing a house isn't much fun on your own."

"My pleasure." Sharon took a long sip of the Merlot. It tasted expensive. She raised her glass. "To great company."

Pete's cheeks reddened. He chinked his glass against hers. "I do enjoy your company, Sharon. I haven't felt so relaxed with someone in years."

She chewed a delicious mouthful and washed it down with the wine. "Same here."

"Do you want to stay over? I know Fergus is back from Edinburgh and they've not got much room, what with the wee one. I've got the space here, even if the rooms aren't quite as I would like them just yet." Pete was aware he was stuttering over his words.

Sharon smiled. "Sure. I'd love to. Now that's out of the way, let's enjoy this fabulous meal."

Chapter 57

As Alice had predicted, Maria Silva was met at the police station by a lawyer with a smart navy trouser suit and what appeared to the DI to be Christian Louboutin heels.

Maria herself was dressed casually, in ripped jeans and a padded jacket. Her expression was sombre. She'd walked into the reception on her own, but Alice wondered if Rosaline Golding was waiting somewhere for her outside in the car. Maria certainly wasn't paying for her own legal representation.

Holly had already spoken with Maria in her native language, asking if she wanted an interpreter present, or for the Spanish consulate in Glasgow to be notified that she was assisting them with their enquiries. Maria shook her head in stubborn refusal. The lawyer, Ms Carmel Cartwright, seemed to agree this wouldn't be necessary. Not if her client wasn't being arrested.

Pete and Holly were conducting the interview. Alice watched the exchange on a monitor in a small, cramped office along the corridor. There was no media suite here, like there was at Pitt Street.

Pete began the interview with some simple information gathering. "Maria Silva, you have been working in Scotland since before the 31st December 2021 and have therefore applied for the EU Settlement Scheme, is that right?"

Maria nodded. "That is correct, I have settled status in the UK now. But I don't know yet if I want to stay."

"Would you return to Valencia? To your family in Spain?" Pete asked conversationally.

Maria shrugged, closely examining her bitten down nails. "I would prefer to go to the United States, or Canada, perhaps."

"Those aren't easy countries to get working visas for," Holly chipped in. "You usually need to secure a job there first. They require lots of references. My sister was looking into it for a while."

The solicitor sighed heavily. "As interesting as this little chat is becoming, my client is not here to discuss working visas. Could you get to the point please?"

Pete nodded, sifting through the notes in front of him. "You started working for the Goldings, at Hill House, in November 2020. You've been a live-in au pair for their three children for almost two years. Where did you work before?"

Maria lifted her head, making eye contact. She clearly felt these were easier questions than she'd been expecting. "I came over to the UK about nine months earlier that year. I had been saving money back home in Spain to start a life here. I had some friends who were working in Glasgow, so I slept on their sofa and worked in some bars in the city. Then I saw an advert on an agency website for au-pair work for a live-in position in Fairlie. Board and meals included. So I applied for it. I got the job. Mrs Golding seemed to like me. I was young and willing to please."

Pete frowned, as if puzzled. "It seems odd to jump from bar work to childcare. Do you have any qualifications in the latter. Have you worked with children before?"

Maria flicked her gaze towards the solicitor beside her. "The agency never said we needed any qualifications. As long as we described ourselves as an 'au-pair' and not a 'nanny'."

Holly leant forward. "Did the Goldings not want to see letters of recommendation from previous employers? References showing you were fit to work with children? They had three tiny kids, one no more than a baby. A respectable family like that would surely want references?"

The young woman began shifting in her seat. She tugged at the rolled collar of her sweatshirt, as if finding the environment suddenly too warm. "I'm used to children. I grew up in a big family, we all had to pitch in to help with the little ones. I explained all this to Mrs Golding at the interview. She was happy."

Holly raised an eyebrow in response, but said no more.

Pete continued his questioning, "What work had you been doing in Spain before you arrived in the UK?"

The solicitor looked annoyed. "How is this relevant, detective sergeant? You are investigating a suspicious death and arson in *Ayrshire* that happened a couple of weeks ago!"

Pete's voice became steely. "Oh, it's relevant, Ms Cartwright. Could your client please answer?"

The woman rolled her eyes, but nodded her consent to Maria.

"I-I was doing bar work, just like I did in Glasgow. After I finished the High School I did a few different jobs, like waitressing and cleaning. There are always lots of opportunities in Spain during tourist season."

Pete made a point of glancing at his notes. "What about between the dates of May and October 2017. Where were you working then?"

The young woman's expression darkened. Her eyes darted about the small room, as if searching for a means of escape. "I can't recall exactly. That's many years ago. I did lots of jobs before coming here."

"Then I'll jog your memory. You were serving in a bar in Almeria, in Andalusia. Your employers were Caroline Torben and Rick Portman. Mr Portman made sure your tax was declared to the local authorities during that period. He remembers you well. There is official documentation to prove you were there."

The colour had drained from Maria's face. "Then that must be true. I struggle to remember all the rubbish jobs I did." She wrung her hands together.

Ms Cartwright narrowed her eyes. "Why is this important, sergeant? Where are we going with this?"

Pete eyed both women carefully. "Caroline Torben is the biological aunt of Leroy Torben, the man found dead just metres from your living quarters at Hill House, Maria. But for most of his life, Leroy believed Caroline was his mother."

The solicitor's body stiffened. "I'm going to need a few moments to confer with my client."

Maria shook her head of dark curls. "There is no need. I did not know this man, or his aunt. I can barely remember this job I did five years ago. You have nothing! Nothing!"

Ms Cartwright looked alarmed at Maria's outburst. "I'm sure there's a logical explanation. Coincidences happen all the time, and as my client has stressed, she doesn't even recall her time working for this couple particularly clearly."

Holly was trying hard not to lose her cool. "But Ms Silva was also seen with her employer whilst she was speaking with Leroy Torben after a football match last year. We have the pictures on CCTV footage. That can't be a coincidence as well, can it?"

Maria slammed her hand on the table between them. "I'm not responsible for what Mrs Golding gets up to. That is her business. You should be asking her about that young football player, not me!"

The solicitor now looked angry. She laid a firm hand on her client's shoulder. "That will be all for now, detective sergeant. My client has been extremely helpful in answering your questions. But next time, if you want to perform an interview, you will have to produce an arrest warrant. From what I've heard here today, you are a very long way from obtaining that."

Pete took a deep breath and sat up straight, trying not to let the frustration show in his strained features.

Chapter 58

The mood in the department was downbeat. Pete and Holly returned to their desks and slipped onto their chairs with barely a word uttered. Even Sharon sensed it wasn't a good time to ask how the interview went.

Moments later, Alice stepped onto the office floor, waving a small, digital cassette in her hand. "Well done you two," she declared. "You really got Maria Silva rattled."

Pete raised his head in surprise. "I thought we'd got nothing, Ma'am. The solicitor totally shut us down."

Alice shook her mane of auburn hair with a grin. "With a brief of that calibre, I thought you were going to face an unrelenting 'no comment' interview. In fact, Maria spoke quite freely. *Too* freely for her solicitor. That's why Cartwright got so annoyed."

Holly looked puzzled. "Did we find out anything useful then, Ma'am?"

Alice rolled up a chair. "Maria has gold-plated legal representation paid for by the Goldings. It's not their au-pair they wish to protect, it's themselves. If they thought Maria was solely responsible for setting that fire and the death of Leroy Torben, I expect they'd have sacrificed her to us by now."

Pete nodded slowly, his clouded expression beginning to clear. "Maria said we should be asking Rosaline Golding about her relationship with Leroy Torben, suggesting the pair had actually had one."

Alice smiled encouragingly. "Before now, Maria has denied ever setting eyes on our victim. Now she's calling him, 'that young football player' and suggesting we should ask her employer more about him."

Sharon finally decided to chip-in. "But the Goldings aren't going to be as loose-lipped as Maria, not after this afternoon's interview. If you bring either of them in for questioning, you really *will* hit a brick wall."

Alice furrowed her brow. "Sharon's right. But at least we know now that there was some kind of relationship between Rosaline and Leroy. We have to keep digging into the nature of that connection."

"A romantic relationship?" Matt asked, looking sceptical.

"No, I don't think so," Holly replied. "Not just because of the age gap. I sense it was something else that connected them. Something Rosaline didn't like."

"It's good to act on those kinds of instincts, Holly," Alice said firmly. "I also happen to think you're right. But it's solid evidence we need. Now more than ever."

Chapter 59

Holly drummed her pink-tipped fingers on the desk. She'd been researching Rosaline Golding's work history online. It seemed that since graduating from the Glasgow School of Art in the early 2000s, the woman had worked as an assistant in a couple of upmarket galleries in the city. But since having children, she'd started up a few small businesses. Particularly after inheriting Hill House on the death of her mother five years earlier.

Holly glanced at the list of businesses registered on the Companies House website. The interior design company was the most recent, but there had also been a party planning enterprise and even an attempt to make and sell goats' cheese. Holly raised her eyebrows at this entry, noting the business had done quite brisk business for a while before Rosaline folded it a year before.

The DC glanced across at Sharon, who she knew was looking into Rosaline's background too. "How are you getting on with your research?" She asked.

Sharon looked up. "Actually, I've discovered a veritable mine of information on Rosaline's family, the Crammonds."

Holly pushed back her chair and moved across to join her colleague. "Oh, yes? All I've unearthed is Rosaline's habit of setting up little hobby-businesses that tend to fold within a few months. Then they started renovating the house ready to do holiday lets. I reckon she gets bored easily."

Pete called from across the desk. "It's Roger Golding who brings in the six figure salary. He may lecture as a Geochemist at the university, but he consults for oil and gas companies, a side-line which is highly lucrative. I've checked both their bank accounts, she gets a healthy allowance. They've got Maria to look after the kids and do the housework. No wonder the woman is bored."

Sharon creased her forehead. "It's odd that Rosaline has been so flighty with her career. Her father was Stephen Crammond. He was a very prominent local business man. He died in 2014. There was quite a lengthy obituary printed for him in the Herald."

Holly looked at her colleague with renewed interest.

"It seems the Crammond family had lived at Hill House for several generations, going back to the early-nineteenth century, even a little before. Except the house was called *Peacehaven* back then."

"Peacehaven?" Pete rolled the name around on his tongue. "It doesn't sound very Scottish. I can see why they changed it."

"It doesn't sound Scottish because it isn't," Sharon explained. "The Crammond family history has been well documented. A local historian wrote a book about them about twenty years back. Zacharia Crammond was born in Peacehaven, East Sussex, England in 1750. He did well at school and when he was old enough, got a commission in the East India Company. Zacharia travelled back and forth from Asia, trading in the new goods they'd discovered out there, like tea and spices. He ended up with his own ship, harboured at Newhaven. By the 1780s, he'd made a decent fortune. According to family legend, he travelled to Glasgow, which was becoming known as 'the second city of the empire', with a view to moving into the flourishing transatlantic trade in cotton and tobacco. Whilst he was here, he was shown a plot of land overlooking the Clyde at Fairlie. He fell in love with it, set about building a house and moved his family there in 1790."

Pete looked thoughtful. "So the Crammonds made their fortune out of the East India Company. Didn't they strip India of their raw materials? I saw a programme about it recently."

Sharon chuckled. "By modern standards, Zachariah Crammond would be viewed as a villain. If there was a statue of him somewhere, folk would be queuing up to pull it down."

Holly laughed along, although she wasn't really sure what her two colleagues were referring to. History hadn't been her strong point at school.

"Once Crammond had built his house, he threw himself into the burgeoning transatlantic trade developing along the Clyde valley. He bought a number of ships and owned his own cotton plantation in Barbados."

Pete whistled. "The guy would have owned slaves. Bloody Hell."

Now Holly understood what they were talking about. She knew how awful the slave trade had been. "The slave trade itself was abolished in 1807 and slavery on the plantations in 1834, but Crammond's properties in Barbados remained in business for another couple of decades after that. He didn't live to see the end of slavery, of course. By this time, his son, William, had taken over the business. Zachariah died in 1820. The slaves were freed, as required by the law, but continued to work in his fields as labourers."

"Doesn't sound much like freedom," Pete muttered.

Sharon sat back in her seat, her eyes gleaming mischievously. "There's tons of information about the family online. The Crammonds made their riches from the British Empire, but they weren't as fortunate as you'd think."

Holly really was puzzled now.

"The reason the family has had so much written about them, is because there's a popular legend, going back to just after the Crammonds set up home in Fairlie, that they are cursed."

Chapter 60

It was dark outside. The windows of the pub round the corner from the police station were streaked with dirty raindrops.

Alice had decided to stay for a quick drink. She wanted to keep morale up in the department, particularly after Victor's disreputable departure.

Sharon was squeezed into a booth beside her boss. Leaning forward eagerly when Matt Singh placed the drinks on the table. "Cheers, Matt." She took a long sup of the 70 shilling ale.

Pete and Holly were on the soft drinks. Both were driving home.

Alice took a fortifying sip of the house red. "We don't really believe in *curses*, do we?"

Sharon raised her eyebrows knowingly at her old friend as she drained more of her pint.

"*No*, we don't," Pete added firmly. "The appearance of a 'curse' is just bad luck with a fancy name. Plenty of families have their fair share of tragedy to deal with." He sipped his coke. "In fact, the richer you are, the more likely tragedy will follow you about. You've got the money to travel, ski and climb mountains. That's when these freak accidents tend to occur."

Alice nodded. It seemed a sensible assessment to her. She certainly didn't believe supernatural forces were at play.

"But the Crammond family really do seem to have been plagued by the most terrible misfortune," Holly said. "After the family built the house, one of the youngest children fell out of a top window where the latch had broken. He was killed instantly. Apparently, Zacharia and Charlotte mourned his passing for the rest of their lives. They had a portrait painted of the boy by Joshua Reynolds. He had to use the younger brother as a sitter. There was no other record of how the boy had looked when he was alive."

Matt shuddered. "That's bloody morbid."

"The painting is in the National Gallery in London," Holly added meekly.

"It's certainly an intriguing family story," Pete agreed. "The grandsons of William Crammond were all officers who served during World War One. Every single one of them was killed on the Western Front."

There was a silence at the table for a moment, whilst they contemplated this shocking loss of life. Sharon broke the spell. "Fortunately, one of the men's young widows was pregnant. She gave birth to Frederick Crammond in 1918. He was Rosaline's great grandfather, and continued the family's name as owners of Hill House, although it was still Peacehaven then."

Holly eagerly took up the tale, her eyes bright with fascination. "The house's name was changed to Hill House in the late fifties by the widow of Frederick's eldest son, Edgar. She claimed in letters to their solicitor, that the name 'Peacehaven' could never be applied to the property, which was 'cursed to its very bricks and mortar'."

"She had very good reason to think so," Sharon added gravely, draining the remains of her ale.

Alice got the distinct impression her officers were enjoying telling this story. She sat back against the hard wood of the booth and allowed them to carry on without interruption.

Holly nodded. "Edgar and Helen's son was killed at the age of nine. He'd been climbing one of the old oak trees in the garden of the house. Nobody knew exactly what happened, but his little body was found broken and bruised by the trunk of the ancient tree.

His head had struck a large, gnarled root and death was immediate. According to Helen's letters, the boy had been her husband's favourite. Exactly a month after the child's death, Edgar Crammond shot himself with a revolver by his study window, overlooking the gardens. After that, his wife changed the name of the house, seeing it as a mockery of the tragedies that had occurred there."

Matt narrowed his brow, wiping the froth of his beer from his moustache. "So, this Edgar Crammond would have been Rosaline Golding's grandfather?"

"Yes," Holly replied, pleased her colleagues were following. "One of Edgar's other sons, Stephen, was Rosaline's father. He married a local woman called Geraldine and Rosaline was born in 1977. Rosaline's parents both died in the last ten years and their daughter inherited Hill House outright."

Alice considered this. "And since Rosaline inherited the place, it's almost been burnt to the ground and a man has very likely been murdered there." She let out a long, slow breath. "I don't believe in curses either, but this family sure have had a shed load of bad luck."

Pete finished his coke, placing the empty glass on a damp beer mat. "Or, all this bad luck mumbo-jumbo makes it seem like the events are part of a 'curse', when in truth it's simply the result of good old fashioned criminality."

"How do you mean?" Asked Matt.

"Well, a child falling out of a window is a terrible tragedy, but sadly these things happen all too often. Also, the death of an entire generation of young men in the trenches was also depressingly common." He leant forward on his elbows. "Then, you have the death of the boy who fell from the oak tree. I've seen the trees that line the gardens of Hill House. They aren't that tall. I don't reckon a healthy nine year-old could be killed falling out of one."

"But he hit his head on a tree root," Holly explained.

"Well, that was obviously what the Fiscal's office agreed had happened, but if I was investigating such a case, I would have at least questioned every member of the household about where they were when the boy had his accident. Why was he playing down there on his own? How did his siblings feel about this particular child being their father's favourite?"

Alice sipped her wine with a wry smile. She was starting to believe that Pete was developing into a very promising detective.

Sharon looked puzzled, however. "Are you suggesting one of the boy's brothers or sisters could have killed him? Out of jealousy?" Her eyes glimmered mischievously. "It could even have been Stephen himself who clunked him on the head, perhaps to inherit the house in future!"

Sharon chuckled at her own suggestion, clearly feeling this was a highly far-fetched scenario. But Alice wasn't so sure. She knew the darker sides of human nature. Jealousy and greed were powerful motives for violence. Sometimes children were the most affected by such forces and the least able to resist them.

Pete continued, unperturbed. "I would certainly have considered a criminal investigation into the death of the boy. Edgar's subsequent death was a straightforward suicide, but it was triggered by the first event. But when it comes to our present-day 'tragedies', there's no doubt they are cold-blooded criminal acts. The fire was arson and Leroy's body deliberately placed there to destroy the evidence of his death. There's nothing supernatural about those events. This myth of a 'curse' is like a diversionary tactic; smoke and mirrors. In reality, these are very human crimes, committed for very human motives."

Sharon glanced at her new lover with curiosity. She'd enjoyed the 'smoke and mirrors' intrigue of the 'curse' myth, but Pete was quite correct. What they were faced with now was murder. It was very important not to get side-tracked from that fact.

Chapter 61

It was reassuring to have Fergus's bulky form in the bed beside her once more. Alice knew he'd have to return to his court case in Edinburgh in a few days, but she'd needed his common sense presence in the house after Victor and John Mitchie's campaign to frighten her out of town.

She turned to face the window, where the pale dawn light was beginning to seep under the heavy curtains. There had been no further threatening calls or attacks on their property. But Alice knew not to be complacent, not until Mitchie was safely serving a lengthy prison sentence.

Obviously sensing she was awake, Fergus shifted his body so he could wrap his arms around Alice's lean figure. "Are you okay?" He breathed into her ear.

"Yeah, just a lot of stuff on my mind, that's all. I can't believe how much Sharon and Holly unearthed about the history of Rosaline's family. We were incredibly lucky some conscientious local historian decided to write a book about them. It prompted a slew of articles in the press. There's nothing the reading public like more than the saga of a rich family who've had awful things happen to them."

Fergus hitched himself up onto an elbow. "Do you really think this family 'curse' business has any bearing on your current case?"

Alice could hear the scepticism in his voice. "No, not really. But it explains something to me about Rosaline's character. She's been hiding stuff from us for sure, but there's something else too. The woman has a kind of melancholy aura that hangs about her. Like she's just waiting for tragedy to strike."

Fergus chuckled. "Don't start getting side-tracked by 'auras' and 'curses'. What on earth would Andy Calder say?"

Alice chuckled at the thought. She knew exactly what Andy would say and it wouldn't be repeatable in front of their young son. She swung to a sitting position and reached for her towelling robe. "Pete Falmer isn't letting the team get sucked into the drama of the story either. He calls it 'smoke and mirrors'."

"He sounds like a very sensible chap." Fergus got to his feet and searched for his glasses on the bedside table in the early morning gloom. "By the way, I saw a flyer for a charity fireworks display happening tomorrow night. I thought we might take Charlie. I don't think he's scared of the bangs any more. What do you think?"

"Yeah, sure." She'd completely forgotten bonfire night was approaching. "Book some tickets if you can. But just bear in mind I may have to work, if something comes up."

Fergus took a step towards her, placing his lips on hers. "I know, darling. But I'll get you one just in case."

She twisted her hair up into a bun, ready to brave the cold bathroom, hoping a hot shower would warm her tired limbs.

"Shall I put the coffee on?" Fergus said from the doorway.

"Great, yes please." She paused for a moment. "By the way, where is this fireworks display taking place?"

"Oh, it's some local football club in West Kilbride." He waved his hand in a general direction to the south-west of them. "I saw the flyer in the library. They want to raise money to improve one of their spectator stands. The ground is on the Law Road, if I recall rightly. I'm sure we can easily park."

Alice stood stock still, her feet numbed by the icy floorboards. She thought perhaps it was important for her to make sure she attended this display after all.

Chapter 62

The air around her felt icily cold, a mist of dampness hung low over the grass. Despite the less than desirable conditions, Caroline Torben had suddenly felt uncomfortable about smoking her cigarette in Victoria's house. She'd taken her morning coffee and packet of Marlborough's out into the small garden instead.

She was dressed in her leisurewear tracksuit and slippers, but the chill was seeping through the fabric and making her shiver. She gripped the warm mug and sucked hard on her fag, not able to savour this early morning treat as she might normally have done.

Caroline had no idea why she'd woken that morning feeling her sister's presence so strongly. She'd been puffing away in the house and treating it as her own since she'd got there several days earlier. But as soon as she'd got out of the double bed her sister had once called her own that particular day, she felt the woman's disapproval press heavily on her chest, as if Vick was right there in front of her, placing a strong, veiny hand to the skin.

She shook the image from her head. Of course she was going to think about her sister whilst she was staying in this house. The poor thing had been murdered within its walls. She stubbed out the remainder of the cigarette on an old country roses saucer she was now using as an ash tray. She hoped fleetingly it wasn't actually valuable and mused if perhaps it would be better to use something else, a jam jar maybe.

The thought was interrupted as she stepped back into the kitchen and pulled the door shut behind her. Caroline finished her cup of coffee and placed it in the slimline dishwasher. She exited the room as swiftly as possible, still not comfortable being in there.

The woman desperately hoped the police would allow her to return home soon. She missed Rick and the warmer climate. But most of all, Vick's house was giving her the creeps. It was like she could imagine both her sister and nephew still being there; sitting at that kitchen table and lounging, long-limbed on the sofa. If the house did come to her in the will, she'd make no delay in selling it. The money would go straight into their bar in Almeria which was in dire need of a refurb.

Caroline was about to go and get her phone so she could do a facetime with her partner before he opened up for the day when the doorbell chimed. She sighed heavily. It was most likely the police again. What more could they possibly want from her?

She approached the door with resignation and opened up. It took her several moments to take in the appearance of the person standing on the doorstep. When she did, Caroline let out a gasp. "Good God! What on earth are *you* doing here?"

Chapter 63

Rosaline Golding sat at the kitchen table with her daughter in her lap. The little girl had wrapped her arms around her mother's neck and had rested her head on the woman's concave chest.

Roger was noisily packing crockery into boxes. "I'm only going to take the stuff we'll need for basic cooking and entertaining in the rented property. The rest can stay here until we return." He straightened up from his labours, placing a hand at the base of his spine. "Once we get the word from the police, I've got our builders on standby to come and totally refurbish the place. It'll be even better than it was before the fire. The house will return to its historic glory."

Rosaline rolled her eyes in frustration. "Why don't we just sell it as it is? Then whomever buys it, probably a developer, can do what they like with the plot?"

Roger looked at his wife as if she was mad. "This house is a classic example of early Georgian architecture. Even the chimneys are worth thousands. Your family have lived here for generations."

The little girl shifted off her mother's knee and proceeded to lead the dog outside for a play, nudging him from his basket, as if sensing an argument might be brewing. Rosaline rubbed her forehead, feeling a tension headache building behind her eyes. "I would have sold the place when Mum died. I never wanted to raise our children here." She waved in the direction of the garden. "As if I want our boys climbing the tree where my great uncle fell to his death? It's bloody creepy."

Roger gaped at her in disbelief. "But that was just an accident! This house, this estate, is far more important than something that happened seventy years ago!" His face was reddening.

Rosaline sighed deeply. "It's not just *one* accident, though, is it? My family are plagued by bad luck. I want my children as far away from this place as possible. Then, maybe, they'll get a chance at a proper life."

"But they love it here!"

Rosaline's tone was quiet, defeated even. "No, Roger. *You* love this house. When we married, there was no question of us living anywhere else. You're obsessed with the bloody place. But I loved you then and wanted to make you happy. Even when I knew this piece of land was more important to you than I was."

Roger gasped. "What do you mean, 'I loved you *then*'? What are you saying, Rosaline?"

Rosaline shook her head sadly. "I don't love you any more, Roger. You're selfish and a blatant social climber. The difference between us, is that I did actually love you at the start. I wouldn't have had children with you otherwise, but I wonder if you ever did love me. I think in some ways, our marriage was always about this damned house."

Roger dropped into a seat opposite, his packing forgotten. "I *do* love you, Rosaline. The children mean everything to me. If we have to leave this place, then so be it. I will do that for my family."

"I expect you do love us in your own way. But it's not enough, not any longer." She finally summoned some strength in her voice. "And it's not your decision whether or not we stay here. This is *my* house and I'm selling it, with or without your permission." She started to laugh; a humourless, hollow sound that echoed around the cavernous kitchen. "Do you know, I haven't even left the place to you in my will? If I die, Hill House goes straight to the children. The money I make from its sale will do too."

Roger's mouth fell open. His face had drained of all colour. He gripped the edges of the thick oak table as if worried he might slump in a heap to the cold tiled floor.

Chapter 64

When she prized her eyes open, against the sticky gunk that seemed to have glued them together, it was obvious she was in a dark place. Her stomach dropped in fear.

Caroline tried to move her legs, only to find they were bound tightly together below the knee. Her arms were secured painfully behind her back with sharp plastic ties and a strong tape was stuck across her mouth. It reached almost to her nose, but she was still just about able to take in air.

Tears sprung to her eyes at her terrible predicament. She felt stiff and bruised. Even without being able to see properly through the gloom, as her sight adjusted, she could tell she was being kept in a small space. A storage room, perhaps. There was a smell. It wasn't unpleasant. It reminded her of wood pulp, mingling with melted plastic. But no fresh air. This room was windowless, the atmosphere stale.

As Caroline's senses adjusted to her environment, she noted it wasn't cold. Which meant she couldn't be in a basement or outhouse, not at this time of year. So, she must be inside a building, and one that was heated. Victoria had always been considered the clever one by her parents. Her sister had spent her childhood with her head in a book. Caroline was more outdoorsy. Always out on the street with a ball until she was old enough to hang about with her pals on the seafront at Ayr, smoking fags and sharing cans of Tennant's lager.

The fact she wasn't the learning type didn't mean Caroline was stupid. She helped Rick run the pub, which involved all kinds of paperwork and spreadsheets. She knew she'd made a fool of herself with different blokes over the years but that was because she craved the love and attention. She sure as hell hadn't got it from her mum and dad.

At the thought of Rick, tears pooled in her gummed up eyes and her nose began to fill with snot. If only she'd remained in Almeria, watching the sunsets from the bar terrace with the only person she'd ever loved. A sob racked her body.

Knowing she couldn't risk obstructing her only free airway, she focused on another emotion instead. Anger. Caroline visualised the way she was tricked into this situation. Her trust was violated by a person she least expected to be a danger. Well, that wasn't going to happen again. She had to think hard about what to do next. She wasn't dead yet, like her sister and nephew, so there was still a chance.

Caroline wasn't going to go down without a fight. Her tears had now dried up. Instead, her eyes were open wide, glinting with determination.

*

Pete was seated at his desk, sipping the coffee Sharon had brought him from the Turkish café. Even though he'd not asked for sugar, the drinks from there always possessed an underlying sweetness, a hint of spice. He didn't really mind.

Sharon leant forward. "Penny for them?" She asked, noting the lines deepening across his forehead.

"I'm just thinking about Maria Silva, about the time when she was working back in Spain."

The DS nodded encouragingly. "Yes, what about it?"

"She was only twenty when she worked as a waitress for Caroline and Rick in Almeria, but she must have been looking for ways to make more money to get her out of Spain. Now, we must assume she overheard Caroline saying something about Leroy, something that caught Maria's interest. That must have led to Maria seeking the young man out when she finally moved to Scotland. This information was valuable to her in some way. She obviously felt it was going to be useful. It may have been the reason she decided to come to Glasgow and not London or Manchester."

"Aye, this was a girl who was escaping poverty, but had no real education or skills. If she didn't want to be cleaning toilets or wiping arses for the rest of her life, she needed another way to make ends meet."

Pete drained the rest of his cup, feeling the caffeine and hidden sugar giving his brain a temporary boost. "Exactly. So what precisely do we think she overheard Caroline saying? It must have been juicy enough for Maria to feel it was worth coming to Scotland for."

Sharon considered this. "It had to be something worth blackmailing someone about. I think she heard Caroline talking to Rick about Leroy. Perhaps she heard her boss saying she wasn't really the boy's mother, how she was tired of pretending to be. That her sister had asked too much of her in pulling off such a deceit and it was a burden too tough to bear. I reckon that would pique Maria's interest."

Pete nodded. "Aye, I can see that. But why would this information lead Maria to the Goldings? I reckon it's Rosaline who has the connection to Leroy there, so how did Maria get to know what it was? Why did she apply for a job with them, of all the other families in Scotland?"

Sharon narrowed her eyes. "Caroline must have said more than we have imagined. She must have said something about the Goldings too. Yet, she's always claimed never to have heard of them before."

Sharon exhaled slowly with a fresh realisation. "Caroline Torben hasn't told us everything."

Pete pushed back his chair roughly. "I agree. Which means it's time to pay our ex-pat friend another little visit."

Chapter 65

Drizzle was working the wipers hard as Sharon and Pete pulled up at the pavement on Seamill Road. They noted Victoria's Hyundai was still parked in the driveway, where it would no doubt remain until probate was finalised.

Pete led the way to the front door. He wasn't looking forward to another couple of hours spent in a fug of smoke. He was tempted to bring the woman straight into the department to be interviewed. Let her manage without her nicotine fix for a while and then see what they could get out of her. If Caroline had kept information back from them, he knew it would be tough to hide his annoyance. She'd led them all a merry dance, even with her own sister laid out on a mortuary slab.

He pressed the bell once more, this time knocking on the glass panel for good measure. Sharon had moved across to peer into the window of the front room. "No sign of life in there. I'll check round the back."

Whilst she was gone, Pete kicked the stone step in irritation. Where could the woman possibly be? She'd not take her sister's car, so the only option was the bus. Perhaps she'd gone shopping and would be out all day. "For Christ's sake," he muttered under his breath.

Sharon emerged from the side passage. "The kitchen door is locked. She may be asleep upstairs, I suppose, but the house looks pretty deserted to me."

Pete cursed once more. Then he turned towards the property next door, remembering Donna Marshall and her swift reporting of the assault on Victoria Braden. He noticed their sky blue car in the driveway too. "Why don't we ask the lady next door?

She's pretty observant. She may have noticed Caroline go out."

"Good idea," Sharon replied. "Our job would be ten times harder without nosy neighbours."

Pete wasn't in the mood for jokes, but he appreciated the attempt to lift the mood. He stepped over the low dividing wall and approached the door, pressing the bell once again.

Donna opened up after a few moments, the chaotic sound of kids' TV blaring in the background. "Oh, hello. Has something happened? I've made my witness statement already."

"It's not to do with Mrs Braden's murder, although we are very grateful for the information you gave us regarding that investigation."

"You've not caught him yet, then?" She added with a jaded tone of voice.

"Not just yet, no. But we're working on it. We were wondering if you have noticed Victoria's sister, Caroline had moved into the property next door?"

"Yes, I heard her moving around in there. The walls are bloody paper thin. It's lucky I didn't call you lot again. Callum persuaded me not to. Then we bumped into her outside. Nice lady, she explained she was Mrs Braden's sister and would be staying until they could have a funeral."

Pete nodded patiently. "I don't suppose you saw Caroline leaving the property today? We have some questions for her but nobody seems to be at home."

Donna shook her head. "No, although it's been quiet for hours over there. I've been busy with the kids. I don't spend my days twitching my net curtains you know." She looked offended.

Donna glanced over her shoulder as a man in jogging bottoms and a white t-shirt, hair wet from a shower was trudging down the stairs. "It's the police again," she explained to the man who was obviously her husband. "They want to know about that Caroline woman, staying next door."

He came up to join his wife. "Oh aye? The woman in pink, eh?"

Donna pulled a face. "Callum calls her that, because she's always wearing a pink tracksuit thing."

"More like pyjamas," the man chuckled.

Pete cleared his throat. "We're looking for her, but there's no life next door."

The man screwed up his face. "She went out hours ago."

Pete felt his pulse rate rise. "Did you see her leave?"

"Oh aye, my shift starts at seven am. This is me just back from the site. It was awful foggy this morning, but I saw her, the woman in pink, get into a car at the end of the drive. Crack of dawn, it was."

"Was she with someone else?" Sharon nearly shouted over Pete's shoulder.

"Someone was driving, but I didnae see them, they were already in the car."

"Do you recall what type of car it was?" Pete was desperately noting the information down.

"It was a wee one, like a Corsa, maybe. The light wasn't great, being foggy and that, but I reckon it was green. Not a bright shade, but kind of murky, like the weather itself I thought."

Sharon clutched Pete's arm. "We'd better get back to the department. Right now."

Chapter 66

It hadn't been easy getting a search warrant granted at such short notice. Alice had been required to call DCI Bevan and ask her to petition the judge on her behalf. The witness statement which described a dirty green hatchback parked on Seamill Road on the day Victoria Braden was murdered, in addition to Callum Marshall's testimony that Caroline Torben was driven away early that morning in a green, Corsa type vehicle had persuaded the judge to grant them access to the Goldings' property, on the basis of their ownership of a Volkswagen Golf in a seagull grey.

Alice braced herself against the dashboard as Pete drove them at speed up the bumpy track towards Hill House. "It's far too early to consider Caroline Torben a missing person," she yelled above the scream of the engine. "But her partner said he's not had his usually daily facetime call from her and she's uncontactable on her mobile, which is unheard of. With what happened so recently to her sister, this seemed to be evidence enough to persuade the judge we need to treat her disappearance as suspicious."

"So he bloody should," Pete replied gravely. "I should have realised the woman was in danger from the start. It's obvious Caroline knew more than she was telling us plods. Sharon worked it out straight away."

"Don't beat yourself up about it. The woman had plenty of chances to come clean with you. When her sister was brutally murdered, she should have had the sense to work out she might be in danger too."

Pete shook his head with frustration. "But maybe Caroline doesn't realise the information she possesses is so important to someone else. The woman isn't exactly 'brain of Britain'." The car swerved onto the sweeping gravel frontage of Hill House. The sun was just setting over the distant water and the light was fading fast. They wanted to find the missing woman before night fell.

Following behind, was a police van with additional officers from Ayr to assist their search. It was a vast property. There were at least five outhouses for starters, not to mention the house itself.

Alice swung open the car door, approaching the side entrance of the south wing of the house, the crunch of her heavy boots announcing their arrival. She hammered on the wood panels.

It took several minutes for the locks on the other side to release. Alice was just deciding they might need the battering ram after all, when the door finally opened.

Roger Golding stood on the threshold. He looked terrible. His hair was ruffled and his face drawn and pale. "What the hell's going on? What do you want? If you've come to arrest us, I'm going to call my solicitor right this minute."

Alice thrust a copy of the search warrant into his hand. "You may well want to call your solicitor, Sir. We have a warrant to search these premises and the surrounding land. Could you gather your family together into one room please?"

Roger gaped at her in disbelief. "You can't be serious!" He scanned the details printed on the paper crumpled in his loose grip. "Jesus wept! You think we may have kidnapped a woman and are keeping her here, in our family home!"

"That's exactly what we suspect, yes."

Pete barked an order into his walkie-talkie and the officers in the van streamed out towards the front entrance.

"If you could open the front door for my officers please, Sir, and ensure the outhouses are unlocked, I'd be most grateful."

The man seemed to have finally absorbed the information he'd been given. "Ye-es. I'll get Maria to open the door. We were having one more night at the house before we move into a rented place. We won't be returning. My wife wants to sell up."

Alice added, more gently. "Where is your green Volkswagen Golf, Mr Golding? We need to examine the car, too."

This request seemed to puzzle him the most, but he silently shuffled across to a cabinet of hooks, passing a set of keys to the detective. "It's parked in the second garage on the right."

"Fine. Thank you for your co-operation. Go and get your wife and children, Mr Golding. Keep them with you in the kitchen until your solicitor arrives. I will want to question you all later."

Chapter 67

The sun had now fully dissolved into the black waters of the Clyde. Night had fallen. Only the occasional flash of torchlight illuminated the set of outhouses.

Alice gulped a deep breath of night air. Her officers had been searching Hill House for a couple of hours. Another team was beating a line through the copse of trees which led to the shingle beach. So far, they'd found nothing.

The fire damaged wing of the house had shown no signs of human life, or a dead body. There were no hidden cupboards or trap doors. She'd done a sweep of the house herself. Alice had even wondered if there was perhaps one of those carefully disguised 'priest-holes' which the clergy had hidden in to evade Elizabethan inspectors.

Pete had explained the house was Georgian, not Elizabethan. The ancient plans were open to be viewed on a local museum website and no such secret rooms existed.

The Golding family had remained seated around the kitchen table the entire time. Someone had lit the Aga and opened the door to provide some heat. The solicitor, Carmel Cartwright, had arrived in her Hybrid BMW X5 half an hour before. The group appeared bewildered by the activity going on around them. Even Maria looked mouse-like and vulnerable.

Alice still had the sting of old smoke and the smell of charred wood lodged in her nose and throat. She decided to join the team examining the set of stables and outhouses rather than return to the fire-damaged main house.

There didn't seem to be an electric light in the stables, so she turned on the torch on her phone instead. A movement in the gloom made Alice start. Then she realised it was the pony, Cinnamon, who was pacing nervously in the darkness. Alice approached her stall and offered her hand to the horse, who slowly moved forward and nuzzled the palm with a wet nostril. "Don't be frightened," she whispered. "We aren't going to hurt you."

The DI felt a sudden spasm of guilt for the disruption her team were causing. They'd found nothing so far, certainly no sign of Caroline Torben being held against her will. What if the woman had simply taken a taxi into the city to do some shopping? They were going to look like fools to the management at Pitt Street if that was the case. That lawyer woman would make mincemeat of them too.

She took a deep breath and shifted away from the pony, allowing the light from her phone to penetrate into the cobwebbed eves and dusty corners. There wasn't much to see in here. Alice moved to the next block. The stalls were empty in this stable. She checked each one, nonetheless, kicking open the half-height doors and sweeping her phone torch across the straw strewn floors. Nothing.

Just as she was about to give up, Alice's narrow beam settled on a door set into one of the walls. She approached the door and slid her hand across it. The material was a cold metal, like steel. Quite out of place in an environment consisting primarily of wood and hay.

She brushed the surface, looking for a handle, discovering a large metal bar bisecting the door. She pushed down on it with all her strength. Abruptly, the door made a popping sound, as if she'd released an air-tight container. Alice felt her heart beat faster. She pushed the heavy door away from her and felt for the entrance with her boot.

This time, when she ran her hands along the smooth walls within, her fingers alighted on a switch. She flicked it on and the chamber was suddenly illuminated by an electric strip on a white ceiling.

The DI slowly took in her surroundings. The door had led to what seemed to be some kind of walk-in refrigerator. White plastic shelving lined the walls and a steel-topped table was placed in the centre, which appeared to be some kind of preparation area. The floor was tiled in grey stone. Alice didn't feel the room was particularly cold. She suspected the refrigeration system wasn't switched on. The place was spotlessly clean and the shelves empty. It looked like it hadn't been used in a while.

Alice called her DS on her phone. Pete was by her side, gazing into the white room, in moments. "What the hell is this place?"

"It's some kind of refrigeration unit, I think." Alice stepped back into the stable and swept her phone torch around. "There! The operating switches are on the outside." She knelt down on the dusty floor. "It's turned off now, but there's a thermostat control to set the temperature."

Pete was scratching his head. "Didn't Holly say something about Rosaline Golding running a goats' cheese business for a while? Maybe this is where she stored the stuff."

Alice nodded, getting to her feet. "That seems likely. But it's certainly large enough to hold a person, isn't it? The only handle is on the outside." She shuddered.

"Well, it's empty now," Pete said levelly. He was relieved that they hadn't found Caroline locked in there. He wondered how much air it held with the door closed.

The two detectives stepped outside the stable. A member of the search team was jogging towards them. "We've found a set of gas bottles in one of the garages, Ma'am. Of a similar size to the one used to set the fire in the house."

"Okay, we need to get a forensic team down here straight away. I'll ring the lab in Glasgow. I want the green car searched from top to bottom for fingerprints, traces of hair, blood, whatever they can find. I also want that fridge examined with a fine-toothed comb. It's been cleaned thoroughly, but the SOCOs will find out if something dodgy has gone on in there."

"What about the family?" Pete asked.

"It's time I had another word with them."

Chapter 68

Expecting anger and recriminations, Alice was surprised to find the Goldings solemnly cradling mugs of tea when she entered the kitchen.

Rosaline glanced up, her expression one of defeat. "I know you told us all to stay here, but we heard the men leave. Maria has taken the children up to bed. It's very late for them."

"That's fine. We're finished inside the house for now. But a forensic team has been called in from Glasgow, to examined the outhouses and your car."

Carmel Cartwright pushed aside her mug. "I hope your justification for this invasion of the Goldings' property is gold-plated, DI Mann. Otherwise, my firm will be lodging a number of serious complaints against yourself and your department."

"I'd like to speak with Mr and Mrs Golding. Maria as well, when she returns. I can take them down to the station for this interview, or we can do it here. The choice is theirs." Alice kept her tone level.

Rosaline got shakily to her feet, gathering up the mugs and taking them to the sink, flicking on the kettle when she got there. "We'll talk to you here, Detective Inspector. Do you take sugar?"

Cartwright shifted her chair noisily. "I really wouldn't recommend that, Mrs Golding. The less you say at this point, the better."

"The better for who?" Rosaline snapped. "This will never be over until the truth comes out. I'm sick of the lies. I'm sick of this ruined house and all the lives it has destroyed."

Alice took a seat at the table. "Milk, no sugar please."

Roger raised his head from his hands. His eyes were bloodshot. "You can ask me questions all you like, but I can't answer them. I'm as ignorant of what has happened here as you are. More ignorant, probably."

Rosaline returned with a tray, she placed a steaming mug in front of Alice, who was enormously grateful. Her mouth felt as dry as the straw she'd been kneeling in. She sipped the scorching liquid. "A woman is missing. Her name is Caroline Torben. She was the aunt of the young man found dead in this house, although for most or all of his life, he thought this woman was his mother. Your au-pair, Maria, worked for Caroline and her partner in Spain for six months in 2017. Then she came here, to the exact area of Scotland Caroline was from."

The lawyer narrowed her brows. "So Maria Silva and this missing woman are acquainted?"

Alice nodded. "Well, Caroline claimed not to have remembered her, but we don't know if that's true, now. Caroline was last seen getting into a small, light green hatchback at 6.30am this morning. She's not been seen since. Her sister was brutally murdered last week. We believed either Mrs Golding or Maria might have taken her. But the woman is not being held here at Hill House. We've searched everywhere. Perhaps she is dead already."

Cartwright shrugged. "It's very circumstantial. I'm amazed you got a warrant granted on the strength of it. Why would my clients wish to kidnap or harm this Caroline Torben?"

"Because the woman knows something. Maria found out what it was and I believe she saw a blackmailing opportunity. It was something to do with Leroy Torben, Victoria Braden and Rosaline Golding."

Roger turned towards his wife, his mouth slack with disbelief. "What is the detective talking about, darling?"

Alice continued, "we found some gas canisters in your garage, Mr Golding. They are a match for the one used to set fire to the north wing of your house. I'm also very interested in that walk-in refrigerator in the outhouse. We have no idea how Leroy died before his body was placed in the fire to be destroyed. Our pathologist could find no obvious cause of death. But if the man had been put in a fridge, whilst he was still alive. Well, death by hypothermia is notoriously difficult to detect in a *post mortem.*"

Before Rosaline could say anything in response, the door leading into the main house swung open. Maria Silva burst through it and flung herself at Rosaline. She pounded her fists against the woman's head and body. "Don't you dare tell them!" She screamed. "Tell them anything and I will kill you!"

Chapter 69

Alice fell into her chair as the sun was rising beyond the grubby windows of the West Kilbride criminal investigation department.

Sharon placed a cardboard coffee cup in front of her. "You don't have to speak. Drink first."

The DI did as instructed, gulping the sweet coffee like it was water. "Thanks. I needed that."

"Pete's gone home to get a couple of hour's kip. You could always do the same?"

Alice shook her head. Her eyes felt gritty and her bones ached, but there was no way she could stop now. Not when a woman was missing and they were so close to finding the answers to two murder enquiries. "Fergus is staying at home today. I'm needed here."

Sharon didn't argue with her boss. She knew it was a lost cause. "There's a PC posted outside Rosaline's room at Ayr Hospital. She's only got cuts and bruises. I expect we can interview her tomorrow. Maria Silva is in the cells downstairs. We've charged her with causing ABH."

"Tomorrow could be too late for Caroline Torben." Alice sighed, polishing off the remainder of her cup.

"What about Mr Golding? He's still at Hill House with the children. We could bring him in for questioning?"

"He told us last night he doesn't know a damn thing. I think I believe him. He can keep for now. It's Maria and Rosaline who hold the key. I know Maria took the children to school in the Golf yesterday morning, but perhaps she had chance to pick up Caroline *before* the school run?"

Sharon made a face. "They left Hill House at 7.15am and arrived at school at the usual time.

There's no way Maria could have picked Caroline up, overpowered the woman and disposed of her body somewhere, alive or dead in 45 minutes."

Alice let out a frustrated grunt. "Maybe it was Rosaline who took her?"

Sharon kept her tone level and rational. "The Goldings' Golf was identified as the car Maria dropped the children off in at Wemyss College prep school car park at twenty to nine. If Rosaline picked up Caroline, it would've had to have been in their Land Rover, which doesn't match with Callum Marshall's testimony."

Alice slammed her hand on the desk. "Dammit! What are we missing? Is there another accomplice?"

"The search team have submitted the gas canisters they found in one of the garages to the forensics department. They may be able to match the brand and type to the one they retrieved from the debris of the fire. A match would be circumstantial, the family could claim it was in the house all along, but it all helps to build a case."

"It certainly does," Alice agreed.

"They also found an old Ford Escort van in another of the garages. It was rusted up and didn't look as if it's been driven in years. There was a logo for a gardening business on the side, with a Glasgow phone number, now obsolete."

Alice crinkled her brow. "It can't have been another of Rosaline's failed businesses, can it?"

Holly picked up on the discussion and abandoned her desk, where piles of papers and printouts were strewn across the surface. It was clear the DI wasn't the only one who'd been working all night. "Ma'am, I've been looking more closely at that book written about the Crammond family. I was able to download the entire thing from the local library website. It was published by the North Ayrshire Historical Society."

"Okay," Alice said encouragingly, although she wasn't at all sure how Holly's endeavours would help progress their case. "What did you find?"

The younger detective rolled up a chair. "The newspaper reports I read only picked out certain examples for their stories. If you read the entire book, you find there were many more tales of tragedy and dodgy-dealing in the Crammond family over the years."

"Oh yes?" Sharon said. She was certainly interested. "Like what?"

"An uncle of Rosaline's was found with thousands of child porn images on his computer in the mid-2000s. He went to prison for a couple of years. But the one that caught my interest the most was a terrible car crash that occurred on the M77 in February 1996. A lorry driver had exceeded his statutory hours on the road. He dozed off at the wheel. So he didn't notice the traffic ahead of him had stopped because of a breakdown on the carriageway further along. His truck ploughed into the line of cars. Four people were killed. The truck driver miraculously survived."

Alice's mind was ticking over fast. "Carry on, Holly. What has this got to do with the Crammonds?"

"In the second car, a young man and his girlfriend were heading towards the city to see a show. The man was called Jonathan Crammond, he was twenty years old. His girlfriend was called Gemma Blake, she was nineteen. The truck rammed their petrol tank and crushed the chassis of the car. The vehicle burst into flames. The police believe both occupants were still alive while the car burnt."

Alice felt bile rise in her throat. "Who was he then, this Jonathan Crammond?"

"I checked with the public records office. He was Rosaline's older brother."

"Christ!" Sharon exclaimed. "How bloody awful for their family."

But Alice was piecing this information together with another tragedy they'd be told about in the course of their investigations. "Does it mention who else was killed in the pile-up?"

Holly shook her head. "No, the book only really focusses on the Crammonds. It's pretty gruesome in places. I'm sure the author has added in some grizzly flourishes which haven't come from official records. In fact, it reads a bit like a horror story in sections. She must have had pretty good sources of information though, to get so much detail on the family."

"You said, *she*. Who was the author of this book?" Alice suddenly remembered Holly saying the entire publication could be downloaded from the West Kilbride library website. Alarm bells began ringing in her brain.

"It was someone called Janice Kirk. It says she was a librarian and archivist at West Kilbride Library at the time. The book was first published in 1998. So it must have been the tragedy of Jonathan Crammond's death which first inspired her to take on the project."

Alice was already on her feet. "Janice Kirk is the manager of West Kilbride library. She worked with Victoria Braden for thirty years. Victoria's husband was also killed in an accident on the M77 in 1996. I'm willing to bet none of this is a coincidence."

Sharon's mouth dropped open. "We need an address for this woman. Right now."

Alice dragged her jacket over her aching arms. "I'm afraid we may have to interrupt Pete's beauty sleep. He's not going to want to miss this."

Chapter 70

Sunlight was piercing through the windscreen of the squad car. Alice lowered her visor, shielding her tired eyes from the glare. Pete was driving them towards an address in Monkton.

The radio crackled into life. Alice grabbed the receiver. "DI Mann," she barked.

"It's Holly, Ma'am. Just letting you know I've sent Matt and Sharon to the library, although it doesn't open until 9.30am. Also, I've looked Janice Kirk up on the DVLA database. She is the registered owner of an Emerald Green, Vauxhall Corsa." Alice swallowed down her frustration at this piece of information only coming to light now, knowing it wouldn't help. "Thanks Holly. Anything else?"

"The woman has never married and doesn't appear to have any children. She lives alone at the address I gave you."

"Cheers. Can you continue researching that road accident from 1996? I want to know everything documented about the other victims of the crash and the driver of the truck."

Alice placed the radio receiver back in its rest. "Shit. Why didn't we look closer into the background of Victoria's boss? We should've found out she drove a green hatchback. We've been on the wrong track all along."

Pete kept his eyes on the road, which was empty this early in the morning. "Why would we? Janice seemed to cooperate with us fully. I thought she was genuinely shocked by the news of Victoria's murder."

"So did I. Maybe I'm losing my instincts."

Pete took a sharp right turn onto a quiet street of small bungalows. "Don't dwell on it. I'm still certain that Rosaline and Maria are involved in this. It just turns out Janice Kirk may be too."

The car came to an abrupt stop outside a neat single-storey dwelling with a compact front garden. "This is it," Pete declared.

*

Alice scanned the property as they approached the front door. There was a single garage to one side. Other than that, the house was small. Perhaps a couple of bedrooms at the most. She knew there would be no hope of gaining a warrant to search the place. They had nothing concrete on the woman except a huge list of coincidences. The DI leant on the bell, not in any mood for social niceties.

Janice opened the door on the chain, eyeing them suspiciously through the crack.

"Ms Kirk. It's DI Mann and DS Falmer. We spoke with you last week about the death of Victoria Braden. We've got a couple more questions. May we come inside?"

The woman narrowed her small features. "I'm just getting ready to go to work. Do you know what time it is?"

"Yes, we do," Alice struggled to maintain her temper. "But this is quite urgent. We are investigating *two* murders, madam."

The door slammed shut and then re-opened with the chain removed. "Well, if you must." She was wearing a knee-length skirt and an untucked cotton blouse. "Please take a seat in the living room. I was just about to do my make-up, as it happens."

"It won't matter if the library opens a little later today, Ms Kirk. We have some officers over there now who can explain to any other staff or customers who turn up in the meantime."

Janice followed them into a cramped room with only enough space for a floral three piece suite and a small TV set. Books were piled on every surface. Pete took a seat. Alice occupied the space beside him. You could have cut the atmosphere with a knife.

Chapter 71

"I have never been late opening the library in the ten years I've been manager. It may be trivial to you, but it certainly isn't to me."

"*Sit down*, Ms Kirk." Alice's tone was steely, like a parent who's finally had enough of a child playing silly buggers.

Surprisingly, the woman did as she was told.

"Janice Kirk, in 1998, you published a factual book entitled, 'The Curse of the Crammonds: The tragedies that plagued a prominent Ayrshire dynasty.' Is that correct?"

The woman shifted awkwardly. "Yes, I'm a bit of an amateur historian in addition to my library work. I've also released a pamphlet on the history of the pier at Wemyss Bay. I've been involved in the Ayrshire Historical Society for years."

Alice leant forward. "When we last spoke to you, you mentioned having read about the details of the death of Leroy Torben in the local paper. The young man's burnt remains were found in the debris of Hill House in Fairlie. This was the family home of the Crammonds. They'd lived there since Georgian times. *Surely*, you must have found this an odd coincidence. One worthy of mentioning to us?"

Janice clutched at her neckline, like she'd done before when they questioned her. Alice wondered if it was a tell; an indication the lies were about to begin.

"Well, of course I thought it was strange. I'm aware of that family's unfortunate history of tragedies from my research twenty years ago. But I didn't really make the connection, no."

Pete nearly let out a snort of derision. "Forgive me, if I find that hard to believe."

Her posture stiffened. "It doesn't really matter what you *believe*, does it sergeant? It's what you can *prove* that's important."

Alice was determined to keep her cool. "How did you come to write the book about the Crammonds? You must have known them very well in order to have access to all the information you provide in the book?"

"Have you read it?" The woman's expression was an odd mixture of pleasure and fear.

"One of my team has. We were particularly gripped by the section on the M77 pile-up of 1996. The crash in which Jonathan Crammond and his girlfriend were killed, along with Greg Braden, who was driving the first car that was struck by the lorry that afternoon."

Her face turned white. "Yes, obviously I knew about that terrible accident because Victoria's husband had been so tragically killed as a result of it. In the course of supporting Victoria through that dark time, it came to my attention the Crammonds' eldest son had also been killed. Someone mentioned the 'Crammond curse', one day in the library, and I suppose my natural curiosity kicked in."

Alice crinkled her face in distaste. "What did Victoria think about you writing a book featuring the horrific accident that killed her husband? She must have objected, surely?"

Janice lifted her chin resolutely. "Victoria was actually very supportive, as were poor Jonathan's parents. They wanted the story to be told. If there wasn't to be any justice served through the court system, then at least the man who drove the truck into those innocent people could be named and shamed."

To Alice's great surprise, the woman's eyes glistened and tears escaped onto her lined skin. She reached into the pocket of her skirt for a tissue.

"So Stephen and Geraldine Crammond, the parents of Rosaline and Jonathan, co-operated with you in the writing of this book?"

She nodded, blowing her nose theatrically. "Yes, I accompanied Victoria to a couple of the court hearings and once to the trial itself. She was a mess during that period. I had to help her dress and wash herself in order to get her there. But we met several family members of the others who'd been killed during the process. It seemed a comfort. That's when I first spoke with Stephen and Geraldine." She shook her head sadly, lost in the memory. "He was so angry, Mr Crammond. His need to see someone punished was very strong. Geraldine was simply lost in her grief, a bit like Vick, I suppose. So when the punishment was so pathetic in the end, it hit Stephen very hard."

Pete looked puzzled. "You said that already – that there was no real justice served for the victims. But the driver was convicted of causing death by dangerous driving, wasn't he? On several counts. He was sentenced to fourteen years with the expectation of serving seven."

Janice's eyes flashed angrily. "Who told you that rubbish?"

Pete's cheeks flushed pink. "I read it in one of the newspaper reports from the time. They'd been transferred from microfiche onto the Herald website in the early 2000s."

"But you didn't check the actual court records, did you?"

Pete felt his stomach contract. All he'd done was check one online source. It hadn't felt as if Victoria's husband's death was of much significance to their investigation then. He tried not to catch his boss's eye. "No, I didn't.'

The librarian flashed him a look of disgust, as if using a single source in a piece of research was the most despicable of crimes. "Six weeks later, the driver's defence team appealed the sentence. The freight company he worked for had been exposed as flouting health and safety laws – forcing their drivers to reduce break times on long journeys. The lawyers argued for mitigating circumstances. In the end, his sentence was commuted to two years suspended, including time already served, plus six months community service." She practically spat out the words. "The man had killed *four people*. In the most grotesque circumstances, and he walked free."

Alice had to admit she was shocked by the low tariff. She'd need to get corroboration from Holly later. "You seem particularly upset by the leniency of the sentence. I know Victoria was your friend, but it seems an acutely *personal* affront to you?"

Janice brushed the question away, "it was an affront to humanity, that's all."

"You also seem to have been far closer to Victoria Braden than you led us to believe. You helped the woman wash and get dressed for court appearances. How the hell could you not have known she was pregnant, for God's sake?"

Janice looked flustered. "That was later! Leroy wasn't born until the end of '98. The court case was well over by then!"

Alice pushed harder. "What about Caroline Torben? Why wasn't she the one accompanying her sister to those court hearings? She was Victoria's closest family."

Janice rolled her eyes in a manner which was slightly manic. "That silly woman? She barely stopped making her slutty way around the dive bars of West Kilbride after Greg was killed. The idea of *her* ever being a comfort to Victoria is a joke."

Alice felt she was hitting a nerve. "Where is your car? We know you drive a green Vauxhall Corsa."

"In the garage, of course. Where else would it be?"

"And where is Caroline, Janice? We also know you picked her up from Victoria's house in that same car early yesterday morning. We have a witness. What have you done with her? What does she know that you're so frightened may come out?"

She crossed her arms over her chest. A spark of satisfaction glinting in her murky grey eyes. "So the silly woman is missing, is she? What a shame. Caroline was never bright enough to avoid ending up in trouble. I'm surprised it didn't happen years ago." She got to her feet. "Now, if you'll excuse me, I've got a library to run."

Chapter 72

There was no way Alice had the authority to make Janice Kirk shut up the library for the day, but to her surprise, the manager allowed them to take a look around the premises, as long as they didn't disturb any of the users.

Alice stalked around the staff seating area, beyond the main floor of the library and opened any door she found. The toilets were empty, as was the tiny kitchen area to the rear of the building.

Pete called over to his boss, "come and have a look in here, Ma'am!"

She padded across the soft carpet to join her DS at the door to a small storage room. It had no windows and was lit by a single bulb hanging from the centre of the tiled ceiling. A photocopier was placed in one corner and the racks of metal shelves contained piles of books which appeared to be fresh from the publishers.

Pete ushered Alice inside and closed the door. He began sniffing the air. "What do you smell?"

Alice knew better than to question his odd behaviour. "That chemical, photocopier smell and the scent of new books. Maybe something musty too?"

"It's stale cigarette smoke," Pete explained. "I've had it clinging to my jacket for the last few days so I'm all too familiar with it."

"Do you think the staff come in here for a fag?"

Pete pointed to a large, red no-smoking sign on the wall beside the copier. "I doubt it. Besides, it's against the law, isn't it?"

Alice swept her eyes across the cramped space. "Do you think Caroline Torben has been in here?"

Pete shrugged. "It's just a hunch. If she has, it wasn't long ago. The smell must have come off her clothes and lingered. If we could get a forensic team in here to look for traces of her, it might prove it for certain?"

Alice shook her head vigorously. "We've got no chance of getting the go-ahead for that. Janice's right. We haven't got nearly enough evidence to apply for a warrant, or even question her further."

Pete lowered his voice, even though they were standing in a cupboard with the door closed. "We could put her under surveillance ourselves though, couldn't we?"

"Yep," Alice replied. "I've already got Matt on the case." She took another look at the cupboard interior, wondering if their missing woman really had been imprisoned here within the last few hours. "For now, we need to get back to the station. There's nothing more we can do here."

As they passed the reception desk, trying to ignore the smug look Janice Kirk was flashing them, Alice picked up one of the flyers that Fergus had seen for the fireworks display at the football ground that evening. She felt a stab of remorse. There was no way she'd be able to accompany them now, not with the investigation at this crucial stage.

She scrunched the flyer into her pocket, striding out of the building without a second glance.

Chapter 73

When Caroline opened her heavy eyelids this time, she knew exactly where she was. Her hands and legs were still tied, the tape still in place across her mouth, although it was loosening slightly at the edges. But the smell and shape of her place of confinement were unmistakeable.

She was in the boot of Janice's shitty little car. The stench of petrol and exhaust fumes were filling her nostrils. In her drowsy state a while earlier, drifting in and out of consciousness, she had even sensed the bumps and jolts of movement. They had driven somewhere. Caroline knew she wasn't in the library any longer.

When her captor had brought her a bottle of water, what felt like hours earlier, turning on the single bulb and illuminating the space she was being kept in, making her realise it was a library storage room and helping her to sit up and holding the bottle steady as the precious liquid slid down her throat, Caroline thought there was still a hope. This act of kindness, quenching her thirst, meant Janice didn't really mean her any great harm. This was just a way to keep her quiet. Persuade her to refrain from sharing what patchy knowledge she had from the police.

That was fine, she was open to persuasion, especially of the financial kind. She would have told Janice that, if the woman had given her more time with the gag removed. But the tape was roughly re-applied, just as soon as Caroline had gulped the final drops of liquid.

It was only now, she realised there must have been a sedative of some kind in the water. Her eyes were gluey and her head pounded like it did with the worst kind of Jerez brandy hangover, when she and Rick shared a bottle after closing up on a balmy, summer night. She had no idea how far she'd been driven for, but the car was certainly stationary now.

Caroline wriggled her body to get the blood circulating in her fingers and toes, as far as was possible with her tight restraints, anyway. Her knees were bent, but she could kick out with her feet and strike what must have been the inside of the wheel arch. The metal felt flimsy beneath the soles of her designer trainers.

It was a long shot, but perhaps the car was parked on the side of a road somewhere. If she kicked hard enough against the bodywork, maybe a passer-by would hear the noise and call the police. She summoned all her strength, striking the panel repeatedly and rocking her body violently in the hope it made the tiny vehicle move in a way that was noticeable from the outside.

She continued the process until exhaustion had overcome her body and her heart was pumping like a jackhammer. Sweat trickled from her brow and ran down her face. She could feel the saltiness of it penetrating through the edges of the tape. A surge of fresh hope gave Caroline the energy to manoeuvre her mouth, poking with her tongue so that one side of the sticky gag had come loose. She gulped in air like it was water in the desert.

Then she realised she could shout. Caroline filled her lungs and let out a barrage of expletives at the top of her voice. When her throat was too dry to continue, her head dropped onto the hard floor of the boot in defeat.

Nobody was coming. Nobody had heard. Silent tears slipped from her eyes. No longer worried about suffocating, Caroline allowed the sobs inexorably rising from her chest to rack her whole body, as the realisation hit her. Victoria was dead, so was Leroy. No way was she going to get out of this situation alive.

Chapter 74

When Alice and Pete returned to the department, the energy coming off the team of detectives was palpable. Holly's desk was even more untidy than before, but she was scribbling notes in the centre of the mess, a look of determination on her face.

Matt had taken the squad car. His task was to park on the road outside the library, waiting for Janice Kirk to go on the move.

Sharon was feverishly tapping the keyboard of her laptop, engrossed in the information filling the screen.

"Pete thinks Caroline Torben may have been kept overnight in one of the storerooms at the library. He could smell her stale fag smoke in the air."

Sharon raised an eyebrow. "Well, at least it means the woman may still be alive somewhere."

"Yes, and we must assume she is alive, until we find a body." Alice turned towards her youngest DC. "Holly, what have you discovered about the crash that killed Greg Braden and Jonathan Crammond in 1996?"

Holly plucked a few stray sheets from the desk, pulled them together and scanned their contents. "The police reports of the RTA were pretty thorough. The Pitt Street traffic division responded, as the accident took place within a few miles of Glasgow. It was 2.15pm when a small white van broke down on the slow lane of the M77. It was obstructing the carriageway, so motorbike police closed the affected lane and diverted traffic into lanes two and three until the tow-truck arrived. The weather was overcast and wet. Inevitably, a line of slow traffic resulted from the diversion. These were the days before dashcams were in use and before most people had mobile phones, so the details of what happened next aren't absolutely clear." Holly took a breath, the events she was about to relay had made her want to cry when she first read about them, but she needed to keep her emotions under control in front of the team. "At approximately 2.45pm, the traffic had come to a standstill. Greg Braden's Vauxhall Vectra was at the back of the queue. Jonathan and Gemma's car was just in front, a small Peugeot, I think. A four tonne HGV, carrying goods from Europe for Mack's Haulage, now no longer trading, was being driven by a 42 year old man called David Murcia. His parents were from Barbados, but he'd been born in Glasgow."

"The driver was Afro-Caribbean?" Pete shot a glance at Alice.

"That's right, he lived in the Cranhill area at the time but was returning from a trip to Hamburg. Later reports showed he'd been on the road for over 12 hours by the time of the crash, when the EU rules stipulated that 9 hours are the maximum that can be driven in one day. It explains why, as his truck approach the stationary line of vehicles up ahead, he failed to slow down. Murcia himself claimed he had temporarily lost consciousness. Had no memory of the crash itself, just waking up in the wreckage."

Sharon tutted loudly. "Was he injured?"

Holly replied, "just a few cuts and bruises. Of course, the cab of the truck was a good couple of metres clear of the cars he struck." Her voice became sombre. "When the front of Murcia's truck hit Greg Braden's vehicle, it was travelling at roughly 50mph, decelerating because Murcia was asleep and had lifted his foot off the accelerator pedal. Braden stood no chance. His car was crushed in seconds. The only solace for his family is that the pathologist and the Fiscal's office ruled his death as instantaneous."

"The couple in front weren't so lucky?" Alice said.

"No, they weren't. The accident investigator reckoned that, contrary to Murcia's claims, he woke up at this point and tried to swerve the truck, this meant he struck both Jonathan Crammond's car, and the car in the adjacent lane. Both had their petrol tanks breached and sparks from the impact of metal-on-metal led to the vehicles catching fire. Murcia managed to bring his truck to a standstill when it rammed the central reservation. Passengers in nearby cars tried to get Jonathan and his girlfriend out, as well as a woman in the other car, she was called Meredith Whiting. But the fire had taken hold too strongly. There was nothing they could do."

Everyone was hushed for several moments. Sharon muttered a prayer under her breath, even though she was barely religious.

Alice broke the silence. "It was an awful tragedy. The families and loved ones of those victims must be tortured by it to this very day. But *we* must keep level-headed. Examine the facts, coldly and clinically. It's the only way we're going to crack this case."

Chapter 75

"Did the fact that Murcia had been driving over the permitted time limits come up at the first trial?" Pete asked.

"No, the original timings submitted by Mack's Haulage recorded Murcia's driving hours to have been 8hrs 42 minutes that day. Several months later, a whistle-blower at the firm, claimed tachographs were being regularly tampered with by managers to allow their drivers to take fewer breaks. Murcia's tachograph was examined by his legal team and was shown to have been altered. Murcia instead, claimed he'd been driving continuously from Hamburg, stopping only for the Channel Tunnel crossing."

Sharon shook her head sadly. "If the guy hadn't take enough breaks, surely that makes the crash even *more* his fault?"

Holly shrugged. "Murcia's lawyers claimed he'd been forced to exceed legal driving times by the bosses. If they were late returning to the depot, they had their pay docked or missed out on future work. This was corroborated by other drivers at Mack's Haulage. The CEO faced criminal charges and the business folded. This evidence provided Murcia's legal team with evidence of mitigating circumstances to put before the judge."

"Sounds like David Murcia had a shit-hot legal team," Alice commented. "I wonder how he afforded that?"

"Apparently, Murcia was a shop-steward for the Glasgow branch of the Transport and Haulage Union. They had a whip round of members to raise money for his defence costs, supported by the

Scottish Express Newspaper," Holly explained. "They raked in hundreds of thousands."

Pete puffed out his cheeks. "That must have been tough for the victims' families to swallow. It must have felt as if everything was stacked against them back then."

"Where is Murcia now?" Alice asked. "He only spent a few months in prison. His suspended sentence ran its course twenty years back."

Holly looked immediately embarrassed. "I haven't got that far yet, I've been looking into the crash and the court case. Murcia won his appeal in early 1997. He's been a free man ever since."

Sharon grinned. "I might just be able to help you there, because that's exactly what I've been finding out about." She reached for her laptop. "David Lyron Murcia was born at the Glasgow Infirmary in 1954. His parents arrived on the Empire Windrush in 1948, eventually settling in Glasgow after David's father got a job at a shipyard." The DS looked smug. "I found a recent article online about the impact of the Windrush generation on Scotland."

"Great," Alice said encouragingly. "Carry on."

"The Herald ran a piece on Murcia during the trial in 1996. It stated he had few qualifications and had trained for his HGV licence ten years before the crash. But his employment at Mack's Haulage had been uneventful up to that time. Murcia wasn't married and had no children. At that point, he lived in a council flat in Cranhill."

"But what about later? What happened to him after the appeal?" Alice was getting impatient, aware that Caroline could still be out there somewhere, in terrible trouble. All this talk of a crash that occurred twenty five years ago could just be a waste of their time.

Sharon looked less sure of herself. "According to council records, he left his flat in 1997 but I can't find any other record of an address after that point. He appears to have been the registered owner of a Ford Escort van from March 1997, but again, no other vehicles were registered with the DVLA after that point. There's no death certificate either."

Pete tossed his pen on the desk. "So, the driver is now completely uncontactable?"

Alice's mind was mulling over something Sharon had just said. "You mentioned Murcia owned a Ford Escort Van? Didn't the search team at Hill House find a vehicle like that in one of the outhouses? It had a logo for a gardening business on the side?"

Sharon's eyes widened. "Shit! I'd forgotten about that!"

Alice leapt to her feet. "Sharon, I want you and Pete to get over to Hill House. Take a look at that van. Make sure you note the registration and the details on the side. Compare it to the DVLA records for Murcia."

Pete grabbed his jacket. "Sure, we'll get going right now."

Chapter 76

Before stepping through the automatic doors at the entrance to Ayr Hospital, Alice checked in with her team. Matt had messaged to confirm he was still sitting in the squad car outside the library. Janice Kirk was inside stacking books on shelves like she hadn't a care in the world.

Pete and Sharon were examining the van at the Goldings' property. Mr Golding seemed to have given up on resisting the police's presence at the house. The detectives had sent photos of the rusted number plate and the faded business decal on the side to Holly, who was feeding the details into various databases.

The receptionist sent Alice to the third floor, where she knew it was visiting time. She'd plucked a bunch of carnations from a display at WH Smiths, paying the assistant and taking it with her in the lift.

The ward was warm and quiet. Alice could immediately see the thin form of Rosaline Golding in one of the huge beds. She looked pale and childlike. The DI pulled the curtain around them as she sat down. "I brought you these," she said brusquely, laying the cheap bouquet on the bedside table, beside a plastic cup of water.

Rosaline nodded. "Thanks." Her face was blotched with purplish bruises. The one around her left eye had already turned a bottle green colour and was swollen like a prize boxer's.

"Your family aren't here?" Alice asked, feeling a sudden pang of sympathy for the woman.

"I told Roger not to bring the kids. I don't want them to see me like this."

Alice pulled up a soft chair. "Rosaline. Don't you think it's time to tell us everything you know? Two people are dead, another is missing. Maria Silva assaulted you in your own home. Surely, this can't be a situation you want to continue?"

Her blue eyes glistened. Tears rolled down her bruised cheeks. "Of course it isn't. But the truth is too awful to bear. Even worse than this."

Alice leant forward. "The truth is never worse than the lies, trust me. You take your punishment and there's a chance to move on, gain some forgiveness."

Rosaline gave a tiny sob. Alice searched on the table beside her for a box of tissues. She handed it to the woman.

"It's too late for forgiveness."

"Let me be the judge of that."

She took a deep breath. "My brother was killed. In a horrible accident. He and his girlfriend burnt to death."

Alice nodded. "I know."

"I was only eighteen myself, about to go to university, make my way in the world. The accident ruined everything." She mopped her tears with a scrunched tissue. "My mother, Geraldine, never really recovered from Jonathan's death. She spent years barely leaving her room. My father and I just about managed to drag her to the courtroom for the trial of the man who caused the crash, although perhaps it would have been better if we hadn't."

"The driver of the HGV that killed four people that day was given a suspended sentence. He only lost his heavy vehicle licence. It was one hell of a lenient punishment."

Pain flashed across the woman's face. The DI knew it wasn't a result of her injuries. "You can say that again. David Murcia was walking the streets within months of killing four innocent people. They died in the most grotesque ways. My father was consumed with grief, but he was also angry. Very, very, angry."

"Was Stephen Crammond a vengeful man?"

Rosaline gave a hollow laugh. "My father was a man who expected to get what he wanted. After the appeal was granted, he wrote to every judge in Scotland. He had every police officer in Ayrshire blackballed from his golf club. But nothing seemed to assuage his boiling rage."

"There were other victims too? Did you meet the families of Gemma, Greg and Meredith?"

"Oh yes, Gemma's family were friends of ours, but they dealt with their grief very privately. Within a couple of years they'd moved away, didn't want the memories of their daughter all around them. Meredith Whiting hadn't seemed to have had much of a family. Her elderly mother was in a nursing home. We never saw anyone connected with her at the trials."

"What about Greg Braden?"

Rosaline's posture stiffened. "We met his widow, yes."

"Victoria Braden, Leroy Torben's mother?"

The woman nodded reluctantly. "She sought us out at the trial, her and a friend, Janice Kirk. Victoria was grief-stricken by her husband's death. She was a shell of a person back then, like my mother. But Janice was angry. She was full of rage and hatred, just like my father."

Alice made a face. "What I don't understand, is why Janice was so worked up about the crash. It wasn't *her* husband who'd been killed. I don't even think she cared that much about Victoria, not really. It doesn't make any sense."

"My father thought exactly the same thing at the time. So, he hired an investigator to find out more about Janice Kirk."

Alice widened her eyes in shock. "That was an extreme thing to do, wasn't it?"

Rosaline managed a wry smile. "My father was a powerful business man. It wasn't unusual for him to check out his opposition. He used his investigator a lot. At that time, he was looking into the background of David Murcia too, in case there was something criminal in his past that the prosecution could use against him. They found nothing."

"What about Janice?" Alice's heart was racing.

"Janice Kirk was working as a library assistant in 1997. She still lived in the spare room of her parents' house. But up until the February of the previous year, she'd spent every Thursday evening in a hotel in Largs. With Greg Braden."

Alice gripped the arms of the chair, trying not to reveal what a revelation this was to her. "Janice Kirk had been having an affair with Victoria's husband?"

"Yes, for about two years." Rosaline ran a hand through her lank hair. "This information made sense to my father. It explained why Janice was so angry. She'd loved Greg, but wasn't even able to grieve openly at his death. They may have had a future together, this had been taken from her. My father then understood her bitterness. He shared it. Jonny was his only son, his heir."

"Did Victoria ever know about the affair, do you think?"

Rosaline shrugged her shoulders. "I don't imagine so. She wouldn't have carried on working with the woman if she had, would she? I always got the impression Victoria was a naïve person, childlike in lots of ways. Certainly unworldly."

Alice thought about the dead woman, with her cleaning fetish and prissy ways. She'd certainly been no match for someone like Janice. She supposed that compared to Victoria, Janice was perhaps more exciting to Greg than his wife. Maybe Victoria's work colleague had set out to seduce Greg right from the start. They were unlikely to ever know now. The important thing was that it explained why Janice was so caught up in the court case against Murcia. Why her hatred for the man had burned so bright.

Chapter 77

Alice glanced at her watch. It was nearly 3pm. She didn't have long. She reached for the jug on the bedside table and topped up the plastic cup, encouraging the woman in the bed to take a sip.

Rosaline gulped it down. "Thanks. You know, it does feel better to talk about this stuff. But then, I haven't got to the difficult bit yet." She grimaced. "It's very bad. The worst, really."

"I've been told the very worst things that a human being can imagine. If you talk to me, confess the stuff you know, I won't be shocked. Not like your husband would be."

Rosaline sighed. "He's a selfish man, unfeeling and spoilt. But you're right. He couldn't get his head around the things I've done, the things I've seen. The children are better off with him than me." Her eyes filled once again.

Alice leant forward, one eye on the ticking clock. "It may not come to that. But you must hurry and tell me. Everything."

*

When Alice returned to the department, she was pleased to see that Pete and Sharon were back. The light was fading outside and Alice thought wistfully about Fergus and Charlie getting ready to leave for the fireworks display; putting on their thick coats, pulling on gloves and scarves to protect against the cold.

"Is Maria Silva still in custody?" She asked the room.

"Yep," Holly replied. "Her bail was set at a couple of thousand pounds. The Goldings are refusing to put up the money or to provide her with a lawyer."

"Good," Alice replied with satisfaction.

Pete pulled out a chair for his boss, noticing how strained her features looked. "Are you okay, Ma'am?"

She nodded. "I've been to speak with Rosaline Golding in hospital. She told me the whole story. It's not easy listening."

Sharon rested her hand on Holly's shoulder. "Thanks to Holly, we now know that the van parked in the Goldings' garage is the same one that was registered to David Murcia in 1997. We have to conclude that after leaving Mack's Haulage, he set up some kind of gardening business. But how the hell it ended up at Hill House or where the man is now, remains anyone's guess."

Alice stayed silent, but her expression was one of deep sadness.

"I think the DI might know exactly why it was there, Sharon." Pete dropped into the seat beside Alice. "Am I right?"

She was about to reply when her phone buzzed in her pocket. The DI fished it out and answered. It was Matt Singh.

The line was crackly, it sounded like he was on the hands free, driving probably. The DI put him on speakerphone.

"Hi Matt, how is it going?"

"Janice Kirk closed up the library about an hour ago. She drove back to her house in Monkton. But now she's on the move again. I'm following her green Corsa right now."

Alice flashed a glance at Pete. "Can you tell where she's headed Matt?"

"I can't be absolutely certain, but I reckon we're on the road that leads to the football ground. The one where the Seamill Shooters play."

Alice exhaled a long breath. "Stay with her Matt. If she changes route, let me know immediately. Otherwise, we'll meet you there."

Chapter 78

The sky was an inky black and the traffic along the Law Road had come to a standstill. Pete struck the steering wheel of the squad car in frustration. "Why the hell is it so busy?"

"It's the only organised fireworks display in the area tonight. Fergus has brought Charlie." Alice could feel her anxiety levels rising. She hoped Janice wasn't planning anything that would risk the safety of the public.

"Should we evacuate the ground?" Pete slid a glance at his DI. "What do we think Janice Kirk might do?"

Alice felt the weight of responsibility pressing down on her chest. The last thing she wanted was to place her little boy in any kind of danger. But Janice had shown no indication she possessed a weapon of any kind. Matt said she got into the car with just her handbag. "No, we can't make that decision just yet. It would only cause panic. I've requested back-up from the station in Ayr. There should be some officers coming along behind us."

Pete nodded. "Okay, but there must be hundreds of people heading for the ground. It's going to be almost impossible to find the woman in the dark."

Alice knew he was right. Before she could formulate a plan, the radio crackled into life.

"DI Mann? It's Matt Singh here."

"Hi Matt. Go ahead."

"I've finally arrived at the football ground. I was directed to park in a field at the foot of the hill. There was so much traffic. I'm afraid I've lost her."

Alice felt her heart sink. "You've lost sight of the car?"

"She was a few vehicles ahead of me, but then the traffic started splitting in different directions to find parking spaces. I tried to keep an eye on the green Corsa, but it slipped out of view."

Alice sighed heavily. "It's okay Matt. We're stuck in traffic ourselves, it's bedlam out here. You'll have to look for her on foot. We'll be with you as soon as we can."

The radio fell silent. Alice gripped the door handle tightly and scanned the road up ahead. She could see the floodlights illuminating the pitch a few yards in the distance. "I'm going to get out and walk the rest of the way. We're getting nowhere stuck here."

Pete looked alarmed. "We've got no back-up yet, Ma'am. There's not much you can do on your own."

"Matt's out there too. I can't let her get away, Pete. Not now I know what she's capable of."

The traffic slowed to a standstill. Alice wrenched open the door and stepped out into the cold night.

*

Alice wished she'd had time to put on some gloves or a hat. Her hands were already numb with the cold. All around her were families wrapped up against the night, wearing brightly coloured wellie boots and with glow sticks worn like illuminated necklaces or swung from tiny hands, leaving streaky neon trails in the darkness. She wondered if Fergus had bought one for Charlie.

She didn't want to push through the crowds, there were already huge numbers of people and causing panic was the last thing she wanted. Fergus and Charlie were in this mass of bodies somewhere.

As she reached the entrance gates, the floodlights were providing a better level of visibility. She waved her warrant card at the volunteers manning the ticket table. They glanced at her oddly as she swept past. Alice scanned the crowds for a glimpse of Janice Kirk. Like herself, a person on their own at such an event would be conspicuous. But there were just too many people. She saw no sign of the woman.

The crowds were making their way through the tall, wire gates into the ground. The first arrivals took the seats in the stands whilst the rest positioned themselves around the pitch side. The grass had been partially covered by wooden boards. In the centre were stacked the large black boxes which contained the fireworks.

Alice thought she could see Tony Stubbs and Martin Quinlan helping the technical team. She made her way around the pitch side, looking frantically for their quarry. She couldn't spot Janice anywhere.

Then Alice noticed Charlie's bright red coat amongst the people seated in the east stand. She peered closer, seeing that her son was perched on Fergus's lap about three rows up. She took the steps two at a time, reaching them in minutes.

When he caught sight of her, Fergus's face broke into a broad smile. "Alice! You made it! Wonderful! Charlie is so excited."

A few kindly people made space for her to join them. She pulled Charlie into a tight embrace, feeling his warm cheek pressed to her cold skin. Fergus leant forward to give her a kiss. He noticed the strained expression on her face. "This unexpected visit isn't purely for pleasure, is it?"

She shook her head solemnly. "No, but let's enjoy the display for a few minutes."

Before he could reply, the sky above them filled with an explosion of light and colour. Charlie's expression was one of awe as yellow stars rained down over their heads, crackling and whizzing. Alice couldn't help but smile at her son's excitement and for a blissful moment, her real reason for being there was almost forgotten.

Chapter 79

Whilst her son was absorbed in the display, Alice used their elevated position to view the surrounding area. It seemed the platform below them was being used for the fireworks, but beyond the gates of the football pitch, in an empty field beneath the Law Hill, a huge pyramid of wood and cardboard and broken old furniture had been haphazardly constructed. A guy stuffed with straw and dressed in a tatty suit was balanced precariously at the top.

Alice turned to Fergus. "Is there some kind of timetable of events?"

He reached into his pocket and brought out a crumpled pamphlet, handing it to her.

She scanned the contents. The fireworks started at 7.15, followed by the lighting of the bonfire at 8pm. She could see there were already people milling around the great pile of combustibles, clearly getting ready to set it alight.

In a final eruption of bangs and sparkles, the display was over. Alice could feel the crowd around them simmering restlessly. She hoped the event would end sensibly and calmly.

Fergus lifted Charlie up onto his shoulders, pointing towards the field beyond. "Look over there. The bonfire is about to get lit," he explained to their over-excited little boy.

Alice watched as three men with flaming torches, touched the flames to the base of the pyramid, until the kindling began to catch fire. The orange glow illuminated the hillside behind. Although they were too far away, she could almost sense the heat on her face.

Charlie's legs began bucking with enthusiasm, as the flames licked higher. Then, just like during the fireworks display, he began calling out the colours he could see. "Pink! Pink!" He yelled at the top of his voice.

"There's no pink in the bonfire, sweetheart," Fergus replied gently. "Just oranges and reds."

"There's pink too!" Charlie replied stubbornly, pointing a gloved finger in the direction of the inferno.

Alice followed her son's gaze, her stomach dropping like a stone. Her son was right. She could see something pink amongst the licking flames and thick smoke and more than that, it was moving.

*

Alice knew she couldn't, under any circumstances, cause a panic within the crowd. She muttered to Fergus that she fancied getting some candyfloss from the vendor outside, slipping away from her family and weaving towards the exit. As soon as she was clear of the throngs, the DI put her phone to her ear.

Matt answered immediately. "Sorry, Ma'am, I've still not located the suspect. The crowds are just too dense."

"Don't worry about that. Where are you?"

"I'm in the field by the car-park."

"Good, because I need you to listen very carefully. You have to put out that bonfire, and as quickly as possible. I'll join you just as soon as I can. I don't have time to explain why."

"O-Okay, I'll do my best."

Alice ended the call, shoving the phone back in her pocket.

Chapter 80

Pete was out of breath, his chest burning with exertion when he reached the field where his colleagues had gathered.

A fire engine, which must have been on standby during the display, had one of its hoses deployed, enabling one of the firemen to extinguish the last of the flames still flickering on the towering bonfire. A St John's Ambulance was also parked up on the grass, a team of paramedics just waiting for the signal to approach their patient. At least, Pete hoped against all hope, that the body his boss had spotted in the flames was actually still alive and requiring medical assistance.

Alice and Matt approached him. "It looks like the fire is nearly out. I think we should go in and search for her, before we send in the medics," she explained.

Pete nodded. "I agree. Let's go now, I don't think we've got any time to spare."

Alice jogged up to the fireman operating the hose. "Can we go in?" She cried above the noise of the gushing water.

He nodded. "But be careful!" He called back. "The structure won't be stable!"

Taking the face masks they were handed, the three detectives approached the smoking remnants of the fire. Matt was shining a powerful torch into the debris. Alice hoped her leather boots wouldn't melt in the still smouldering embers, as she stepped gingerly through the collapsing structure of sticks and soggy boards.

Despite the mask, Alice found herself coughing and her eyes stung, but finally, she noticed a glint of pink material amongst the detritus. She signalled to her colleagues.

Alice began elbowing aside lumps of charred wood until she found the long, human form that had been rolled onto the base of the bonfire. Tufts of blond hair were visible and the pink of a velour tracksuit. The woman's legs and arms had been bound, but despite the covering of smoke and soot, Alice could tell they'd found Caroline Torben. "She's over here! Help me carry her the hell out!"

*

Alice and her fellow rescuers had just been seen by a doctor at the emergency department at Ayr hospital. None of them were suffering any ill-effects from the smoke they inhaled.

Pete was slotting coins into the coffee machine. He approached Alice and Matt where they sat on plastic seats in the waiting room with three cups perilously balanced in his hands.

Alice took hers gratefully. "Thanks. I know we've been given the all-clear by the docs, but my throat still feels like I've swallowed razors." She had just heard that Fergus and Charlie were safely back home and allowed herself to relax just a fraction.

Matt chuckled, sipping the scorching liquid. "Yep, I'm going to be talking like Rod Stewart for a few days, that's for sure."

Pete dropped into the uncomfortable seat beside them. "Any news on Caroline?" His face was smeared with soot, but the deep worry lines were still evident beneath the grime.

Alice sighed. "The medics at the scene said she'd actually been right in the centre of the bonfire, which meant the flames hadn't reached her properly yet. But she's inhaled a hell of a lot of smoke. They reckon she was also heavily sedated, so they won't know the extent of her injuries until she's completely come round."

"It's an irony that a woman who chose to inhale so much smoke in her daily life was almost killed by it in the end."

Alice wasn't sure she could see the funny side of it just yet. "I wonder if that's why Janice did it, put the woman in the fire? An ironic death for a silly woman she hated?"

Pete shook his head. "It's too similar to Leroy Torben's fate for it to be that simple. Fires are just an extremely good way of getting rid of bodies. Janice must have found out there was a huge funeral pyre being lit practically on her doorstep this evening. It was too much of a temptation to resist taking advantage of."

Matt make a face. "But how the hell did she manage it? How did she transport Caroline to the football ground and then shift her body into the bonfire without anyone noticing? I mean, I was on her tail, for God's sake, she couldn't have known I'd get lost in the traffic chaos?"

Alice drained her cup. "She was desperate. Janice knew we were onto her and it was just a matter of time before we found Caroline. She had to get rid of the woman and fast. The support team located and examined her car. It looks like Caroline was being kept in the boot. Her captive had made a bloody good attempt to get out of it too."

Matt shuddered. "Poor Caroline."

"According to the organisers, right up until the bonfire was lit, their volunteers were bringing wheelbarrows full of old wood and furniture, even mattresses, to make the fire as big as possible. Janice must have grabbed a wheelbarrow, rolled Caroline into it, and then tipped her onto the bonfire. She would have known the woman was still alive. It's absolutely evil."

Matt crushed his plastic cup with feeling, tossing it into a nearby bin. "I'm so sorry I let her get away, boss. It's my fault Janice Kirk isn't in custody now."

Alice sighed. "I should have had more officers than just you on surveillance. But we didn't have sufficient proof to warrant the budget back then. It's nobody's fault. Besides, Caroline has been found and she's alive. That is all that matters right now."

Matt seemed to accept these words of reassurance.

Alice got wearily to her feet. "Now, I suggest you both go home and get a few hours of sleep. We'll have a busy day tomorrow. Besides, I've got to buy some candyfloss from somewhere, otherwise I'll have to face a very disappointed little boy."

Chapter 81

Caroline Torben was sitting up in her hospital bed, gulping down her second glass of water. "Take it easy," the nurse said tolerantly. "Your poor stomach has been badly irritated by all those sedatives pumped into it. Best to give it a little rest."

The patient rolled her eyes behind the nurse's back. "If you'd inhaled half a bonfire, you'd be necking the clear stuff too."

Pete suppressed a smile, waiting for the nurse to leave before saying, "how are you feeling, Caroline? You've been through one hell of an ordeal."

The woman coughed violently, as if to answer his question. Finally, the hacking ceased. "My throat's as dry as a desert and my chest is full of smoke. I've got some minor burns to the soles of my feet, where my trainers were starting to melt, but apart from that, the doc said I'd make a complete recovery."

"I'm really pleased. We were very worried about you for a while."

Caroline frowned deeply. "You and me both. I thought I was a goner, that's for sure. She's a psycho that woman, absolutely nothing behind the eyes."

"Did Janice Kirk tell you why she had kidnapped you?"

She took a deep breath which seemed painful. "Janice turned up on the doorstep of Vick's house at the crack of dawn. I'd not set eyes on her in years. Although, she had been a good friend of Vick's back in the day, or so I thought. She told me to come with her to the library, that she'd got some important information about my sister's will. Hinted she'd witnessed a copy of it and could show me who Victoria had left her money to, including the house."

Pete noted how clever Janice was, knowing this was exactly the kind of bait that would make Caroline bite.

"So, I got my coat and joined her in the car. She drove us to the library. It was a couple of hours before she needed to open up. Janice said she'd fetch the documents but first she'd make us both a nice cup of tea. Well, I drank the tea whilst I was waiting for her to come back with the document. That's the last I remember, until I woke up bound and gagged in the storeroom."

"She'd drugged you."

"Yep, and she did it again before moving me into her car boot. I thought if I kicked and wriggled and made enough noise, a passer-by might hear me and call you lot." Her eyes glistened with tears for the first time in recalling her ordeal. "Your detective inspector told me the car was in Janice's garage the whole time. Nobody was ever going to hear me."

Pete took her hand and squeezed it. "So why did she imprison you, try to kill you?"

Caroline dabbed her eyes with a tissue. "She thought I knew something. When she came to feed me water, she kept muttering about not being able to trust me to keep quiet. If I was more reliable, she could've let me go."

"What is it that you know? You've got to tell us. This woman is incredibly dangerous, we've got to stop her."

She blushed, looking suddenly uncomfortable. "I had a lot of time to think while I was strung up like a turkey in the boot of that car. It happened a good few years ago now, but I reckon I may know what Janice was so worried about."

Chapter 82

Despite getting a few hours of precious sleep, Alice hardly felt rested at all. She supposed there'd be time for R&R when this was all over.

Pete and Matt didn't look much better but the ladies in her team at least looked bright-eyed and bushy-tailed. Sharon could be relied upon to recognise when it was time for a caffeine hit. A tray of coffees and pastries awaited the detective inspector as she entered the office floor that morning.

She picked up a cardboard cup on her way to the front desk. "Morning everyone. I hope you managed to get some sleep last night?"

"It sounds like the rest of you had plenty of excitement," Holly commented, she looked a little disappointed not to have been involved.

But Alice was relieved, she needed at least some of her team to be fresh for the day. "You could say that. The good news is that Caroline Torben is going to be fine and she's already provided Pete with a signed statement."

A smattering of applause rippled round the room. Alice was glad to see her officers were genuinely pleased the woman had been found alive. "The bad news is that Janice Kirk remains at large. We have her car in the pound, where it will be examined thoroughly by forensics. When we do arrest her, we'll have a water tight case of kidnapping, ABH and attempted murder to charge her with."

"She must have left the fireworks display last night on foot," Matt added. "Could she have walked home to Monkton?"

"We've got officers watching her house and the library. There's been no sign of her turning up at either yet. We have her image circulating amongst local police patrols and an all-ports warning out against her. Although, her passport is still at her house. We'll find the woman eventually."

"So, what has this whole business been about?" Sharon asked in exasperation. "You were going to tell us what Rosaline Golding revealed to you when we found out Janice had gone on the run?"

Alice took a gulp of coffee and rested her weight on the desk. "Rosaline and her family met Victoria Braden and Janice Kirk when they all had loved ones killed in the M77 crash in 1996. Stephen Crammond and Janice Kirk were particularly enraged by the meagre sentence eventually handed out to the driver of the HGV, David Murcia."

"But *why* was Janice so angry?" Sharon asked.

"Because Janice had been having an affair with Greg Braden for two years before the crash."

The other officers let out a collective gasp.

"Yep, and Rosaline doesn't think Victoria ever knew about it. Which explains why they remained friends afterwards. Victoria and Geraldine Crammond were prepared to move on from the disappointment of Murcia walking free from court, but Janice and Stephen were not. Mr Crammond was a businessman with money and connections. He continued to try and find ways to punish David Murcia through legal means for several months after the appeal. But to no avail. At first, Rosaline thought her father had let the matter drop, then, one day in October 1997, she found out he hadn't let it drop, not at all."

"He took matters into his own hands?" Pete suggested.

Alice nodded. "Rosaline hadn't been told anything about her father's plans. She'd had to defer her entry into the Glasgow School of Art to look after her mother, who spent most days in her bed at this stage, just over a year after she lost her son. One day, Rosaline was tidying her mother's room, when she spotted a man working out in the garden. He was chopping branches off the old oak trees that lined the garden with a powered saw of some kind.

She came downstairs and found Janice and Victoria seated at their kitchen table, with her father opposite them. When she entered, they looked up at her, their expressions guilty. Rosaline knew they'd been plotting, like the three witches in Macbeth."

"Victoria was involved too?" Pete's tone was surprised. He remembered the prim and proper widow who had also grieved the loss of her only son.

Alice nodded solemnly. "Rosaline thinks Janice poured poison in her friend's ear, telling her how David Murcia had taken everything from her; her husband, her financial security and more than that; her chance of ever having a child. It was clear to everyone at the time that Victoria would never dream of re-marrying, even though she was only in her early thirties."

"So this group wanted revenge on the man?"

"Oh yes, it had become an obsession, certainly for Stephen and Janice. Rosaline's father had a private investigator on speed-dial, he knew Murcia had struggled to find work since the accident. He'd been stripped of his HGV licence. The man had started a small gardening business, one man and a van. This seemed like an opportunity to lure him to Hill House, where it was remote and secluded."

Holly shuddered. "They wanted to murder him?"

"By this stage, Rosaline said that revenge had become an inevitability for each of them. It was as if they were caught in some kind of limbo from which there was no escape until Murcia was properly punished." She finished her coffee, her mouth still feeling parched. "When Rosaline found them in the kitchen, her father told her she must leave the house and pretend she'd never seen the women there that day and certainly not the workman in the garden. He insisted, became angry with his daughter when she refused. But Rosaline was adamant, she wasn't going to leave her mother. Whatever they had planned, they'd have to do it with her present.

Rosaline was secretly hoping this would make her father give up his crazy idea, see how mad it was. But he didn't. The three of them continued with their plan as if the young woman wasn't even there.

Stephen had given a false name to Murcia, when he booked his services in the garden that day. He had no idea he was on the property of the family whose son he had killed in such horrific circumstances. They hoped that he wouldn't recognise Janice, who had only been to the trial on one or two days."

"Was it Janice who killed him?" Sharon asked in surprise, thinking of the bulky frame of David Murcia seen clearly from his photos in the press, compared to the slight figure of the librarian.

"In a way, yes," Alice continued. "She prepared him a cup of tea. She balanced it on a saucer and carried it down the garden to where Murcia was hard at work. He put down his saw and accepted the drink. She waited while he finished it, taking the empty cup back up to the house. Within ten minutes, Murcia had collapsed to the ground unconscious. The tea had contained crushed Ketamine and lots of sugar, to disguise the taste."

"The horse sedative?" Sharon asked, knowing it was now a popular drug of choice on the streets of Glasgow.

"Yes, Stephen knew plenty of horse trainers. It wasn't difficult for him to get hold of the drug." Alice contorted her features in disgust. "What happened next has haunted Rosaline for twenty five years. She stood at the kitchen window, almost mesmerised by the awful events unfolding. She supposed her father and the other women improvised, using the tools at their disposal. When Murcia was incapacitated, they calmly walked down the garden to where he lay, like they were taking an afternoon stroll. Stephen picked up the man's chainsaw and protective mask and proceeded to dismember Murcia's body, whilst the women simply stood and watched."

Chapter 83

When Holly returned from the ladies toilets, her face was as white as a sheet.

"Are you okay?" Alice asked.

She nodded, obviously not trusting herself yet to speak.

"Where did they bury the body?" Pete asked.

"According to Rosaline, it was beneath the furthest oak tree in the line," Alice replied. "I've sent a forensic team out to dig for traces of it this afternoon."

"Wasn't that the same tree where the body of Stephen's brother was found? How odd to bury him there?" Sharon commented.

Alice shrugged. "The place obviously had significance for Stephen Crammond."

"Somewhere he'd committed a crime before," Pete added with feeling. "It's clear the man was a psychopath."

"Driven mad by grief perhaps?" Matt suggested.

"I think Janice and Stephen were both perfectly capable of murder, even before they lost people they loved. Victoria I think was just weak, easily manipulated by a stronger character than her," Pete said wearily.

Alice was inclined to agree with him.

"What about Victoria's sister? Did she know about the murder?" Holly asked.

"No, she didn't know the details," Pete explained. "She told me earlier this morning, that when she was back at the bar in Spain, she got a strange phone call from Victoria. It was about five years ago, very possibly when Maria Silva was working for them. Victoria was in a panic. She was telling Caroline that someone had come looking for David Murcia, had knocked on her door and asked if she knew where he was, a journalist she thinks. Caroline told her she knew it had stirred up bad memories but not to worry about it, because she didn't know what happened to him, did she? The man had left Glasgow and never come back. He had no family and few friends, so nobody knew or cared where he'd gone to.

But Victoria wouldn't be consoled. She kept telling Caroline she knew where Murcia was, that he was at Stephen Crammond's house. Caroline thought her sister had finally cracked. She told her to fix herself a brandy and calm down, to tell the journalist nothing, to keep whatever she knew a secret, like they'd kept the secret about Leroy being Victoria's son. How that had worked well for them all these years. Nobody had ever suspected. Then she ended the call. The next time they spoke, her sister never mentioned the hysterical incident again. But now, Caroline thinks Maria must have overheard the conversation."

Alice grimaced. "If Maria overheard all that, she would have had an awful lot of material she could use for the new, far more lucrative business she'd decided to branch out into."

"Blackmail," Sharon said with a shudder.

Chapter 84

Alice checked with the desk sergeant that Maria Silva had been allocated a duty solicitor. She would be scheduling her official questioning for later that day. When she returned to the office floor upstairs, she found her colleagues waiting for her, eager expressions on their faces.

"I want Holly and Pete to question Maria. You are going to need a set of well-prepared questions. She isn't going to have the hot-shot Carmel Cartwright by her side this time. I have a feeling she's going to want to dish the dirt on the Goldings. But first, you're going to need to know exactly what Rosaline told me about the young woman in the cell downstairs." Alice rolled up her chair.

"This is only Rosaline's side of the story," Pete added, in the interests of balance.

"Yes," Alice replied, "but I got the feeling she was ready to confess. She's been carrying a heavy burden of guilt for a long time. I believe what she told me was the truth as she saw it."

"When did Maria first come to Scotland?" Sharon asked.

"She arrived in Glasgow two and a half years ago. Maria continued to work in bars and restaurants in Spain until she'd saved enough to travel. But she'd never forgotten the information she'd picked up from her time at Caroline and Rick's bar. Even from one side of the conversation, she knew that Leroy Torben, the boy her boss had always referred to as her son, was in reality the child of Caroline's sister.

Maria also knew that someone who nobody in the UK could trace, a man called David Murcia, was at the property of someone called Stephen Crammond. For someone as crafty, or desperate, as Maria, this was all she needed. After arriving in Glasgow and kipping on the sofa of friends, the first people she decided to seek out were Leroy and Victoria. She wanted to know if there would be any money to be gained in telling Caroline's sister she knew their little secret."

"Did she approach Victoria Braden?" Holly asked.

Alice shook her head. "It wasn't difficult to find Leroy, his name was unusual and she knew Caroline came from West Kilbride. She searched for his name on social media and found out he played for a local football team and that he worked at Rossmore Garage. Maria knew what he looked like from a football team photo on Instagram. She waited one day outside the garage and followed him home, taking the same bus.

When Maria saw the shabby semi-detached house and the old Hyundai on the drive, she knew there wasn't any real money to be made out of Victoria Braden. She sensed there were bigger fish to fry in this story she'd heard. But she felt sorry for Leroy. He was the same age as her, and Maria felt he deserved to know the truth about his parents. Leroy wasn't someone who'd been given many privileges, much like herself. It wasn't fair that he'd been lied to, but she left it at that."

"Maria turned her attention to the Crammond family, instead?" Pete suggested.

"Yes, Maria was working in bars for minimum wage and was getting restless to make some proper cash. She searched the name, Stephen Crammond online and discovered he'd lived at Hill House, Fairlie. The man had been dead for a few years, his wife more recently, but his daughter and her family now seemed to live in the property. She could tell there was money in this Crammond clan. The house looked huge from pictures posted in Google images.

When Maria performed a search on the Golding family, the daughter's married name, she discovered, to her great delight, that they were looking for a live-in au pair at Hill House."

"She applied for the job like a shot, I bet." Sharon frowned with distaste.

"Yes, she did. Rosaline and Roger were getting desperate by this stage. There didn't seem to be any suitable young people who wanted to live in such a remote place as Hill House. Maria seemed keen and hardworking. They gave her a month's trial and she stayed on. But as time went by, Rosaline said Maria started to become insolent towards her. She would take expensive food from the fridge and wine from the cellar and barely apologise for it. When Rosaline finally confronted her about the unacceptable behaviour, Maria told her she could do as she wished. She knew what Rosaline's father had done with David Murcia at Hill House."

"That must have come as a nasty shock," Matt said with feeling.

"It certainly did. Of course, Maria didn't know the details at all, but she was fishing. The look on Rosaline's face must have said it all. She asked what Maria wanted to keep quiet. The au-pair said she wanted more money and to keep living at Hill House for as long as she wished. Rosaline agreed and began paying her privately. But part of the deal was that Maria wouldn't tell Roger what she knew. As far as he was concerned, Maria was simply their au-pair."

"So, Roger never knew about any of it?"

"No, and he still doesn't know much, I expect. It's going to come as a terrible blow."

"But what about Leroy? How did he end up dead?" Sharon looked puzzled.

"Maria had contacted Leroy by email, not long after arriving at Hill House. She discovered he had a work account on the garage's network. She began a correspondence with him. These conversations must have been lost along with his phone and laptop, incinerated in the fire, I expect. Maria was young, attractive and a similar age to Leroy, it can't have been difficult to gain his trust.

I don't believe she meant him any malice at this stage, she just wanted him to know the truth. She didn't have any friends in the area, was probably lonely. Blackmail is a lonely business. She began suggesting to him in messages that he should find out who his birth dad was. That he should ask Victoria to give him more information, that she sensed his aunt had something to hide. She hoped the young man would get the truth out of Victoria that he wasn't really Caroline's son.

Eventually, Leroy took the bait. He went searching through Victoria's room when she was out. He found a box under her bed with dozens of newspaper clippings about the car crash that killed Greg. But also about the trial of David Murcia, and later, a newspaper article from an investigative journalist, speculating as to what had ever become of the man, who'd disappeared without a trace in 1997."

"So the plan backfired on Maria. She wanted Leroy to know Victoria was his real mother, but not to find out all about the trial and the disappearance of the truck driver," Pete added.

"Yes, and worse than that," Alice explained, "Leroy found a photo in an old copy of the Herald, with all the families of the crash victims standing in a group outside the courthouse during the trial. He recognised Janice Kirk, his aunt's boss, standing amongst them. Leroy decided to ask *her* what it all meant, not trusting his aunt would tell him the full truth."

Chapter 85

"Well, Janice wouldn't have liked that," Sharon said matter-of-factly.

"No, according to Rosaline, she didn't. Leroy came to see her at the library, with all sorts of questions about the time he was born and the car crash. Janice fobbed him off as much as she could, but it had unnerved her, how keen he was to rake up the past.

Within a few days, Janice had decided to contact Rosaline again, for the first time in twenty-five years. She wanted to warn her that someone was digging into what happened back in '97. Rosaline invited Janice to the house one afternoon. They were discussing Leroy. But Maria was listening. She joined the women and admitted it was her who had tipped Leroy off about the strange circumstances of his birth.

Janice was livid. She was also angry to discover Maria seemed to know so much about their secret. But they quickly decided between them, that it was Leroy who had become the problem, the issue that needed to be dealt with. Maria's silence could be bought."

Holly felt overwhelmed with sadness. "That poor boy. He'd been lied to all his life and when he tries to find out about his heritage, he signs his own death warrant. It's tragic."

"Did Rosaline really go along with all this? I mean, I know Janice has a screw loose, and Maria is out only for herself, but Rosaline has young children, something of a conscience, surely?" Pete shook his head sadly.

"You're right, Pete," Alice continued. "Rosaline thought they could persuade Leroy to leave the past alone. Her idea was to contact the young man and offer to help him trace his roots – pay to get a DNA ancestry test done, that kind of thing. It's why Rosaline decided to sponsor the football club where he played. She'd already approached him after a Friday night training session. It's why she tried to talk to him again at the semi-final in July. She'd been introducing herself as an old friend of the family, suggesting she might sponsor Leroy personally, as he had so much talent and potential.

But Leroy was suspicious. He'd recognised Rosaline from the photo in the paper of the families of the crash victims. She'd not changed all that much. Her approach just made him more curious."

"So Janice had to take more decisive action," Sharon said with a note of anger.

"Janice suggested they invite Leroy to Hill House, talk to him together, try to persuade him to let the issue drop, perhaps explain a little of what happened, but not everything. The day when Roger was away at a conference seemed perfect. They planned to offer to pay for a DNA search that might track down Leroy's real father, give him the money, there and then. Rosaline thinks Janice already suspected who his father was, but that was irrelevant, her real plan was to get rid of the young man anyway." Alice sighed wistfully.

"Maria messaged him to see if he would meet her that Wednesday afternoon. She had already built up a certain trust between them. Leroy told his boss he had a doctor's appointment but he met Maria instead. He brought his laptop along because he wanted to show her what he'd already found out about his aunt and the crash.

The au-pair drove him to Hill House. Janice and Rosaline were waiting. The children were kept well out of the way. Rosaline said there was no plan, not on her part anyway. They talked with Leroy all afternoon, explaining the trauma of the accident and the trial that followed, assured him it had nothing to do with his parentage. That they would help him answer those questions. Leroy wouldn't let the issue drop. He was even speculating at one point whether David Murcia had been his father.

Janice realised the situation was getting out of hand. As the evening drew in, she poured their visitor another cup of tea. Into it, she'd dissolved a number of sedative powders. The young man drank it eagerly. Within half an hour, his head was slumped on the kitchen table.

Maria put the children to bed whilst they discussed what to do. Janice said they needed more time to figure out what to do with Leroy. They needed somewhere to keep him until they came up with a plan. To Rosaline's shame, it was she who suggested the walk-in fridge. The woman swore to me that when they dragged Leroy inside and locked the door, the fridge had been switched off, much like Pete and I found it the other day. But as they were leaving, Janice must have stooped down and turned on the switch."

Holly gasped. "That woman is evil."

"They returned to the kitchen and continued to talk for hours, over a bottle of whisky. Rosaline claims they'd decided to offer Leroy a big package of money to keep him sweet. He was saving for a new car, so they'd buy him one. He'd never been abroad, so they'd send him to Ibiza for a weekend. All the time, Janice must have known the boy was slowly dying. Because by the time they went back to the stables to check on him, a few hours later, young Leroy had frozen to death."

Chapter 86

"Jeez," Sharon genuinely shivered, despite the warmth of the room. "Leroy must have died of hypothermia. I hope he was still unconscious when it happened."

"So do I," Holly added. "It's just so sad."

Alice nodded. "There were recriminations for a while, about who had turned the refrigeration system on, but Rosaline said it didn't matter much. They'd all known that if they weren't going to the police about what happened twenty five years before, then Leroy needed to be silenced. Permanently. Besides, they only had until morning to decide how to get rid of the body. Roger would be returning by lunchtime.

It was actually Rosaline who came up with the idea of the fire. They didn't have time to dig a grave and anyway, she thought Roger would notice the disturbed ground. By this stage, Rosaline was growing to hate the house, she thought it might be an excuse to finally leave.

The plan was set. They used one of the gas cylinders from the garage, hooking it up to the old stove in the north-wing and leaving the valve open. Janice set a sort of make-shift timer by lighting some fuel in a wire bin and waiting for the gas leak to explode. They placed Leroy's body in the centre of it all, along with his phone and laptop. The explosion and resultant fire was meant to incinerate any traces of him and the devices."

"It was a big risk for Rosaline and Maria to stay in the house, and the *children*, too," Matt stated.

"They didn't have any other choice," Alice sighed. "They had to make it look like an accident. Even if the authorities found out it was arson, who would suspect the people who were in the house when it happened? Especially with their own children. Maria volunteered to stay in the north-wing, then she could keep the fire going if anything went wrong. Rosaline was to keep the children as far away as possible from the flames. Janice drove home under cover of darkness.

The plan almost worked. They knew the smoke alarms would go off eventually and they had to get out of the house when they did and call the fire brigade, otherwise it would seem suspicious. But it was wet that morning and the fire engines arrived very quickly. The fire didn't burn for as long or with as much intensity as they'd hoped. In reality, it takes incredibly high temperatures to burn a human body to ash."

Holly's face had turned a sickly green again. "If the fire had been allowed to burn on, we may never have found Leroy's body at all."

"No, and that's how our job goes sometimes. A murderer makes a mistake and then we become involved, simple as that."

"What will Rosaline and Maria be charged with?" Matt asked with curiosity.

"If we find the remains of David Murcia in the garden, Rosaline will be charged with two counts of accessory to murder, arson and insurance fraud. Maria will be charged with a single count of accessory to murder, arson and with blackmail against the Goldings. They'll both go to prison for a long time. With the forensic evidence we have and Rosaline's testimony, the case is water-tight."

Chapter 87

Sharon was about to ask about Janice Kirk's charges when the phone on the DI's desk began to ring.

Alice dived to answer it. She listened intently to the caller, jotting down notes at the same time. She placed the receiver carefully in its cradle. "That was one of the PCs who I sent to check with the bus station and the taxi companies in the town, for any sightings of Janice Kirk last night. Apparently, one of the taxi drivers he spoke with had a fare last evening from the football ground. A single female, late fifties, who was caked in mud and sweat. He almost refused to take her, until she offered him double the money in cash."

Pete jumped to his feet. "Did he provide the location he drove her to?"

Alice waved the scrap of paper. "Better than that. I've got an address. It's in Wemyss Bay."

Pete grabbed the paper and scanned the address for himself. "Shit. She went to Donny Jones's house."

*

The drive would take them half an hour, but the traffic was thick. Alice drummed her fingers on the dashboard as they jerked their way long the A78. They had a couple of local uniforms placed in a squad car outside the property in Wemyss Bay in case anyone came and went in the meantime.

"Do you think Donny is in danger from Janice?" Pete turned to his boss, shifting his eyes from the road for a second.

"I think everyone's in danger from Janice Kirk. Let's just hope she's gone to this man because she needs him to shelter her, not for any other reason."

Pete gulped. He hoped exactly the same. "They worked together at the library for years. Donny was her boss. Hopefully that means she considers him a friend?"

Alice liked Pete's optimism but she suspected that for people like Janice, they didn't really have true friends, just people who could serve a function for them. If they stopped being useful, they became expendable.

Finally, the queues ahead seemed to disperse and Pete was able to put his foot down. The scenery flashing past Alice's window should have been uplifting, but on this occasion, she could only concentrate on the relentless approach of the tarmac ahead.

They arrived at the house just before 12pm. Alice nodded to the policemen positioned in the car outside as they approached the gate to the Jones property. Pete pushed it open and they climbed the steps to the front door.

Donny Jones appeared swiftly at their knock. The man looked confused and stressed, but was otherwise physically unharmed.

"I'm DI Mann and this is DS Falmer. Is Janice Kirk here, sir?"

He nodded tentatively, his voice lowered. "She arrived on my doorstep last evening, in an awful state. Her shoes were caked in mud, she had nothing but her handbag. Not even a coat. I asked what on earth had happened but she wouldn't tell me. Still won't."

"Is she still on the premises?" Alice asked, hope tightening her chest like a band.

"Yes, she's in the spare room. Been in there practically since she arrived. I haven't even been able to tempt her with breakfast and I made blueberry pancakes, too."

Alice stepped over the threshold. "Could you wait in the sitting room please, Mr Jones."

He looked puzzled, but did as he was told.

The detectives approached the only closed door in the bungalow. Alice knocked firmly. "Janice! Are you in there?"

A muffled sound came from within. Alice nodded to Pete and turned the handle, making sure her stance was solid as the door swung open and hit the wall.

Janice Kirk was seated on a neatly made single bed. She was still wearing mud splattered nylon trousers and her feet were in laddered tights. Her light blue cotton jumper worn over a cream blouse was stained and her hair was a tangle of ash grey. She glanced up at the officers, a hint of amusement in her expression. "Expecting me to make a run for it, were you?"

Alice felt the anger surge through her tired body. "Janice Kirk. I am charging you with the murder of David Murcia, Victoria Braden and Leroy Torben and with the kidnap and attempted murder of Caroline Torben. You do not have to say anything. But it may harm your defence if you do not mention when questioned something which you later rely on in court."

The woman rose to her feet and offered her wrists to Alice. "Don't you want to cuff me first?"

"That won't be necessary," she replied, through gritted teeth. "Why did you come here, Janice?"

The woman let out a hollow laugh. "I'm not a fool Inspector Mann, I know when the game is up. I've got nothing but the clothes I'm standing up in, my house will be surrounded by police and I've the kind of savings you'd expect from a provincial library manager. I was waiting for you to come for me. Also," she said with a glint in her soulless eyes. "I thought if the secrets were finally coming out, you may as well know them all."

Alice wondered what the woman meant, but wasted no time in ushering her down the steps and out to the waiting squad car. Pete and the uniforms would take her straight to Pitt Street. Janice Kirk was too big a fish for their little police station.

Donny Jones had joined her on the driveway, watching as his old friend was assisted into the rear seat of the police car and driven away at some speed.

"Could you come back inside, Detective Inspector? I think there's something I really need to tell you about."

Chapter 88

The sitting room was spacious and pleasant, with a wonderful view across Wemyss Bay. Alice accepted a cup of tea from her host and watched him carefully as he took the armchair opposite.

"I heard what you charged Janice with. I can't get my head around it. All those people? I'd hardly think her capable?" He smoothed a hand over his bald pate.

"I can't talk about the charges Ms Kirk is facing. Now, what was it you wanted to tell me?" She sipped the tea, it was most welcome.

He cleared his throat awkwardly. "I don't really know how to frame this, but I think I may have been the father of Leroy Torben."

Alice almost spat out her mouthful. "What do you mean?"

He sighed heavily. "It was twenty-five years ago. Anton and I had been a couple for quite some time. The truth was that we were keen to have a child. But back then, two men adopting wasn't heard of in this country."

Alice nodded, allowing him to continue.

"I'd known Victoria and her husband wanted children but they'd never managed to conceive. I'd given Victoria plenty of time off for doctors' appointments. Then she lost her husband in that awful car accident. Poor Victoria was devastated. She told me once that the worst part of it was that the chance for her to ever have a baby was gone. She knew she'd never marry again but it was Greg who had the medical problem, not her." He grimaced at the memory, placing his floral mug on a side table. "I waited until she was looking better, more settled. This was maybe a year after the crash. Then, I suggested she have a baby with me and Anton. She would carry the child, obviously, and Anton and I would bring him or her up here, in this lovely house, with walks on the beach and lots of love. Vick would have been in the child's life too, she would have been as close as a mother to the baby." The man's eyes glistened with moisture.

"What did Victoria think of the idea?" Alice wondered how anyone in her position would react to such a suggestion.

"She was more enthusiastic than I had predicted. She wasn't offended at all by the idea. She came here a few times for dinner and we discussed the practicalities, even devised a kind of contract. One thing Vick was adamant about though. She wanted *me* to be the biological father, not Anton."

Alice was suddenly confused. If Anton had been Leroy's dad, it would have explained everything.

"It was because she knew me so well I suppose, thought I was a gentle, thoughtful man. The kind of person she wished her future child to be."

Alice thought this care over the child's potential genes ironic, as a few months before these discussions, Victoria had taken part in the brutal, cold-blooded murder of a man. But she said nothing.

He suddenly blushed, right to the top of his scalp. "We set aside a weekend, back in the early months of 1998. I supplied Victoria with a vial of my, ahem, semen. She took it home with her. We had read some relevant publications in the library during break times. Victoria didn't need much in the way of equipment. She did the 'procedure', by herself."

"So what happened?"

"Well, we waited a few months and Victoria took a test." He looked Alice directly in the eye. "It was negative. She showed me herself."

"Did you actually seen her pee on the stick?"

"Well, no, she disappeared off into the staff toilets and came out with it. But I trusted her, you see."

Alice sighed, knowing this to be a mistake many people made in their lives.

"Anton and I were very disappointed, obviously. But then, my mother died and I took it very badly. Anton helped me through my grief and, to be honest, we forgot all about our baby plans."

"Then, Victoria's sister gives birth to a little boy, about nine months later."

Donny nodded vigorously. "Yes, well, it did seem a huge coincidence. But then, I swear Vick never looked pregnant during all those months and then, when I saw the baby, well, it set my mind at rest."

"Because the baby was mixed race."

"Yes, because the baby was mixed race. I never really thought about the episode again, not until your two officers arrived on my doorstep. I mean, I still don't think the child could have been mine, but I've been thinking about nothing else these last few weeks. If Victoria really was the child's mother, then he could have been mine, couldn't he?"

Alice nodded. "I'll send an officer over here in the next few hours to take a DNA swab. We'll compare it to Leroy's and then we'll know, once and for all." She got to her feet. "Now, if you'll excuse me, I've got a lot of work to do."

Donny accompanied her to the front door. "If he was mine, why did she do it? Why go to all that trouble to convince everyone the baby was Caroline's? Why lie to me and Anton?"

"Because she desperately wanted a baby, Mr Jones. Not one to share with you and your husband. A baby she could keep in *her* house, within *her* family. You provided her with the perfect opportunity to get one."

Chapter 89

Pete helped Caroline Torben to her feet. He pulled back the curtains around her cubicle and gathered together her bags. "Now, do you need a wheelchair to get down to the lobby?"

The woman glanced at him as if he was mad. "Of course not. I'm not an invalid." As if on cue, she coughed violently. "I just need to get this bloody smoke cleared from my lungs. The Mediterranean air will help."

Pete couldn't help raising his eyebrows at this comment.

"I know, I know. I've spent the last forty years filling my lungs with toxic smoke, it's a bit rich of me to be complaining about it now. But I promise you, DS Falmer, I'm never touching another ciggie, not for as long as I live. I'm going to make my Rick give up too."

Pete smiled, he wasn't sure he entirely believed it. He picked up her bags. "At least let me help you get your stuff downstairs."

"Okay, if you insist." Caroline linked her arm through his, leaning some of her weight on his broad form.

Pete wasn't sure the woman needed this much assistance, but he was happy enough to oblige. He was just relieved she'd survived her ordeal, one the detective counted himself partly responsible for.

"Donny Jones, the man who was Victoria's boss back in the late nineties, has submitted a DNA sample to be compared with Leroy's. He said he provided a vial of sperm to your sister in early 1998. They'd planned for Victoria to have a baby for him and his partner, but she told him the insemination had been unsuccessful. Now, he thinks she may have lied to them."

Caroline shuffled along the bright corridor in silence for a few moments, taking this information in. Finally, she nodded. "I think that sounds plausible. If Vick had stolen her boss's baby, she'd have been very keen to keep it a secret. If I said the baby was *mine*, it would've put him off the trail. Quite clever, really."

"Yes, it was, but I don't see how it could have been the case, because Leroy was mixed race and Donny Jones is as white as the driven snow. My boss and I had wondered if the baby might have been David Murcia's? Victoria may have seduced him, in order for him to give her the child that the man had prevented her from having by killing her husband?"

Caroline tutted loudly. "There's *no way* Victoria would have had that man's baby. She *loathed* him." Her voice cracked. "Leroy wasn't Murcia's child. He was a lovely boy."

Pete didn't argue, not wanting to intrude on the woman's grief.

"Besides," she went on, when she'd recovered her composure. "There's no reason why Donny couldn't have been Leroy's dad."

Pete crinkled his brow. "How come?"

Caroline shot him a look, as if he had just come down in the last shower. "Because mine and Vick's mum was black, that's why. Her parents were born in Guyana and she had skin as dark and silky as the finest mink. Beautiful, she was."

Pete stopped walking. "What? But how come you and Victoria were so pale-skinned?" The detective suddenly felt a complete fool, and an ignorant one at that.

"Our father was of Irish descent and had a great mop of ginger hair. Victoria was a little darker than me, but we both took after the Celtic side. They say, don't they, that these traits can skip a generation. They certainly did in the case of our Leroy. The picture of our mother he was, I always told Victoria so."

Pete said nothing, but began walking again, supporting the woman beside him as they approached the lifts to the ground floor.

Chapter 90

Alice had lit candles for their visitors and placed some bowls of nuts and crisps on the coffee table, mostly for Sharon's benefit.

Fergus entered their living room with a freshly opened bottle of wine. "Charlie's fast asleep, all that stimulation has knocked him out!"

Pete chuckled from his seat on the sofa, accepting a top-up to his glass. "He can join the club, it seems kicking a ball around the garden with a toddler is more tiring than you'd think."

Sharon nudged her boyfriend's arm. "You need to build up your stamina," she joked.

Alice smiled. Today was the first time in weeks that she'd relaxed with Fergus and Charlie. She was still exhausted, but happy.

Fergus perched on the arm of Alice's chair. "So, it was Janice Kirk's bail hearing today. How did it go?"

Pete glanced at his boss, as if looking for permission to talk shop on a social occasion. Alice shrugged her shoulders, as if in defeat. "The judge refused to grant bail. I'm not surprised. The charges against her are just too serious."

Sharon gulped the smooth wine, trying her best to savour it. "Yep, Janice, Maria and Rosaline will all be on remand until the trial. It doesn't matter how expensive Mrs Golding's lawyers are, they are all going to prison for many, many years."

Alice agreed. "The remains of David Murcia were found in a shallow grave on the perimeter of the woods at Hill House. We've managed to find a relative in Barbados to compare the DNA with."

"Speaking of DNA, have we had the results back on Leroy's paternity?" Pete asked.

Alice answered this question. "They came back from the lab this morning. Donny Jones was definitely his father. They've sent a letter out to him to confirm."

"Imagine that," Fergus whistled. "To have had a son for all those years and to only find out after he had passed away."

"It's tragic," Alice agreed.

Sharon placed her glass on a coaster and scooped a handful of nuts. "The thing I don't understand, is why Janice had to kill Victoria Braden? Leroy was dead by this time, so surely their secret was safe?"

Alice frowned. "I think that after Leroy's death, Victoria had begun to unravel. She must have suspected his death had something to do with their violent secret. I think she spoke with Janice about coming clean. Perhaps Victoria's conscience had finally come calling. With Leroy gone, she might as well confess everything to the authorities."

"Well, Janice couldn't have had that," Pete said with feeling.

"No, from the evidence we've gathered so far, Janice purchased a four inch kitchen knife and went to Victoria's property on Seamill Road with the express purpose of killing her. The dining room window was easy enough to break. Janice came gloved up for the job. Victoria put up a bit of a fight, but not enough to overpower her boss."

Sharon tutted. "So much bloodshed. I suppose once she'd started killing, it became easier. Maria must have told Janice she'd got all her information from Caroline's phone call back in Spain. Janice must have decided Victoria's sister was a liability who knew too much. We kept questioning her, so it was bound to come out in the end."

Pete felt that pang of guilt once more. "Well, Caroline is safely back in Almeria now. She sent me a postcard, addressed to the station, would you believe. *14 days without a fag*, it read."

The others started laughing and Pete joined in. Alice placed her glass on a side table to stop the wine spilling over. Her first case with her new team had been a tough one. But they'd made it through. Perhaps she'd stick around for a few more.

Three months later

Roger Golding stood at the top of the slope and surveyed his domain. It was mid-winter and the trees in the copse had shed their leaves, meaning the view down to the water was even clearer.

He puffed up his chest with pride. The ugly hole the police had dug all those months ago had been filled in and a new sapling planted there. Although there had been no insurance money in the end, Roger had used all his considerable savings to rebuild Hill House.

He employed skilled local craftsmen and the best designers to bring the gutted shell of the north-wing back to its previous glory. Rosaline was in prison. She'd be in there for decades to come. His wife may have left the deeds to the house to their children, but that was fine. Jacob loved it there. He had his pony in the stables and, in time, Roger would buy two more, for Cassie and Joe.

Hill House may have belonged to the Crammonds for all those generations, but it was *his* now. His children were Goldings and their stewardship of this piece of land would mark a new era for the place. Maybe Roger would even bring a new wife to live here too, once the divorce was finalised. Not Anne from the office, but someone younger, who may give him more children, in time.

He had many plans for their future in this house, which he'd fallen in love with the moment he visited on that Spring day fifteen years earlier. Hill House would be the great estate it was always intended to be. What a legacy that would be to pass on to his children.

If you enjoyed this novel, please take a few moments to write a brief review or give a rating. Reviews and ratings really help to introduce new readers to my books and this allows me to keep on writing.
Many thanks,

Katherine.

If you would like to find out more about my books and read my reviews and articles then please visit my blog, TheRetroReview at:

www.KatherinePathak.wordpress.com

To find out about new releases and special offers follow me on Twitter:

@KatherinePathak

Or on my Facebook author page: Katherine Pathak

Most of all, thanks for reading!

If you enjoyed this book, have you read any of the original DCI Dani Bevan series?

Against A Dark Sky

Book 1 in the DCI Dani Bevan series

They died thirty years ago, but the case is not closed...

Five walkers set out to climb Ben Lomond on a fine October day. Within hours, the weather has taken a turn for the worst. The group find themselves lost on the mountain. Two of the climbers manage to make it back down and call for help.
The following day a body is found. One of the female climbers has been strangled and another man is missing without trace.
DCI Dani Bevan is called to the Loch Lomond town of Ardyle to lead the case. It quickly becomes clear that Bevan must dig into the events of a similar tragedy which occurred on the hills thirty years earlier in order to find the killer.
This investigation requires the DCI to face up to the ghosts of her own tragic past, and to endeavour to put them behind her, once and for all.

On A Dark Sea

Book 2 in the DCI Dani Bevan series

A missing girl.

A broken marriage.

Who can you trust?

When fourteen year old Maisie Riddell goes missing from a Glasgow High School, DCI Dani Bevan knows she needs to act fast, particularly as the Headmistress is the wife of her DS, Phil Boag. But as the inquiry into the girl's disappearance deepens, Bevan finds herself caught in the fall-out from a broken marriage, unsure of whose word she can really trust. The DCI is required to take her search to Norway, in order to discover the truth about Maisie's secret life.

Meanwhile, Bill Hutchison's unauthorised investigation into a brutal murder in Stonehaven places him in terrible danger. With Dani wrapped up in the Riddell case, who is there left to help him...?

A Dark Shadow Falls

Book 3 in the DCI Dani Bevan series

Never invite evil into your home…

DCI Dani Bevan finds herself dragged into the disturbing case of Eric Fisher, a man accused of slaughtering his own family in a case of domestic homicide. But when a spate of violent burglaries breaks out in the area, whilst Fisher is on remand, Dani wonders if the man's claims of innocence are as crazy as they first thought.
The DCI quickly becomes caught up in a race against time to stop a terrifying serial killer, who appears to be one step ahead of Dani's every move.

A Dark Shadow Falls is perhaps the darkest of all the DCI Bevan investigations. It is a police procedural which uncovers dark secrets and a deadly obsession with the bloodiest episodes in Scottish history.

There are 14 books in the series so far, all available from Amazon!

Printed in Great Britain
by Amazon

13771029R00194